W9-BGD-751

WITHDRAWN

WINTER OF DISCONTENT

**Center Point
Large Print**

Boyle County Public Library

**This Large Print Book carries the
Seal of Approval of N.A.V.H.**

WINTER OF DISCONTENT

JEANNE M. DAMS

CENTER POINT PUBLISHING
THORNDIKE, MAINE

This Center Point Large Print edition
is published in the year 2005 by arrangement with
St. Martin's Press.

Copyright © 2005 by Jeanne M. Dams.

All rights reserved.

The text of this Large Print edition is unabridged. In other
aspects, this book may vary from the original edition. Printed in
Thailand. Set in 16-point Times New Roman type.

ISBN 1-58547-611-0

Library of Congress Cataloging-in-Publication Data

Dams, Jeanne M.
    Winter of discontent / Jeanne M. Dams.--Center Point large print ed.
    p. cm.
    ISBN 1-58547-611-0 (lib. bdg. : alk. paper)
    1. Large type books. I. Title.

PS3554.A498W56 2005
813'.54--dc22

                                                    2005000238

To Barb and Mark,
who never let me get by with a thing,
this book is gratefully dedicated

ONE

I LOOKED AT THE CALENDAR AND SIGHED. NOT ONLY A Monday, but December eighth. Exactly seventeen days till Christmas and I had done almost nothing. No cookies had been baked, no cards sent, no presents bought, let alone wrapped.

It's true that I'm a chronic procrastinator, but this time I had a good excuse. Recent events, including a fairly narrow escape from being murdered, had taken up a good deal of my time and every bit of my energy.

However, excuses notwithstanding, Christmas was going to be here in a little over two weeks, and I wasn't going to be ready, not unless I got my act together immediately. I poured myself the last cup of coffee in the pot, checked to make sure that my husband was happily occupied with his memoirs, and sat down to make a list.

Half an hour later I kissed Alan on the top of his head as he sat absorbed in front of the computer. "I'm going shopping. I may not be home for lunch. There's soup in the fridge."

He muttered something. I knew he'd really heard me and would remember what I'd said when he got hungry and I wasn't there. I patted his shoulder fondly and went out the back door, clapping an old plaid tam on my head.

It was an incredibly beautiful day for December.

The temperature was at least fifty, the sun was shining brightly, and the jasmine on the south wall of my house was in full, fragrant bloom. Perverse creature that I am, I resented the weather. My soul, nourished by more than sixty years of life in the Midwestern United States, insisted that there should be snow. It was a foolish longing. We seldom got much snow here in the part of southeastern England I'd adopted as my home.

Never mind. By the time I got back home I'd be glad enough of dry feet and warm hands and would, I hoped, be imbued with the somewhat frenetic Christmas cheer forced upon me by the merchants.

I knocked on my neighbor's back door. Jane Langland, my best friend, was often willing to accompany me on my jaunts, and I find shopping much less tiring with company.

I was greeted by Jane's bulldogs. I'm never sure how many she has. Soft touch that she is, she's forever bringing home a new one from the animal shelter and then placing it in a good home, so the population varies. They are all invariably good-humored, gregarious, and extremely interested in the way I smell (perhaps because I have two cats). I patted the nearest ones, shoved away the too-curious ones, and waited until Jane herded them all out of the way and motioned me into her pleasant kitchen.

"Sorry. Miserable beasts," she said in fond tones that belied her words. "Coffee?"

"Thanks, but I don't have time to stay. I'm off to do

my extremely belated Christmas shopping, and hoped you'd come with me."

"Well." She considered. "Laundry folded, washing-up done, no committees today—right. Why not? Want to stop at the museum in any case."

She looked at her feet as she muttered the last remark, and I tried hard not to smile. "Do you have a present for Bill?"

"No. Need to talk to him." She spoke gruffly and stumped out into the vestibule. She pulled a sweater off a peg. "Coming, then?"

"How has Bill been?" I pursued as we walked past my house. It's at the end of the street, which is a dead end terminating with a gate into the Cathedral Close. The quickest route to the High Street and most of the shops is through the Cathedral. "I haven't visited the museum lately."

"Hmph! Blinking fool!"

I took this to refer to Bill, not me. And I was pretty sure I knew why she was upset. "So he still won't come to live with you?"

"Hah! Sensible thing to do, with both of us lonely, and nearly eighty, and him an old crock who can barely walk. Not taking proper care of himself."

"Well, I've said before and I say again, I think there's a reason. Don't look at me that way! I don't think he's suddenly lost his fondness for you, so it must be something else. Maybe he doesn't like your house. Maybe he doesn't care for dogs. Maybe he hates the idea of living so close to the church bells.

9

Maybe he's just afraid of losing his independence."

"Hmph!" said Jane again. I thought she was going to say something else, but she shook her head and closed her mouth firmly.

I was thoughtful as we took the shortcut through the Cathedral and out again and turned onto the High Street. Jane had told me, in bits and pieces, about her decades-old romance, and I found the story infinitely pathetic.

She and Bill Fanshawe, neighbors in Sherebury long ago, had known each other from infancy, but love had blossomed when they were just eighteen, in 1943. They desperately wanted to marry, but that was a bad time for romance. Their families insisted they were both too young and times too uncertain. Bill had enlisted in the RAF as soon as he was old enough, promising he would marry her as soon as the war was over and he came home.

But he hadn't come home when the war was over. His plane had been shot down over Germany and Bill taken prisoner. His prison camp was liberated in due time, of course, but under the harsh conditions his injuries had never healed properly. A broken leg, badly set, left him crippled and unable to work at his previous factory job. Even after English doctors did the best they could, he was unfit for factory work and untrained for any other job that could support a wife. Jane had begun her teaching career by that time, so she was earning a little. Bill doggedly worked at what-ever menial jobs he could find while he studied history at Sherebury University. They both lived with their parents and tried to save, but the post-war austerity programs made life hard and saving almost impossible.

Then, in the early fifties, Bill's father was offered a better job in Norwich. The family moved, and Bill, unable to support himself, had little choice but to go with them. In the bigger city, Bill, too, was able to find a better job, his knowledge of history leading to work in the city's museum. The two lovers tried to keep up a correspondence, but since neither had the time or the money to travel to see the other, the letters became unsatisfactory and eventually lapsed. Jane lost touch with Bill except for the occasional Christmas card. Neither married. Time went by.

It was in the mid-nineties, as I recalled, that Bill retired and decided to return to Sherebury. He found a comfortable little flat in what had been a wool merchant's grand house in the seventeenth century. He had finished his degree and become a curator of some note by that time, so when the small Museum of Sherebury moved into the splendid old Town Hall and lost wispy little Mr. Pym, its old curator, Bill was a logical successor. He settled in happily and began to see Jane now and then.

The trouble was, they'd both become set in their ways. If they'd hoped (as the gossipy little town, eagerly awaiting developments, certainly hoped) to take up where they'd left off, they were disappointed. A late-life romance did not develop. But they still shared many of the same interests and enjoyed each other's company. The town held its collective breath and kept hoping, until a major rift developed.

The trouble arose when Bill fell on the stairs getting to his flat, which was on the top floor of the old house. He wasn't hurt, only shaken up, but Jane was extremely upset. Being Jane, she tried to take charge. Bill, with the old weakness in his leg, had no business climbing all those stairs, she insisted. In fact, he had no business living alone at his age.

When she had recounted the conversation to me, I had refrained from saying that she lived alone, in a house with many stairs, and that she was the same age as Bill. I wasted my tact. It seemed that Bill had pointed out that very fact. Jane had then changed tactics and said there was no sense in both of them living alone. She would be more than happy to have him move in with her, as a paying guest if he liked, and they'd be there for each other in case of illness or other disaster.

Well, that put the fat in the fire. Bill backed off like a scalded cat. I thought, personally, that he took the suggestion as a backhanded sort of marriage proposal, and was scared to death of the idea. I didn't say so to Jane, of course. She was mortally offended, and became even more upset when Bill up and moved to Heatherwood House, a retirement home in a beautiful old manor house on the edge of town. At one blow he had rejected her, dealt with all her objections about his unsafe living conditions, and distanced himself from her physically as well.

Jane Langland is one of the kindest people I know. She's also one of the stubbornest, and I'm well equipped to recognize the trait. She didn't give up. She called on him at the museum every chance she got, raising some new argument. I suspected that they secretly enjoyed the quarrels a good deal, and I was looking forward to watching them spar today.

Not yet, though. Shopping came first. List clutched in my hand, I steered Jane firmly in the direction opposite the Town Hall.

Two hours later, only halfway through my list, I was more than ready to stop for lunch. My feet hurt, my arms were weighed down with packages, I had a headache, and I was starving. So much for Christmas spirit. "Jane, let's go to Alderney's. It's about halfway home, and even with your help, I can't carry all this stuff much farther. Besides, they have wonderful food and I don't have much at home."

"Better idea. Town Hall's just across the street. Pop in there and leave your parcels."

"That *is* a good idea! And maybe Bill will come to lunch with us, if his assistant is there today." I glanced slyly at Jane, but she refused to meet my eye.

We staggered across the street. Jane opened the heavy old oak door and I negotiated the half flight of stairs to the level where the museum occupied the space vacated some years before by the city offices. The architects, with Bill to advise them, had done a lovely job with it. The building retained its Elizabethan dignity, and the artifacts of centuries of Shere-bury history were displayed attractively.

The desk he usually occupied in the corner was vacant, and there was no sign of his assistant.

"Jane, he must be upstairs looking something up, and I positively cannot climb any more stairs." Bill, I knew, had been doing a lot of work lately in the store-rooms, pulling out odd bits and pieces that had been donated to the museum years ago and trying to make some sense of them.

"HELLO-O!" Jane's stentorian bellow raised some dust motes that eddied in the sunlight coming through a leaded-glass window. There was no other response.

"Old fool's fallen asleep up there. Suppose I'd best wake him."

Jane made for the stairs while I sank gratefully into a chair. Jane's older than I, but better able to climb stairs, especially when my arthritic knees are acting up. I often think it's unfair that I feel about thirty-five on the inside, but the outer shell sometimes seems to be approaching a hundred. I leaned back as far as the rather hard chair would allow and closed my eyes. I'd have time for forty winks before Jane persuaded Bill to leave his work and come to lunch with us.

She came back before I'd reached even the edge of sleep. "He's not there," she announced.

Her tone of voice roused me. "But—he'd surely never leave the place unattended. He must have gone to the loo."

"Knocked. Then peeked in. No one."

This was unexpected. Bill Fanshawe was fanatically reliable. He viewed the museum's collection as virtually his own property, and guarded it jealously. He would never have walked off with the doors unlocked. I tried to make my weary brain function properly. "Maybe he isn't here at all today, and his assistant has done something foolish—gone off for a sandwich or whatever, and left the museum open."

Jane, prowling restlessly, reached Bill's desk and did some rummaging. "No," she said, holding up one of the papers. "Schedule for the week. Bill's here alone today."

I looked at her blankly. "Well, then, where is he?"

TWO

WE DID THE OBVIOUS THINGS FIRST. "WHERE DOES HE usually go for lunch? Do you know?" I asked Jane.

"Usually brings a sandwich and an apple and a flask of tea." Jane opened a bottom drawer of the desk and produced a plastic bag with food in it. The tea flask was on the desk, some of the tea poured out into a mug. The mug was about half full, and was stone-cold.

So we searched. We searched the whole building, including the basement storage area and the attic, my knees protesting loudly. We found stacks of old documents and artifacts, file cabinets, shelves, display cases—all the things one would expect to find in a museum. In the basement and attic we found, also, evidence that spiders, mice, and bats had enjoyed the hospitality of the City of Sherebury. We opened the secret room in the attic (the one that everyone in town knew about) and found an inhabited mouse's nest. That wasn't the high point of my day.

We did not find Bill Fanshawe.

Exhausted, we retired back to the main room of the museum, collapsed into chairs, and tried to collect our thoughts.

"Could he have run out to get something he urgently needed? Some—oh, paper clips or something?" I asked hopefully.

"Not without locking up. Always locked up. Be back by now, anyway."

That was reasonable. Jane and I looked at each other. I nodded slowly. "Something's happened, then. He's fallen, or become ill, and someone's taken him to the hospital without bothering about closing up the museum."

Jane got up without a word, went to Bill's desk, and picked up the phone. In quick succession, she phoned Sherebury's one hospital, Bill's doctor, and the St. John's Ambulance Service. After each call she shook her head.

I bit my lip. "Maybe he was feeling so ill he went home and forgot—"

Jane looked exasperated. "I tell you, he wouldn't forget. This museum is his life."

"Well, we can at least see if his car is here. And we

can call Heatherwood House."

Jane knew Bill's car and where he usually parked it. While she went out to check, I called the retirement home. He wasn't there, and Jane came back to report that his car was in its usual place.

"Did you think to feel the hood?"

"Cold."

I sighed. "Then it's time to call the police, isn't it?"

Neither of us had wanted to admit that the matter might be serious, but it was looking more and more that way.

"Won't be any use. Won't consider him a missing person so soon."

"You could be right, but I'll bet if I have Alan call we'll get some action." For my husband is the retired chief constable of the county of Belleshire, in which Sherebury is located, and his influence at police headquarters is still considerable.

But Alan, when I made the call, wasn't home. I'd told him I'd be out for lunch; he probably took advantage of my absence to run some errands. I hung up on the answering machine, pondered a moment, and then dialed the police myself.

I was lucky enough to reach Inspector Derek Morrison—Detective Chief Inspector, to give him his full title. He was a friend and virtually the only man I knew on the force anymore. He listened patiently, even though he deals only with major crimes.

"Well, you know there's very little we can do at this point, officially, that is. Unofficially I can ask our people to keep their eyes open. I agree it's somewhat puzzling, but people do sometimes behave in unexpected ways."

"I know, but—"

"Dorothy, I do understand your concern. Have you considered the possibility that he may simply have wandered off? I hate to mention it, but people his age do, you know."

I was glad Jane couldn't hear him. "I doubt it, in this case." My tone had become somewhat frosty.

"All right, I'll tell you what. It's well past time I found some lunch. Suppose I take a little jaunt out to Heatherwood House. They might have some suggestions. Meanwhile, try not to worry too much. I'm sure he'll turn up."

I hung up the phone and turned to Jane. "No good, really. He was kind, but a little patronizing."

"Suggested Bill had got lost? Old, absentminded, all that rot?"

"More or less."

Jane snorted. "I'm more likely to get lost than Bill is. So are you."

"I get lost all the time. I admit it. It's your wretched medieval street system. I'm used to nice rectangular blocks. However, I agree about Bill. Now, look. We're both tired and hungry. I think we need to take a little time to replenish our energy and think sensibly about what to do. Is there a key on the premises anywhere, do you think? I hate to leave the place unlocked again."

"Don't know about a key. We need the assistant."

"The assistant . . . oh, the *assistant!* Bill's assistant."

Jane turned once more to the desk. An appointment calendar lay to one side. She found the address book at the back and made a call. After a few barked commands she hung up.

"Said he had to go to class. Coming here instead."

Jane has that effect on people.

We sat, growing more and more restive while waiting for the assistant to arrive, and when he finally came, I wasn't sure the wait had been worth it. The boy, a Sherebury University student named Botts or Potts or something like that, was amiable and willing but not especially capable. His primary duties were to fetch and carry for Bill, and fill in when Bill had to be away. I'd never actually had a conversation with him, but the few times I'd seen him in action, so to speak, I had discovered that he apparently knew almost nothing about the collection, and very little about serving the public. He was no use at all in helping anyone with research.

He was, I had learned, reading history at the university. One wondered what they were teaching him.

However, when we explained the situation to him, he was more than happy to mind the store while we went to find lunch. "We may not be back before closing time," I warned him. "Can you lock up?"

"Oh, yes, there's a key right here." He opened the top desk drawer and pawed through it. "Oh. Well, p'raps in here." He tried another drawer.

Jane raised her eyes to the ceiling in a long-suffering expression and pushed me out the door. "Best find Bill," she said in a stage whisper that I'm sure young Potts, or Botts, could hear. "Young pup'd let anyone walk off with the lot."

We had a quick sandwich and tea at a café across the street. The sandwich wasn't especially good, but our minds weren't on food. I asked if Bill had been there. Well, he might for once have decided he was sick of his own sandwiches, mightn't he? But no one at the café had seen him for several days. Jane and I went over Bill's disappearance, and over it, and over it again. We could find no logical explanation.

"It's simply impossible," I said, finally. "He didn't go anywhere of his own free will, because his car's there and he would never have left the museum unlocked and unattended. Agreed?"

Jane nodded morosely.

"He didn't simply wander off in a daze, because his mind's still quite sharp. Agreed?"

Another nod.

"And there's no possible reason for anyone to kidnap him, or anything ridiculous like that. He has no money to speak of, he has no criminal background—there's just no *reason* for someone to abduct him!"

Jane sighed. "Things happen. No reason."

"Yes, but to a harmless elderly man in the Museum of Sherebury? There are surely lots better targets. But look, I said something a minute ago that gave me an idea. We don't actually know much about Bill's life after he left Sherebury, or even in the war. Is it possible that something happened, maybe a long time ago, that would make him vulnerable now?"

"Bill?"

The incredulity in her tone carried conviction, but I persisted. "Okay, maybe it's far-fetched, but he *was* in the war. There are still some strong feelings about that, even after all these years. What if he saw something he shouldn't have, and suddenly ran into someone . . ."

Her look of disbelief stopped me. "Well, maybe I haven't thought it out well enough. I still think there's a possibility lurking somewhere. But unless we can figure out what it might be, there's only one other idea that makes any sense, and I'm afraid I don't like it much at all, but—"

"Stroke, bump on the head. Thought of it already. Something to destroy his memory. Only possible thing."

"Well, then," I said, rising, "we have to try to find him. He can't have gone far if he's ill."

It would be tedious to detail all the places we looked. We started near the museum. There's a rather nasty little alley between the Town Hall and the shop next door. There were rubbish bins and lean stray cats and disagreeable smells and, I was very much afraid, an occasional rat scurrying out of sight. That was all.

We tried the buildings nearby. We tried a pub that

21

Jane said Bill frequented. We tried perhaps a dozen other increasingly unlikely spots. Everyone was friendly and helpful. No one had seen Bill that day.

We had to give up, finally, out of sheer weariness. The museum had closed, my parcels inside. It didn't seem to matter much. I couldn't have carried them all home, anyway. It was all we could do to walk home unencumbered.

When I reached my front door with its inviting little porch, I raised my eyebrows at Jane. Wordlessly, she preceded me inside. We dropped onto the soft couch in my parlor and uttered groans in unison.

"I may never get up," I moaned.

Jane grunted.

Alan had built a small fire in the grate. I wished I could feel as pleasant and cozy as it looked.

Alan appeared in the doorway. Bless the man, he had glasses in his hands, glasses containing amber fluid. "I heard what's happened," he said. "Derek phoned. I thought you'd need a restorative." He handed each of us a glass.

I took a healthy sip of my bourbon and then sighed. "Derek wasn't much help. Alan, we're really worried. Anything could have happened to a man his age, and we've looked every place we could think of. He's simply vanished."

Jane sipped her scotch and glowered. She muttered something under her breath about police. It didn't sound complimentary.

Alan left the room for a moment and returned with

a glass of his own. He sat down by the fire. "There are rules about these things, as both of you well know. There's very little the police can do under ordinary circumstances. Derek knows you're both upset. That's why he rang up."

Jane glared.

Alan continued. "He said he'd promised you he'd check with the Heatherwood House people, and he did just that. He said they were quite cooperative, and more than a little concerned."

"And no one had the slightest idea where Bill might be."

"I'm afraid not. The staff did organize a search around the grounds, in case Bill had come home in someone else's car and fallen somewhere. They also sent a staff member to drive the road into town, because it was just barely possible he'd tried to walk home. And they checked the hospital again. No one is taking this lightly, I do assure you."

"Except the police," Jane said.

Alan was patient. "They have to follow procedures, Jane. I understand how you feel, but—"

"No, you don't." Jane set her glass down with a thump and was out of the room faster than I'd have believed she could move.

I struggled out of the soft depths of the sofa and started to follow her.

"Leave it, love." Alan's voice was almost sharp. "She won't listen to sense just now. She's angry and scared. I do understand how she's feeling, of course, even if she doesn't believe it. So do you. We've both lost a spouse."

"I'll never forget what it felt like, wondering if Frank was going to make it. It's the not knowing that's the worst."

"Indeed. But just now she wants to be alone with her fears. I'll talk to her tomorrow, unless Bill has turned up by then."

"I hope he does." But I didn't believe it, and Alan's sigh told me he didn't, either.

That night the weather changed. We went to bed, tired and despondent, about ten, with the windows wide open and a light blanket over us. Sometime in the middle of the night I woke huddled up against Alan's back. He is a man of comforting bulk, tall and solidly built, and he's usually nice and warm to cuddle up to. Not now, or not warm enough. I realized I was both cold and cramped. A chill wind was blowing the curtains into the room. The cats had crowded against us for warmth, pinning us down. I fought free of them and the blanket, closed the windows, and tossed a comforter on the bed.

I didn't sleep for some time, what with the cats and Alan rearranging themselves, and my last waking thought was of Bill, perhaps out in the cold December night.

THREE

The weather was even worse the next morning. A determined rain, mixing at times with sleet, was washing away all remnants of autumn. I woke late to the welcome smell of coffee, but my eyes had barely popped open when I thought again of Bill. I put on my warmest robe and hurried down to the kitchen.

I didn't even say good morning to my husband, who was making toast. "Alan, if Bill's out in this—"

"I know, love. I've rung Derek. Bill's not turned up, and they're launching a real search. It's been nearly twenty-four hours, now, and the weather changes the scenario. They'll find him."

He spoke with the confidence of forty years of policing. I didn't answer, but I thought plenty. An elderly man, a fall, perhaps a broken hip, pneumonia . . . the familiar story.

After picking at my breakfast for a few minutes, I scraped my chair back from the table and stood up. "I'm going over to talk to Jane. She'll be frantic."

"I've already talked to her."

"Oh?" Of all the responses in my repertoire, that one is probably the most annoying. Said with the intonation I used, it implied anger, disdain, disbelief, a whole range of emotions in one syllable. When I was a teacher I used to use it with particularly naughty and insubordinate schoolchildren. I didn't recall that I'd

25

Boyle County Public Library

ever used it before with Alan.

"She was here an hour ago," Alan replied evenly, "angry and distraught. She demanded I phone Derek."

"And?" Same tone.

"I told her I already had."

"Oh." I took a deep breath. "Alan, I'm sorry. None of this is your fault, and I'm being hateful. But I'm afraid I don't have quite your faith in the police."

"I do assure you, as I have assured Jane, that they will do all in their power—"

"I know, I know. They won't neglect their duty. But, Alan, they're young, at least relatively. They think of Bill as an old man, probably senile. They'll look for him in places where he might have wandered. Even the staff at Heatherwood House is thinking that way. You told me they were searching the grounds yesterday. And they, of all people, ought to know Bill isn't like that."

Alan made a visible effort at patience. "People change, Dorothy. When they're Bill's age, sometimes they change suddenly. He might have had a stroke, or a heart attack. Something might have happened to confuse and disorient him."

"I know. And that's what I was thinking yesterday. But they haven't found him in any of the likely places. This isn't a huge town, Alan."

"What are you suggesting?"

"You're going to think it's silly."

Alan refilled my coffee and waited.

"All right." I sat back down and took a good sip of

coffee before I could work up the nerve to go on. "I think it's possible that he has—oh, the expression sounds so melodramatic—that he has met with foul play."

Alan didn't smile. He probably knew I'd throw something at him if he did.

"He was in the war, Alan. He was taken prisoner. Is it completely impossible that something that happened way back then has caught up with him now?"

"For example?"

That, of course, was the weak point. "I don't know. I don't know enough about the war. I was too young to have more than the vaguest idea of what was happening, and of course we in America didn't have a clue, anyway. I realized, the first time I came to England, in the 1960s, and saw all the bomb sites, that you over here experienced the war. Except for our soldiers, and of course the civilians living in Pearl Harbor, we only read about it. But I have a good imagination"—Alan did smile a little at that—"and I imagine that there are still some secrets floating around, and some strong feelings."

"Certainly there's still a good deal of classified material. As for strong feelings—well, we do have long memories, it's true."

I thought of a story that had been told me long ago. It concerned two ancient churches in the fen country of East Anglia. By the 1980s the congregations had become so small that it was necessary to combine the two parishes into one. Now the fen country, centuries before, had been an important battleground of the English Civil War. Oliver Cromwell and his men with their short, round haircuts had cut a wide swath, lopping the heads off countless statues in the churches and wreaking other destruction. However, there was strong Royalist support in certain areas.

It happened that one of the parishes under discussion in the story was historically Cromwellian in sympathies, and the other Royalist. At a parish meeting in the latter, one of the old men of the congregation had stood during the discussion of the merger and shouted indignantly, "What? Go to church with them Roundheads?"

The Civil War ended—officially—in 1649. Yes, the English have long memories.

I finished my coffee. "I'm still going over to talk to Jane. She doesn't think much of my idea either, but I can't just sit here and wait for someone to find Bill. There must be something Jane and I can do. He's been gone too long now, and it's cold out there, Alan."

He nodded. "Wrap up well if you're going out in it."

My husband doesn't always agree with me, but he's long since stopped trying to tell me what to do. I often think I don't appreciate him enough.

Even to dash next door, I put on a full set of waterproofs, including wellies. This rain meant business. I didn't bother even to knock until I was inside the back door. Civility is one thing. Sense enough to come in out of the rain is another.

"Jane, it's me," I shouted over a tumult of bulldogs.

"May I come in? I mean, I already am in, but do you have time to talk?"

Over the frenzied barking I thought I heard a voice in the kitchen.

Jane was sitting at the kitchen table, an untouched cup of coffee in front of her. She looked awful. Her usually ruddy face was gray. There were purple smudges under her eyes. She was wearing the clothes she'd had on yesterday, and looked as though she had slept in them. If she'd slept. She looked up, muttered something, and let her head droop again.

This would never do. I'd seen Jane angry, combative even. I'd never seen her defeated.

I shooed the dogs out of the room, plugged in the kettle, removed her coffee cup, and found the teapot.

"Don't want any tea."

"Well, you're going to have some, so you might as well resign yourself. What did you have for break-fast?"

She shook her head.

"This won't do, you know. It won't help Bill to worry yourself into a state. You can't think on no sleep and no food, and you need to do some productive thinking."

"Why?"

"Because Bill's somewhere, and I don't think the police are going to find him. I don't think they're looking in the right places. You've got to help me think where the right places are."

"Tried yesterday."

"Yesterday we didn't know for sure he was missing." The kettle shrieked. I made the tea and poured her a cup, with lots of sugar and milk. "Today we know. We can start to look in earnest, if you'll help me work out where."

I made her drink the tea while I boiled an egg and made toast, and after she'd eaten she looked a little better. A little. Not much.

As I cleared away the dishes, I began my pep talk. "Look, Jane, I know how you're feeling, but—"

"No." She raised her head and looked me in the eye. "Anyone you cared for ever gone missing?"

"Yes. My husband. And not just missing, but dead. Jane, the hours I spent in that hospital waiting to hear how Frank was doing after the heart attack . . . yes, I do know how worried and scared you are."

She held up a hand in a gesture of apology. "Sorry. Didn't mean to be rude, but . . . not just worried and scared. Helpless. Old."

That stopped me. I put the dishes in the sink, carefully, so I wouldn't break them—or myself. I sat at the table. A silence fell.

"You don't know, yet," said Jane after an eternity. "Not old enough. Don't know how people look through you. Talk about you as if you weren't there. Smile politely when you make a remark." She spoke in a monotone.

I found my voice. "I can't imagine anyone treating you condescendingly, Jane. You're so forceful, so vital."

"Never used to do," said Jane. "Terrified them, I did."

I waited for a satisfied chuckle. It didn't come.

"Used to be a character, now I'm a nuisance. Haven't had the decency to die. Worse for Bill out in that bloody awful place."

Jane never swears. I gulped. "Heatherwood House? It seems like a lovely place, and the staff—"

"Kind. All of them. So bloody kind."

"Oh." A chill ran through me.

I'd tried not to think about what lay ahead for me and Alan. We were both healthy, we weren't all that old, Alan had family to help out. I'd clung to those thoughts, tried to keep at bay the terror of old age.

I've never been afraid of dying, but the thought of living too long does terrify me. When Frank died unexpectedly in his early sixties, I'd thought I faced a future entirely alone, childless and bereft. Then Alan came into my life, along with Alan's family of children and grandchildren. I was able, for a while, to put off uncomfortable thoughts.

But every day, every hour, brought us closer to the time of our lives when anything might happen. Physical weakness was more than a possibility. My knees were already in bad shape, and would only get worse. Knee replacement? Confinement, perhaps, to a wheelchair?

Alan had always taken good care of himself, but one read every day about much younger men, fit and healthy, dying of heart attacks or strokes or undiagnosed cancer or a hundred other things. What if Alan became ill, too ill for me to care for him?

Then there was my worst fear of all, mental decay. If I should begin to see the signs of Alzheimer's in myself, or worse, in Alan, then what horrors faced us? Living in a place where people were kind and looked after all our needs? And treated us like sweet children?

There were other sorts of places, of course. Places where the staff were not kind, where they neglected the inmates, treated them like naughty children. I had visited such places in the States, nursing homes reeking of stale urine. The residents lined the halls, slumped in their wheelchairs, tied in with bandages. Some dozed. Some cried out constantly, asking for help or calling for loved ones. The staff would tell me their cries were meaningless, that the "poor old souls" didn't know what they were saying, that a response was useless. I had wondered even then if that was the truth or just a convenient fiction.

But those were nursing homes and the residents all had dementia to some degree. Surely a retirement home was a different sort of environment. I wrenched my thoughts back from the scary future to the worrisome present.

"Bill still drives, though," I argued. "He has his independence. He has a job. Doesn't that make a difference to people's attitude?" I had to fight it, fight the possibility that Jane was right.

"He's old. We're both old. One foot in the grave. Out of the loop. And single. Makes it worse."

I usually have a lot to say, but there seemed to be something wrong with my throat. I swallowed several times.

Jane gave me an unreadable look, got up, and put the kettle on. She copes better with other people's distress than with her own.

A fresh pot of tea helped. So did the brewing interval, time enough to get my emotions under some kind of control and my thoughts in some semblance of order.

"Jane, you were right. I didn't understand completely, but I'm beginning to. You're afraid of the whole situation, not just Bill being missing. And you think that your age, and his, will keep people from paying enough attention. Are people really that callous, though?"

"Not callous. Ignorant. Think they know who Bill is, what he is, when they haven't a clue."

"All right, then. We can't make them older and wiser all of a sudden, and we can't make them know Bill better. Maybe we can't even get them to listen to us. So we'll just have to use our own resources. And don't look at me that way. We do have resources. You know Bill well, and you know this town as well as you know your dogs. As for me, I don't have either of those advantages, and besides I'm something of an old crock. I may have fewer birthdays behind me than you do, but my knees would argue the point. But even if my joints don't work very well, my mind is just fine, thank you. I can contribute ideas, lots of them. And my tongue works double time. I can ask questions."

Jane didn't look impressed. I played my ace.

"And if you don't think much of that list of assets, I've saved the best for last. Alan."

She sat, stony-faced, and said nothing.

"Jane, he knows the police, he's brilliant, he's no spring chicken, and he's on our side. What more do you want?"

"I want my friend, Bill."

And a tear coursed slowly down her weathered cheek.

FOUR

I WAITED, PRETENDING NOT TO NOTICE. I'D NEVER SEEN Jane cry. She would hate to be patted on the shoulders and told, "There, there." I debated about leaving. Would she be embarrassed? Tough, resilient Jane, reduced to tears?

But it was, after all, only the single tear. She turned away from me, blew her nose, and stood up. "All right."

Jane not only speaks in shorthand, she thinks in it. "Um-m-m?" I said brilliantly.

"Ready to go."

"Whoa! You've turned a page. Go where?"

"Museum," she said impatiently. "Last place we know he was. Place to start."

I was so happy to see her jolted out of her despair, I

didn't state the obvious: that we had been all over the Town Hall yesterday and found nothing. "We'd better drive, then. It's pouring cats and dogs."

"No place to park. Have Alan drive us."

So Alan obligingly got out the car and drove us the short distance. "Right," he said as he let us out of the car. "Do you have the mobile?"

I nodded. I always keep the cell phone in my purse, even though I seldom use it.

"Ring me when you're ready to come home, or if you need help. I'll be here. If the line's busy I'm working on the problem myself. We have to find Bill soon. This is filthy weather."

What he didn't say was that every passing hour made it less likely that Bill would be found alive. He didn't have to say it. Jane and I both knew.

"What are we going to do, now we're here?" I asked.

"Ideas are your department, remember?"

Well, I had said something like that, hadn't I? I pulled myself together and tried to look intelligent.

"All right, then, we talk to the assistant. What *is* the kid's name, anyhow? I keep forgetting."

"Tubbs. Walter Tubbs."

"Oh. I knew it was something like Potts. Poor boy. I can imagine what the boys must have called him at school."

"Good job he's not fat."

Jane was herself again, determined to keep a good Britishly stiff upper lip. Good for her. I hoped I could live up to her example.

The assistant was at Bill's desk when we opened the door to the museum proper. It had apparently not been a busy day so far. His string of paper clips reminded me of the chain that encircled Marley's Ghost.

He jumped up when he saw us. "Miss Langland! Any news?"

"No." Jane was brusque. "Thought we might pick up some ideas here."

The boy's shoulders slumped. "I thought so, too, but I haven't found a thing. I hoped he might have left me a note, but if he did, I haven't seen it."

Bless the child, he was worried. Now I had to come up with a way for him to help. He worked with Bill two or three days a week. Surely he'd be able to tell us something.

"Mr. Tubbs, my name is Dorothy Martin—"

"I know. Mr. Fanshawe told me about you when you were in once. He said you always wear hats." He held out his hand. "And please call me Walter. I somehow haven't quite got used to 'Mr. Tubbs' yet."

"Delighted to meet you, Walter. Now, we're here to see if there's any hint at all about where Bill might have gone. No, I know you've looked, but there's an approach we haven't tried yet. At least, maybe the police have, but if so I don't know about it. I'd like to figure out, if I can, what Bill might have been doing yesterday morning before he disappeared."

"Ah, the old 'retrace his steps' ploy," Walter said in a creditable Inspector Clouseau accent, with a momentary grin. "But I can't help much. All I know is that he's been working a lot on the old acquisitions, things people gave the museum donkey's years ago. Most of it is pure rubbish, you know. Love letters, family albums, war medals, things of no possible interest except to the family. But Mr. Fanshawe has to sort through all of it to make sure there's nothing valuable, and then write letters to the donors explaining why we can't keep their family treasures. It makes a lot of work."

"Hmm. There could be something in that, I suppose. Do you have to type the letters for him?"

"Sometimes. Usually it's only a form letter, and he can do that himself easily enough on the computer. I do the touchy ones, when it has to be rather lengthy and especially tactful. I'm rather good at that sort of thing, funnily enough, and I'm a decent typist."

He reminded me of a Labrador retriever, not wildly competent but eager to please. I smiled at him. "I expect you are. Have you had to do any of those special letters lately?"

I suppose I had some vague idea about a family that had become irate at Bill's rejection of their donations. Incensed by what they perceived as an insult to their family honor, they had . . .

"No," said Walter. "Nothing. I've just been doing the usual dogsbody routine: filing, showing visitors where to find things. Dead boring." He held up his chain of paper clips with a grimace. "I should be doing other things, really. There's a special exhibition coming up in a few months, and lots of work connected with that. But Mr. Fanshawe never lets me do anything very important, and he'd be annoyed if I made mistakes. I don't know quite what to do, actually."

I felt sorry for him. Maybe he seemed incompetent because he'd never been given a chance to show what he could do. I pulled off my yellow plastic hat and ran a hand through my hair. "Well, I can't help you there, I'm afraid. I don't know the first thing about running a museum. All I can do is try to find Bill as soon as possible." I was rapidly running out of ideas, but I could follow up on my earlier notion about Bill's background. "What about—um—has any of Bill's work lately been about World War II memorabilia?"

Walter looked at me pityingly, and even Jane snorted, worried as she was. "Nearly all of it," said Walter. "Makes sense, doesn't it? War ended sixty years ago, more or less. So most of the old soldiers are dying, or they died a few years back and their families threw out their things. Unfortunately, a lot of it comes here instead of going in the rubbish bin. Although it's usually only a stop on the way."

I sighed. Well, I never thought this was going to be easy. I ran my fingers through my hair again. "All right. I suppose the next thing is to go upstairs and look around. Bill does have an office up there? I mean, it isn't simply a storeroom? I didn't really notice yesterday."

"Well, there's a desk and a chair and a lamp. Most

of the rest is filing cabinets and boxes. I don't know what you might be looking for, though."

"I don't either. There has to be something. There has to be a *reason*. People don't just disappear into thin air."

They did, though. Not often, but every police department in the world has a thin file of cases about people who just disappeared, a year ago, ten years ago, a hundred. They walked out the door and were never seen again, dead or alive. We had to go on the assumption that Bill wasn't one of those cases, that there was a sensible reason for what had happened, and if we could work it out, we'd know where to find him.

We hoped.

So we trooped up the stairs, Walter leading the way with Jane trudging sturdily behind. I made a poor third, holding tightly to the banister and wincing every time a knee cracked or threatened to give way. I was really going to have to see if something couldn't be done about those knees, once more important things were out of the way.

The second floor of the Town Hall, when it was the center of Shrebury city affairs, had been a single large room for mayoral receptions, smallish public meetings, and various other functions. When the museum had taken over, a wall had been built to divide the room in half. Shelves and filing cabinets had been installed in one of the halves. A museum always needs a good deal of live storage space. The other half had been left as it was, since there would still be occasion for receptions. We walked through the elegant half and into Bill's work space.

As I had expected, the room was a mess, but it was what I thought of as a purposeful mess. As every housewife knows, there is a stage of tidying up when things look much worse than they did to start with. Order is being produced, but the casual eye perceives it as a disaster. I thought I could see here evidence of sorting and even, occasionally, of controlled excitement. One could almost hear Bill saying of one find or another, "Here! Look at this!" even as he dismissed most of the junk as just that.

I stole a glance at Jane. If Bill's personality came through here to me, who knew him only slightly, how much more powerfully it must be evoked for her. If she was in distress, however, she hid it well, setting her mouth into a firmly blank expression.

"He won't let me put anything away," Walter said apologetically. "He says he knows where everything is. The cleaners aren't even allowed in."

"Well, you're going to have to help us look. At least you know something about the work he was doing. You might be able to spot something missing, or something that shouldn't be here."

"Well . . . I can try. But I'll have to go downstairs if anyone comes in."

"No one's likely to take a sudden notion to go to a museum on a day like this. Would you choose to be here if you didn't have to be?"

Walter grinned and began somewhat aimlessly to turn over piles of papers. "Tell me again what I'm looking for?"

"I don't have the foggiest idea. Something that doesn't fit the pattern. I get the feeling Bill is pretty methodical. There are piles, after all, even if they do look a bit haphazard."

"Oh, he has his methods. He's been sorting things by family, and by date, and by historical significance. That's to say, everything related to the Whosis family would be in one pile, and everything related to the Queen's accession in another—"

"And if they overlap? If Mr. Whosis, or Lord Whosis or whatever, happened to be in on the Coronation in a big way?"

"That's where it gets tricky, of course. I think then he photocopies documents and puts one in both piles, as a cross-reference."

"It all sounds exhausting, but it gives us enough idea of Bill's system to make a start. Walter, if you'll bring a couple of chairs upstairs and find someplace to put them, we'll begin looking for anything that doesn't seem to belong."

Of course, in my house, I thought as I settled down with a formidable stack of papers, things are constantly getting put where they don't belong. It means nothing except that I was thinking about something else at the time. I joke about it, claim I have no memory and can lose something in fifteen seconds flat.

Thinking about Bill and the problems of aging, I decided I wouldn't make that particular joke again. It wasn't really so very funny.

The papers I was going through weren't easy to read. Many of them were handwritten, and I've always found English handwriting somewhat difficult. The stack I'd chosen apparently had to do with the Lynley family, squires and benefactors of Sherebury for hundreds of years. The main family had died out long ago, but some of their distant relations still lived hereabouts, and apparently some of them had been taken with a fit of attic-cleaning. The documents they had seen fit to donate to the museum looked to me to be of no value whatever, but if Bill had planned to throw out the whole mess, it would have occasioned one of the super-tactful letters Walter specialized in.

Certainly there was nothing in the stack that shed any light whatever on Bill's disappearance. Sighing, I put the Lynleys back where I'd found them and started on the next pile.

We worked most of the day. Walter braved the rain at lunchtime and went out for sandwiches and coffee. We ate them almost silently and got back to work as soon as we'd finished.

I was beginning to doubt we'd get anywhere. It all felt so futile. Here we sat poring over long-dead papers and artifacts, while a living, breathing man was lost somewhere. I called Alan in the middle of the afternoon, even though I knew he would have called me if there had been any news. "Nothing yet, love. At least we know a lot of cold, wet places where he isn't."

Small comfort.

By four o'clock there was so little light from the windows that it was hard to work. The electric lights in the room weren't at all bright. The museum probably did that deliberately, to keep old objects from fading, but it certainly made the place gloomy. My neck and shoulders were aching and my morale had sunk to rock bottom. We were making no progress at all, except that the room looked a little neater than when we'd begun.

"Jane, let's call it a day. We were both wrong. This isn't a reasonable place to search. We could spend a week in here and never even know if we'd found anything that mattered."

Jane grunted and pushed herself back from the desk, where she'd been exploring the drawers. "Wonder what this is doing here?" she said, pointing to something in the top drawer.

"What? Have you found something?" My voice was sharp with excitement, my fatigue forgotten.

"Nothing that matters. Just wondered why Bill has an atlas of the States in his desk."

I pulled the book out. It was one of the big road atlases, the kind that Rand McNally puts out, with two pages devoted to each state, sometimes more for the really huge ones like Texas and California. It looked new.

"Here, let me see that," said Walter.

"Was he planning a trip to America, then?" I asked Jane.

"No. He was planning—we were planning—" Her voice cracked and she stopped, then took a deep breath and began again. "Wasn't going to tell anyone. We're planning to be married."

FIVE

"BUT—BUT I THOUGHT—"

"Thought we'd quarreled. We did. Made it up. His idea to get married. Said Heatherwood House wasn't his sort of place. Wanted to get out of it, wouldn't live in my house unless we made it legal."

I tried to knit together the fraying threads of my composure. "Well, that's—that's wonderful." It sounded flat. I tried again. "He's a lovely man, Jane. I hope you'll be very happy." If we find him. I didn't say it aloud, but of course I didn't need to.

"That's why I know he hasn't taken French leave. We were to be married today."

"Oh, *Jane!*" My voice broke. I looked at Jane, but her face was stony. Did she want sympathy? Probably not. She was holding on to her composure by a thin thread.

"But why didn't you tell anybody?" I asked, trying not to sniffle. "Alan and I would have wanted to be there, and lots of other people would, too."

"See a pair of old fools tie the knot? Pah! Better

entertainment on the telly."

"Well, you've let the cat out of the bag now. Where were you being married? In the Cathedral?"

"Registry office. Didn't want a fuss."

"Oh. Then there were no arrangements to be canceled. Unless—did you plan to go away?"

"A wedding trip? Not at our age." Jane's tone did not invite further questions, so I didn't mention the atlas.

"Well, you realize you've let yourself in for a big party when the day comes."

"If."

"No. When. We can't lose hope, Jane. Look, he's a sensible man. Something's happened, that's certain, but he isn't a child."

"Crippled." She was determined not to let herself be sweet-talked into optimism.

"All right. He's got a bum leg and he's not young. But he's smart. Unless somebody's killed him, for some unimaginable reason, we'll find him."

"Hmph."

The rain had slackened off, but we were too tired, and too dispirited, to walk home. I called Alan and he picked us up. As I got in the car, I queried him with a lift of the eyebrows. He shook his head.

We offered Jane a drink once we got home, but she preferred to go home and brood alone, so Alan and I sat in front of the fire with our bourbon and our cats. We told each other what we'd done all day. It wasn't much, either of us.

"I've rung everyone I thought might help," Alan said, setting down his glass with a sigh. "Not a glimmer. Derek's searching in earnest now. Bulletins are out, and I believe there's to be an appeal on the evening news."

"Alan, it just occurred to me—has anyone searched his old house? Where he used to live when he was a boy? If something happened to confuse him, a stroke or whatever, he might have gone there, mightn't he?"

"Derek did think of that. The house is long gone. It was near the university; the fine arts building is there now. And yes, they did ask people in the building, and no, Bill hasn't turned up, muddled or otherwise. I'm afraid things aren't looking hopeful. Poor Jane."

I'd told him her startling news. "Yes, I think she's pretty shattered, though she's trying to keep her cool. She really expected to find something at the museum, and to tell the truth, I did, too. All we came up with was this." I nodded toward the atlas on the tea table. I'd brought it home simply to give myself the illusion of something to do.

"Odd thing for Bill to have." Alan frowned.

"That's what I thought. That's why I was interested. But there's nothing stuck inside, no dog-eared pages, nothing to tell us what he might have been doing with it."

"Is it marked at all?"

"I don't know. I never thought to look. Why would it be?"

Alan shrugged. "I've no idea. But if it is, it might give us a lead."

"I suppose you're right. No, you *are* right. It's just that I've read so many papers today, dusty things in bad handwriting and by a bad light, and my eyes positively tear at the thought of reading any more."

"Hand it over, then, love. I'll take it into the study and have a look while you do something about dinner. Unless you'd rather eat out?"

"I'm too tired to change clothes. I'll thaw something." I dragged myself into the kitchen and searched the freezer, thinking as I did so that it was now only a little over two weeks until Christmas, and I had absolutely nothing in the house to cook for a festive dinner.

There wouldn't be a festive dinner unless Bill was found.

I didn't feel like cooking, and the only ready-cooked food I could find was the remains of a pot of soup I'd made on the first chilly day of fall. It hadn't been wonderful then, but I'd thought as I'd frozen it that I'd add a few things later, doll it up a bit. I was too tired now, and besides I didn't care. I knew, rationally, that food mattered, but I couldn't make myself believe it. When it was hot and I'd dragged out some rather stale crackers to go with it, I called Alan in.

He made no complaint about the meal. Either he realized I was in no mood for criticism, or he truly didn't notice. I suppose if a man has spent quite a lot of his life eating quick meals when and where he can find the time, often from the police canteen, he loses his critical palate. At any rate, he spooned up the soup obediently while I toyed with mine, making desultory conversation. When he had put down his spoon, he cleared his throat.

"I found some markings in the atlas."

"Oh? Notes, you mean?"

"No. They're rather odd, really. I hadn't time, of course, to go through the whole book, and the markings are very faint, but all of them—all I could find, at any rate—are on the map of Indiana."

"But, Alan, that is odd! Surely Bill's never been to Indiana in his life."

"Not using this atlas, at any rate. It's the current edition."

"So what are they, the marks, I mean?"

"They're in blue pencil, very faint, as I said, and they're underlinings of certain towns. Or villages, I should think, by the size of the type."

"Could they be places he wanted to visit? Maybe he was planning—I mean, maybe they're honeymoon ideas. Jane said they weren't going on a trip, but Bill might have had plans he hadn't told her about."

"Well, I'd have no idea, of course, knowing next to nothing about the state. Perhaps you should take a look."

With relief, I left my soup and went with Alan to his study. The atlas, open to the Indiana pages, was spread out on the desk under a good light. I sat down to take a look.

After a minute or two I looked up at my husband. "Alan, this makes no sense at all. These are tiny places, all of them. I imagine the biggest attraction in town is the grain elevator. Why would anybody want to visit Donaldson, Indiana? Or Tiosa? Or Spring Grove, or Laketon, or Rolling Prairie, for heaven's sake? I was a lifelong Hoosier till I moved here, and I've never even heard of most of these places. The only one I've ever been to is Rolling Prairie, and that was because I got lost one time, wandering around the northern part of the state."

"There wouldn't be an historical thread, perhaps? Bill's an historian. Let's see—something to do with Indian wars, perhaps?"

"I have no idea. To tell the truth, I was never much interested in American history, beyond the high points. I know a little about the Indian tribes that lived in the southern part of the state, near Hillsburg, because I had to teach it in fourth grade, but as for battles! The only one I can remember at all was called the Battle of Tippecanoe, involving an Indian they called The Prophet, who was the brother of someone named Tecumseh. And I don't even remember the details of that one, but I know where it happened, and it wasn't at any of these places." I tapped the map. "If Bill is following some kind of historical trail, he knows a whole lot more of the history of my home than I do."

"That isn't impossible, of course, but I admit it's unlikely. What else could there be? Does he have a hobby, do you suppose? Something obscure, like collecting—um—arrowheads?"

I held up my hands in despair. "Alan, these are little farming communities, all of them. If there ever were any arrowheads around, they would long since have been plowed back into the soil, or found by the kids in the town. When I was little, I used to find an arrowhead occasionally, but I don't think any child I taught for at least the last twenty years ever found one, even when we did local history and they were thinking about the Indians." I yawned desperately. "I'm sorry, I just can't think. I'm too tired, and I'm too worried about Bill. Maybe I'll be brighter in the morning."

"You're too worried to sleep, probably. Take a pill, love, or you won't get any rest at all."

I almost never need a sleep-aid, but I keep a supply of the over-the-counter stuff in the house, just in case. Alan was right. That night I needed something that would turn off my mind, with its visions of nice old Bill, out in the cold and wet, in trouble . . .

I took the pill and knew no more until Alan woke me next morning with a cup of steaming, fragrant coffee. The sun was shining as brightly as if it had never stopped. I wished I were feeling as clear of mind and spirit.

The first words out of my mouth were, "Any news?"

Alan shook his head. I felt like turning over and burrowing back into the soft, comfortable world of sleep, but it was hopeless. My train of thought had already picked up speed and would certainly not let me get off.

50

I was hungry. I felt guilty about it, as if not eating would be more appropriate, but I'd had very little yesterday and I wanted food. Alan had fried bacon and scrambled some eggs, so I ate an abundant, if hasty, meal, and then went straight to Alan's study to confront that atlas again.

I did everything I could think of to try to wrest meaning from the markings. I made a list of the hamlets that were marked. I consulted the index at the back of the book for population figures. I noted the counties involved. Nothing seemed to form a pattern.

Pattern. Feeling silly, I put some tracing paper over the map and tried several connect-the-dots routines to see if a picture appeared. It didn't, at least not any that I could recognize.

Well, maybe there was some sort of code hidden here. I counted numbers of letters in the names of the towns. I tried letter substitutions. I tried acrostics. I tried scrambling the letters. I even entered a few of them into a crossword diagram to see if any of the names took on a different meaning in combination.

Nothing.

I created routes from one town to the rest, circular routes, zigzagging routes, even alphabetical ones, starting first at one town, then another, through the whole list.

Could the highway numbers have any significance? Or the names of the roads, where they had names? What about the rivers? Were there significant connections?

I came up with a big, fat zero.

At last I threw down my pen in disgust, got up, and stretched. "I give up," I said to Alan, who had come into the study to bring me some coffee. "Bill was playing games, I guess. Maybe he had a new pencil and was just doodling. Maybe he collects place names and liked these for some reason."

"Hmm." Alan put the coffee down and looked at the open pages. "It would have been interesting if he'd marked some of the bigger towns near these ones, wouldn't it?"

"Why?"

"Take a look." He pointed with my pen. "Here, near Rolling Prairie. What a name, incidentally."

"It's nothing like as bad as some English ones," I said indignantly. "What about Upper Piddle? Or Lower Slaughter? Or my very favorite, Oswaldtwistle Moor?"

"You made that one up."

"I did not. I knew someone who knew someone who lived there. It's in Lancashire; look it up for yourself."

"At any rate," said Alan, dismissing this frivolity, "your delightfully named Rolling Prairie is quite close to New Carlisle. That must have been settled by the English, wouldn't you think? And here's Rochester, and Richmond, and North Manchester . . . English place names, or versions of them, dotted all over the map, some of them quite near the villages Bill marked."

"You're right." I looked more closely. "And look

52

here. There are others, too, Dublin and Edinburgh—and look! European ones! Alexandria, and Frankfort—that's pretty much like Frankfurt—and Versailles. They pronounce it Vur-sales, by the way."

Alan winced.

"Yes, I agree. But you're right, it's interesting. In fact, Alan, every single one of these places is very near a bigger town with a British name, or a European one. That simply can't be a coincidence."

"What do you reckon it means? If anything?"

I sat back, my momentary elation gone. "I haven't the slightest idea. Are we back to honeymoon plans, after all?"

"Seems rather convoluted, doesn't it?"

"Yes, and silly, as well. I think it's time to get Jane back into the act. I want to know how she's doing, anyway."

I phoned Jane and asked her over for lunch and consultation. She came in the back door as I was fixing sandwiches, and she looked awful. Again I wondered if she'd slept at all.

"You haven't heard anything?" I asked, though it wasn't really a question.

She shook her head.

I wondered if I could get her to take one of my pills after lunch. She was going to be ill if she kept this up.

I came straight to the point. "We're going to have a bite to eat, and then I want to show you something curious about that atlas. Have a seat; we'll eat in the kitchen."

She shook her head. "Show me now."

There is a time to insist on knowing what's best for someone else, and a time to give way. I led Jane to the study, showed her the markings and the adjacent towns, and asked if Bill had said anything that might give a clue to their significance.

She studied the pages for a long time before she shook her head. "Didn't say anything to me. But might have, to young Tubbs. Let's go."

This time I did insist on lunch, and made Jane eat something, too. When she had half a sandwich inside her, and had looked at her watch for the seventeenth time (I counted), I took pity.

"All right. Off to the museum and Walter. You'll let us know, Alan, if . . ."

He nodded. "The moment I hear."

SIX

JANE AND I FOUND LITTLE TO SAY TO EACH OTHER AS WE trudged across the Cathedral Close. Speculation was futile, and we didn't want to talk about our fears. I saw the dean coming out of one door of the Cathedral as we went in another. I was tempted to hail him, but I feared that his kind sympathy would shatter Jane's fragile composure. She had let me see her cry once. That, for Jane, was a lifetime's allotment. Let her maintain her dignity as long as she could.

"Do you suppose they've searched this place?" I

ventured to ask as we traversed the shadowy south aisle. "It's full of nice medieval nooks and crannies."

"Bound to've. No reason he'd come here, anyway. Bill's not religious."

"Mmm." I wondered briefly how well that boded for their marriage. Jane is quiet about her beliefs, but they are important to her.

I dismissed the thought. Just now other worries loomed larger on the horizon. I tried to shove another thought aside, as well. Even if Bill wouldn't go to the Cathedral of his own volition, there might be good reasons for someone to bring him here. So many hiding places in a fifteenth-century building . . . but Jane was right. The police would have looked here. We went out of the church into the hard bright sunshine.

"Jane! Will the museum be open?" I put a hand on her arm as we turned into the High Street. "Young Tubbs can't neglect his university work indefinitely."

"Don't know. We'll get in somehow."

The building was open, however, and Walter Tubbs was sitting at his desk. This time there were books in front of him and he seemed to be studying. He looked up when we entered, and blinked at us.

"Oh, it's you. Sorry. I was in the fourth century." He gestured at the books. "Roman Britain and all that. They're building roads and drains at the moment. Not frantically thrilling, but I've an essay due tomorrow. Have you heard anything about Mr. Fanshawe?"

"No, but I suppose no news is good news." Walter

didn't look impressed by the cliché, and neither did Jane. I realized it had been a pretty stupid thing to say, and changed the subject. "Walter, we've come with more roads for you to look at, modern ones this time." I took the atlas out from under my arm and thrust it at him. "Or at least, the places the roads lead to. This is the book we found in Bill's desk yesterday, and we found some markings in it. We wondered if you'd have any idea what they're all about. Open it to the Indiana pages and have a look."

He studied it for a few moments and then looked up, bewildered. "I suppose he was planning to go and see these places. But I don't know why, or when. He hadn't said anything to me about a trip to America. I'll take a closer look, if you'd like to leave it with me."

He was speaking about Bill in the past tense. I hoped Jane hadn't caught it. "I suppose we might as well. We don't seem to have learned anything from it, and you just might come up with something if you think about it for a little while. Or more likely, if you don't think about it. At least that's the way my mind works." I was babbling. I took a deep breath. "Of course, the markings don't have to have any significance. Maybe he was just doodling."

"He did that a lot. Mostly on his desk pad, though. I wouldn't have thought he'd deface a book."

That was an aspect that hadn't occurred to me. Yes, it *was* odd that a curator would write in a book. A modern book, true, and one whose lasting value was limited, but still . . . "Well, he did write in this one. For whatever reason. Or wait! I don't know why we're assuming the marks are Bill's. We found the atlas in his desk, but that doesn't necessarily mean he made the marks."

"I think he did, though. He had a thing about blue pencils. I don't know anyone else who uses them."

"Ah. Well, we may never know why—um, maybe we'll only know when we can ask him."

This time Jane did notice. She looked at me, her face dull with misery, and then turned away.

I bit my lip. There was nothing I could do to comfort her, nothing, apparently, I could do to help. I'd tried every way I could think of to find Bill, but nothing had worked. I exchanged a look with Walter; we both shook our heads.

"Well, Walter, I suppose we've bothered you long enough. You're putting in an awful lot of extra time here, aren't you?"

"It doesn't matter. I don't really have anyplace else to go. I mean, I can study here better than where I'm living. And I'm happy to be here, if it's any help to Mr. Fanshawe. I only wish . . ."

We both wished. Wishing didn't help. "It's nice of you, all the same. Will you be here tomorrow, then, in case we think of something?"

"I have to be. There's some kind of donors' meeting in a few days, and I need to try to get ready for it. I saw it in Mr. Fanshawe's diary."

"Diary? He kept a diary?"

Walter looked puzzled. "Of course."

"Not the journal sort," Jane explained to me. "Calendar. Engagement book."

Walter still didn't understand, but I didn't enlighten him about the differences in our common language. "Yes," he said. "Quite a nice one, black leather, with his initials. Anyway, I don't suppose I'll be much use to the donors, but I thought I should be here. People like that can get awfully waxy if they feel neglected."

"Surely they'll know about Bill, wouldn't you think?"

"Probably. But I don't know who's to be there, exactly. The note in the diary simply says 'Donors.' It might be two people, or a crowd. So I can't phone them to make sure they know about Mr. Fanshawe, and . . ." He trailed off again.

I felt sorry for him. He sounded forlorn, and very young. I tried for a moment to imagine being eighteen or so, with no better place to go than a small, not very exciting museum. "I'm sure you'll deal with them just fine," I said briskly, and smiled at him. "By the way, I left a lot of bags full of stuff here the other day and forgot all about them. Do you have them?"

He produced the bags. I bundled everything together as comfortably as possible and headed for the door. "Come on, Jane. Home. You can help me when some of these threaten to fall out of my arms."

She followed silently, slowly, as if reluctant to leave. I could sympathize, but there was nothing more we could do there. I intended to spend the afternoon trying to catch up on Christmas, and then I was going to try to get Jane to take a sleeping pill, by bullying if nothing else worked. Maybe if I thought about something else for a while, and Jane got the first good rest she'd had in days, one of us might have a bright idea.

"I gave him that diary," she said as we walked home. That was all, but all her fear and worry were somehow condensed into that single sentence.

Alan and I put up the Christmas tree that afternoon. My heart wasn't in it. The tree was a small one, English style, that fit nicely on a table by the bay window. We'd picked it out a week ago, and I'd looked forward to decorating it. Now it was just a chore. I tried hard to get into the mood, but I kept thinking about Jane and her Bill. I'd hardly known him, but she was my best friend, and the poor woman was coming apart at the seams. She was trying to cling to the hope that he was still alive, but I could see that hope waning. As for me, I felt as useless as I ever had in my life. I was supposed to be kind of good at figuring things out, and I hadn't come up with one single good idea.

Every time the phone rang, I jumped, hoping it might be good news, fearing it might be bad. And every time it was no news at all, just friends or Alan's family calling about inconsequential matters. They were kind, pleasant, and friendly. I could have screamed at every one of them.

I wrapped some presents that evening, rather listlessly, and then went over to Jane's with one of my magic pills.

She was sitting in her kitchen waiting morosely for

a pot of coffee to steep. Even the bulldogs were subdued, reflecting their mistress's mood as animals so often do.

"Late for a visit," she growled.

"I know. I'm sorry, but I'm worried about you. I mean really worried, Jane. You're going to be in really bad shape if you don't get some sleep. Have you ever taken a sleeping pill?"

She shook her head and reached for the coffeepot. Gently, I stayed her hand.

"Jane, listen to me. How many times, when I've been upset, unhappy, beside myself with worry, have you held my hand and dried my tears, figuratively, at least?"

"Mmph. Didn't do anything much."

"Yes, you did, and you know it. And not just for me, but for virtually anybody in this town who was in trouble. You've bullied us, cajoled us, fed us, done whatever was needed, and always for our own good. Now it's time I did something for your good. Please, for my sake if not for your own, take one of these tonight. They're not narcotic, but they work. You'll sleep well, you'll feel better in the morning, and you'll be ready tomorrow to help me do whatever needs to be done. I can't do this all myself, Jane. Please."

That was a cheap shot, but it did the trick—that, or the quite genuine quaver in my voice. Wordlessly she accepted a pill out of the bottle and swallowed it with a swig of the water I provided.

"Now what?" she growled. "Do I fall over in five minutes?"

"No, you get ready for bed, take a warm bath, read a little—whatever will relax you. In about half an hour you'll be really sleepy and want to turn out the light. I'll look in on you tomorrow. And thanks, Jane."

I slipped out, mission accomplished, and went to bed early myself. I tried, before I dropped off, to think hard about all I'd learned at the museum, in the hopes that some part of my brain would keep working on the problem after my conscious mind had set it aside.

I also said a fervent prayer for Bill, wherever he was, and for Jane.

Maybe it was the prayer that did it, or perhaps my mind did keep on working. At any rate, I woke very early on Thursday, long before dawn, with an idea. It was so urgent an idea that I woke Alan, who was still snoring peacefully.

"Mmph?"

"Are you awake?"

"Mmph."

"Alan, do wake up. Really, I mean. I want to talk to you."

"I'm awake."

He wasn't, though. He's mastered the art of talking in his sleep on such occasions. So I got up, made coffee, and fed the cats, all in a fever of impatience. I made all the noise I possibly could, and it worked. He appeared in the kitchen just as I was about to take coffee up to him.

"There you are, finally."

He looked pointedly at the kitchen clock, whose hands hadn't quite made it to six-thirty.

"I know, but I have an idea, a really good idea, and I need you to call Derek and get things moving."

He took the cup of coffee I thrust into his hand. "This is about Bill?" He sounded fully awake now.

"What else? Listen, something I heard yesterday started me thinking. Bill's assistant at the museum was talking about Roman Britain, and the roads and sewers and things the Romans built, and it reminded me. Isn't there a system of Roman sewer tunnels under Sherebury?"

"Yes. Well, they were Roman originally. They were enlarged considerably in medieval times, and then later—"

"Yes, okay, but the point is, where can you get into them?"

"There were once entrances from most of the important buildings in town, I believe, but they've been blocked off. The tunnels aren't at all safe, you know. They haven't been shored up for hundreds of years, some of them."

"Was there an entrance from the Town Hall?"

"Certainly there used to be at one time." Alan put down his coffee cup. "Are you thinking what I think you're thinking?"

"Why not? If there was once an entrance, even if it was boarded up, it could have been opened again. After all, Bill saw to a lot of renovations when the museum opened. He could have found plans and discovered the entrance."

"Dorothy, even if the entrance exists, why would Bill have gone there on Monday?"

"How do I know? Maybe he wanted to get a better look at the tunnel, with an idea to using it for storage, or opening it up as a part of the museum. It's part of Sherebury history, after all. I don't *know* why he might have gone there. I just think it's a possibility worth exploring. He hasn't been found anywhere else, after all, and everyone's just about run out of suggestions."

Alan considered that. He began to nod slowly. "You're right, love. It may be far-fetched, but we can't neglect any possibility. I'll ring Derek."

I prepared a very quick breakfast while Alan made the call, but we would have had time to eat it twice over before the inspector was finally found. He'd been called out very early on an important drugs case and hadn't returned to the office. The sergeant on night duty assured Alan she'd have Derek ring up as soon as he was able.

He did better than call. He turned up on our doorstep.

"I was nearby when they reached me on the mobile," he said when I answered the doorbell, "so I thought I might as well pop in."

"Come in, Derek. I'm really glad to see you! And you look awfully cold. Would you like some coffee, and have you had breakfast?"

"Yes, I would, and no, I haven't."

So I made more toast and boiled another couple of eggs while Alan told him my theory.

Derek, bless his heart, took it seriously. "You may have something there. I ought to have thought of it, but I didn't. The planning office has a map of the old tunnels. Suppose I go and fetch it and meet you at the museum."

We were very near the shortest, darkest day of the year. I shivered in the foggy predawn gloom as I waited for Alan to get the car out of our minute garage.

"Not propitious weather," he commented when I got into the car.

"No." I pulled my woolly orange hat down over my ears and wished I were in California, or Spain, or my own front parlor. Anywhere warm.

I was still shivering when we reached the museum. The car hadn't had time to heat up. "I hope the place is open," I said as I got out. "It's so early. I hadn't thought of that."

"Young Walter must be at work already," said Alan, trying the front door. "It's unlocked."

There were no lights in the front hall, but of course the museum wasn't officially open yet. Perhaps Walter had left them off on purpose, or a lightbulb had burned out. We felt our way up the half flight of stairs to the museum entrance.

There were no lights on there, either. A streetlight outside one of the windows did little to dispel the inky blackness of the room. "Alan," I whispered, clutching his arm. I'd thought I'd overcome my childhood fear of the dark, but I didn't like this.

Alan put his hand over my arm and moved cautiously forward. "I'll find a light. Walter must be working upstairs. I think there's a lamp on Bill's desk—oh!"

"What? What is it? Alan?"

He took a step back, pulling me with him. "Stay there. Don't move."

"Alan, you're scaring me! What *is* it?"

"I don't know yet. We have to have light. I'm going to let go your hand, but *don't move*."

I stood as one petrified while Alan very cautiously moved away from me. I heard him patting what I thought was Bill's desk, and then there was a click, and a dim lamp cast a circle of light around the desk.

I gasped.

Walter Tubbs lay slumped across Bill's desk, and something was very wrong with the back of his head.

SEVEN

"DON'T TOUCH HIM. DON'T MOVE." ALAN'S VOICE HAD overtones I had never heard before. This was Chief Constable Nesbitt, not my husband. I stayed where I was and concentrated on keeping my breakfast where I had put it.

Alan, moving with a catlike lightness surprising in

so large a man, stepped over to Walter and put two fingers on the side of his neck.

"He's alive," Alan said quietly. "Only just, I think. I'll ring for help, but I'm afraid we'll have to compromise the scene somewhat. The boy needs immediate attention." Quickly he went through the ABCs of first aid—clear the airway, check for breathing and circulation—and then picked up the phone and dialed 999.

It seemed hours before the ambulance and Derek arrived, almost simultaneously. I didn't wait to be asked to leave. Much as I wanted to help, I realized I would only be in the way. These people knew what they were doing, and would do everything they could for Walter. My business was to keep from destroying evidence, and I could do that best somewhere else.

But where? Back in the car? Alan had the keys, and he was busy helping.

My eyes lit on a table just inside the museum door. A small book lay on it, a dusty, tattered paperback with the words "Medieval Sherebury" on it. I looked more closely. Could this have been something Walter had found?

No, probably not. When I adjusted my bifocals, I saw that there was a stamped marking: "Sherebury Planning Commission." And in small print under the title were the words "A Plan of the Roman and Medieval Tunnel System."

This must be the book Derek had brought with him! Without an instant's hesitation I picked it up and carried it out of the room.

Derek and his crew had turned on lights as they came in. I leaned against the stair rail in the foyer of the museum and squinted at the map. The light out here was dim and the print in the book was faded, but I persevered.

The book, or pamphlet really, was like a tiny atlas, dividing the city of Sherebury into eight sections, with a detailed, large-scale map of each. The tunnel system and its entrances were marked in what must once have been bright red ink. It had faded to a dirty yellow, but I could make out, barely, the tunnel that ran right under the Town Hall. At the bottom of the page was some tiny print. I fumbled in my purse for the small flashlight I always carry and turned it on the book.

Ah! There it was, the entry numbered 7: "Town Hall. Entrance in northwest corner of cellar. Covered by paneling, with latch."

I made my creaky, arthritic way down to the cellar.

It was a real cellar, originally a wine cellar, probably. One story below the basement level of the building, it was accessible by a rather nasty, cobwebby enclosed staircase. I had been there once before on a tour of the building, and I didn't relish the thought of going down again. I cannot bring myself to like spiders or any reminder of their presence.

This time, however, the cobwebs were less bothersome. Oh, a few were in evidence, but they didn't brush my face in that disgusting, shivery manner. Either someone had been doing some housekeeping down here, or someone else had passed here very recently.

I quickened my pace.

I remembered that the cellar itself was rather splendid, more like the crypt of a cathedral. It was really cellars: several large though low-ceilinged rooms with Gothic-arched roof and stone walls and floors. The wine racks that had originally lined the walls had been removed, but the oak paneling behind them had not. The paneling covered the walls from floor almost to ceiling, and amazingly had not warped very much over the centuries, as I recalled. The cellar, unlike many of its kind, was remarkably dry.

I remembered a good many odds and ends had been stored here the last time I was down. Now, as I discovered when I found the switch to the single dim bulb hanging from the ceiling, the room was nearly bare except for dust.

Now to find the northwest corner.

Yes, but which northwest corner? In this room, or another? And for that matter, which way was northwest? I've never been wonderful about directions, even aboveground. In a place where there are no windows I'm lost. I cast my glance and the beam of my flashlight rather helplessly around the room I was in. It had five sides, rather than four, and every corner looked exactly like every other.

Wait, though. Were those footprints in the dust?

The dust had certainly been disturbed in what looked like a path from where I stood to one of the corners. It was hard to tell by the feeble light whether I was seeing footprints or not, but the hairs on the back of my neck twitched uncomfortably, and I felt my mouth going dry.

I hadn't even told Alan where I was going.

I should have turned tail right then, I suppose. I almost did. The police were right upstairs, after all. Let them take it from here. I didn't like this place. My claustrophobia was reaching out its clutching, suffocating tentacles, and my nerves were stretched taut.

But the police were dealing with a boy who was badly hurt and might die. If Bill was down here, hurt, and I delayed long enough to climb several steep flights of stairs, he might die, too. I could just take a look. I was on my guard, after all. And no one would be lurking down here, surely.

I wasn't convinced, though. My feet moved most unwillingly toward the corner. If a mouse or, horrors, a rat had appeared I would have screamed the place down. The flashlight in my hand trembled as I played the light over the paneling, trying to see some sort of secret spring.

It turned out to be not very secret. The paneling was carved in rectangles, not anything fancy like linenfold, and a bottom corner of one rectangle had a square cut out of it, about four by four inches. I put my hand into the recess, trying hard not to think about spiders, and found a metal ring that turned.

The section of paneling opened with a creak of rusty hinges that sounded like every horror movie I'd ever seen. I gripped my flashlight until my knuckles were white, gulped once, and called into the black hole, "Bill?"

No sound came out. I cleared my throat and tried again, but I couldn't hear any reply over the pounding of my heart.

This was ridiculous. I had either to muster the courage to go into that awful, black place, or hightail it upstairs and get help. Taking several long, deep breaths, and trying to hold my flashlight steady, I crept forward.

The cobwebs were very much in evidence here. I stuck my hand out as far in front of me as I could, moving the flashlight in circles to brush them from the ceiling, before I went very far. Then I shone the light on the floor, in case there were stairs in that blackness.

The first thing I saw was another flashlight, lying on the stone floor a few feet inside the doorway.

The next thing was a foot.

My breath came in shallow gasps. I wondered briefly what a heart attack felt like, but the thought passed out of my mind instantly. With the utmost reluctance I moved the beam of the flashlight to play on the face of the man on the floor.

On Bill's face.

That broke my fear. Sorrow and pity washed over me in a rush, wiping out any other feeling. I knelt stiffly on the hard flagstones and put my hand to his face. "Bill?" I whispered.

But the touch had told me that Bill would not

answer. The cellar was cold, but not that cold. Bill's face held the chill, not of a cold room, but of the grave.

I knelt a moment longer and said a prayer for Bill, and for Jane, and then slowly got to my feet. I knew I must not disturb the scene any more than I already had, but I needed to try to make sense of this dreadful thing. I could see no visible injury to Bill. There was no blood on the floor, nothing except dust, scuffed by his feet and mine. If there were any other footprints, they were beyond my discerning. His hands—I looked more closely, shining my flashlight on them. They showed no signs of a struggle, no broken fingernails that I could see, no scratches. His right hand lay partly under his body and—yes! There was something in it! A piece of paper?

I took one step forward, and then stepped back. No. This was a matter for the police. It was time, and past time, to go and get them. And then my job was to tell Jane.

It seemed to me that I had been gone for hours, but in fact only a few minutes had passed since I left the main room of the museum. No one had missed me. They had taken Walter away, to the hospital, I hoped. The room was a scene of intense, but controlled, activity. Men and women with cameras and measuring tapes and small plastic bags made careful rounds. Lights had been set up, illuminating the scene with a dazzling glare. Alan stood off to one side, conferring with Derek. I wanted to rush to him for comfort, but I

71

knew I mustn't trample over the crime scene any more than I already had. I stood in the doorway and waved, and when I caught his eye, I beckoned to him.

He came to me at once. "What's wrong?"

He has always been able to read my face. "I've found Bill," I said, and the tone of my voice told him the rest.

"Derek," said Alan. His voice was quiet but commanding. I think that for a moment he truly forgot that he wasn't Derek's boss anymore. Derek forgot, too. At least he moved to Alan with alacrity and the air, if not the actual gesture, of a salute.

"We have a serious complication, Derek. Tell him, Dorothy."

I told him. I think I was crying by that time, but it didn't matter. Alan had put a comforting arm around my shoulders, and I was able to be coherent.

"You're certain he's dead?" asked Derek.

I nodded, shivering. I didn't want to talk about why I was sure. "I left the door open. You won't have any trouble finding him. And I didn't go in any farther than I had to. I really did have to, Alan. He might have been alive. I know I might have disturbed something, but—"

"Hush, love. It's all right. We'll take over now."

"Don't leave me!" It was almost a wail. The instant it was out of my mouth I would have given anything to take it back. Was this any way for a policeman's wife to act? Where was my much vaunted independence?

Alan tightened his hold. "I won't. Don't worry. It's all right," he repeated.

I swallowed. "I don't mean to keep you from what you have to do, but I want to know—well, I guess I want to know how Walter is." That was a sop to my pride, of course, but I really was worried about him. At least I had been before my discovery of Bill overshadowed other concerns.

"There's nothing I need do here. Derek has everything under control. I'm a supernumerary anyway. Nothing quite as bad as an old general who won't quit, eh, Derek?"

"Not at all, sir. You know we're always happy for your help, but perhaps your place now is with your wife." He was being very formal, and very careful of Alan's feelings.

"Oh, get on with it, man!" He gave Derek an apologetic half smile, and led me to a bench on the landing. "Now, as to young Walter. He's not good, I'm afraid. They won't know exactly the extent of his injuries until they take a good look, at the hospital."

I shuddered. "The back of his head looked awful."

"Yes, he was hit pretty hard. His skull was cracked, I think. But actually that may be all to the good. There'll be swelling, and that crack may allow the skull enough movement that the pressure on the brain won't cause too much damage. If not, they may have to open up the crack, or open the cranium elsewhere to relieve the pressure. That's the real danger."

"Will he have permanent brain damage?"

"I don't know, love. Nobody knows yet. If they can minimize the swelling, there's apparently a pretty good chance for recovery, but the ambulance crew thought he'd been lying unconscious for quite a long time. That could be bad."

I nodded. It helped to think about Walter and not about poor Bill. "He said he was coming to the museum today to prepare for a meeting with some of the donors. I suppose he could have stayed late last night, working."

Alan frowned. "I don't understand."

"Well, the meeting, the appointment, had been made with Bill, of course. Walter said it was set for a few days from now. He didn't say exactly when. And Walter couldn't figure out who all was coming, but he thought he ought to turn up, in case some of the people—whoever was coming—hadn't heard Bill was missing and kept the appointment. And Walter's a conscientious boy, if not terribly bright. He probably wanted to try to find out who was coming, learn a little about them, or what they had given, or something. Bill's filing system isn't—wasn't—oh, dear! I don't know how to talk about him."

"I know, love, I know. It's a bad thing. Did you get any impression about how Bill died?"

"Alan, there wasn't a mark on him. Not that I could see, anyway. I'd swear he died a natural death. But what on earth was he doing burrowing around down there in the tunnel?"

"We may never know, Dorothy. The only thing I

know for certain right now is that something very odd is going on around this museum, and I intend to find out what. I didn't know Bill well, but Jane is a friend, and poor Walter is just a kid. They don't deserve this."

I got up, stricken. "Jane. Alan, we have to go to Jane."

EIGHT

JANE TOOK THE NEWS BETTER THAN I HAD FEARED SHE would. She was barely awake, for one thing. It was still early, and the pill I'd talked her into taking the evening before had worked well. She looked a little groggy when she answered my knock on her back door, although she had a cup of coffee in her hand.

Alan was with me. I think that was Jane's first clue. She looked at us with no expression, and then stood aside and gestured us in.

Alan was marvelous. He waited until she had poured us coffee, unasked, and sat down, and then said, "Jane, it's about Bill."

She put down her cup and looked at him. "Go ahead," she said gruffly.

"I think you have an idea of what I must tell you."

She sat silent for a moment, and then sipped some coffee, her hand shaking. She cleared her throat. "Dead, isn't he? Has been all along."

"I'm afraid so. We don't think he suffered at all."

"Exposure?" She was keeping her voice steady.

"No. He wasn't outside. He'd gone to the tunnel under the museum, and must have had a heart attack."

"You found him?"

"I did," I said, my voice cracking a bit. "He looked quite peaceful, Jane." He'd looked awful, dead and cold and horrid. I wasn't about to tell Jane that.

"Why'd you go down there?"

"What Walter said about Roman Britain reminded me of the tunnels, and I just thought Bill might have gone there for some reason. I really don't know why the idea entered my head. It was just that he wasn't anywhere else, and . . ." I trailed off. I was babbling again.

"Have to ask Walter."

I looked at Alan, hesitating. Let him make this call. He'd known Jane longer than I had. "Yes," he said finally, "we will ask him, but not just now. He's been hurt, and is in hospital."

"Hurt how?" Jane's voice was sharp.

"A blow to the back of the head. We don't know much more than that. Now," said Alan, briskly changing the subject, "would you like to come and stay with us for a while? We've plenty of room."

"No." Jane's eyes were dry, her face stiff. "Dogs need a run. I'll be all right."

I was about to argue, but Alan squeezed my hand and shook his head at me. "That's a good idea. A brisk walk, and then come over for breakfast. Come, Dorothy."

He hustled me out the back door. I protested the minute we were out of earshot. "Alan, should we leave her alone?"

"She's grown up, love. She knows what's best for her. Remember how angry she was when she was talking about Bill's caregivers and their smothering kindness. Treat her like a sensible adult."

"You're right, but—oh, darn it, it's hard!"

"It is. You note I did shelter her from the details of the attack on Walter's life."

"You think that's what it was? Not just some sort of robbery attempt gone wrong?"

"We don't know, of course. The place was pretty well ransacked."

I made a shocked noise.

"Yes, I thought you didn't notice. It was dark when we went in, of course, and then we had eyes for nothing but Walter. In any case, they were subtle about it. Nothing tossed about or broken, but lots of things in slight disarray. It didn't look like robbery, more like someone hunting for something."

"And they hit Walter so they could do it."

"They probably thought they'd killed him. Certainly they stayed for some time after he was knocked out, and didn't try to help him. Dorothy, if you hadn't had your bright idea, if he hadn't been found when he was, his brain would have gone on swelling, and he would have died."

"So maybe I helped him, even if it was too late for poor Bill?"

"Exactly. Now"—as he opened our back door—"suppose you lie down for a bit while I keep an eye out for Jane's return."

I did as Alan suggested. I felt as though I'd been hit over the head like Walter.

Well, no, I didn't, of course. Poor Walter's life was in danger, or might be, and I lay there in a comfortable bed feeling sorry for myself because I felt tired and discouraged.

And guilty. If only I'd had my bright idea about the tunnel sooner! Bill might still be alive. Walter might not have been hurt.

I turned over and pummeled my pillow, which refused to cooperate. Lying on my front made my knees hurt. And my back. I turned to my side and pounded the pillow again.

If Walter died, it would be my fault. Where did I get off thinking I was some kind of detective? Anybody with an ounce of sense ought to have thought of those tunnels ages ago.

Nobody else did, though, did they?

Well, no, but . . .

And you don't know when Bill died. It might have been instantaneous.

True, but . . .

And punishing yourself won't accomplish a thing. Your martyr's hat is getting a trifle threadbare. Throw it out.

I often have conversations with myself, but this time the voice of reason spoke quite distinctly in Alan's

78

accents. I sighed, gave him a mental salute, and went to sleep.

I woke after an hour or so. I'd had plenty of sleep the night before, after all, and closing my eyes at this hour of the day never did much for me. But I woke somewhat refreshed, and certainly in a better mood.

I went down to the kitchen and started a pot of coffee, and then went in search of Alan. He was in his study, but not, this time, at his computer. In fact, he was just finishing a phone call.

I barely gave him a chance to cradle the receiver. "Have you seen Jane? Is she all right?"

"As well as can be expected. She came back with the dogs about fifteen minutes ago. She wouldn't have breakfast, just popped in to tell me she was driving to the hospital to see young Walter."

"Oh, dear! I hope he's not—I hope he's better."

"I rang up. He's still unconscious, but they're working on bringing down the swelling. They seem cautiously optimistic."

"How did you find out all that? I've never known a hospital to give anybody any information about a patient except the one-word description of his condition. You know, 'critical, serious, guarded'—those words that don't really mean much."

"A policeman has certain privileges. Even a retired policeman. I've learned quite a lot in an hour on the phone."

"Well, come and have a cup of coffee with me and tell me everything you know."

"For a start," he said when we were settled at the kitchen table, "you'll want to know about that piece of paper that was in Bill's hand when you found him."

"Oh!" I sat up straighter. "I'd forgotten all about it, to tell you the truth. I'm slipping."

"Not surprising, under the circumstances. But I think you'll be quite interested in what Derek told me."

"For heaven's sake, Alan!"

"Yes, well, all right. I could draw this out, of course, but I won't. Bill was holding a letter, an old letter, by the look of it. There is no date, but the paper is creased and dirty, and somewhat yellowed and chipped and so on. There's no name of sender or addressee, no return address, and no signature. In fact the last sentence on the page is incomplete, so it looks as though what we have is the first page of two or more. But the text of the letter is of interest, because it contains—are you ready for this?—the place names that Bill marked on that map of Indiana."

"But—I don't understand. Was the letter written to Bill? Suggesting some places he ought to go, maybe?"

"It was headed 'Dear Waffles.' I asked Jane, when she was here a few minutes ago, whether Bill was ever nicknamed Waffles. She thought not."

"It's an awfully old-fashioned kind of nickname, anyway," I said thoughtfully. "The sort of thing one might find in a Dorothy Sayers novel, or even P. G. Wodehouse. Ever so frightfully public-school, what?"

Alan grimaced at my imitation of an upper-class British accent.

"And Bill wasn't that sort at all," I pursued, "and he was just a child in the thirties. On the other hand, what would Bill have been doing with someone else's letter, down there in the catacombs?"

"Search me. That, of course, is what Derek is trying to find out. One of the things. Do you want to hear the rest of my news?"

"I haven't had time to deal with this bit yet, but go ahead."

"Well, you remember I said the museum looked as though the intruders were looking for something?"

"Intruders? There was more than one?"

"Plural for convenience. We don't know yet how many there might have been. At any rate, Derek and his people have been searching through the mess, trying to work out what ought to be there and isn't. And so far, two things seem to be missing. One is Bill's diary. Sorry, 'engagement calendar' to you Yanks. They can't find it anywhere."

"But that could be really important! If we knew who Bill had seen on that last morning—"

"Exactly. That's why Derek put particular emphasis on finding it. Now it's still possible they may find it. Walter might have taken it home with him, or it could be in that rabbit warren of an office upstairs. They'll keep looking."

"It's certainly suggestive, though. That it's missing, I mean."

"It is. And the other thing that's missing—care to hazard a guess?"

I thought hard, and then looked at Alan with dawning comprehension. "The atlas?"

"Got it in one. The atlas. That carefully marked atlas with all the place names—the same place names that are in the letter. Now what do you make of that?"

NINE

WELL, I COULDN'T MAKE ANYTHING OF IT AT ALL. So Alan and I sat over our coffee, brewing another pot, until we had ingested enough caffeine to keep a grizzly bear awake all winter. We got ourselves thoroughly wired, but we didn't come up with anything very useful.

We began hopefully enough. "All right," I said briskly, stirring sugar into my coffee, "let's start with the missing stuff. Why would someone steal an appointment book and an atlas? Maybe—maybe Bill kept his address book in the back of his calendar, as I do. Maybe—um—someone wanted to look up addresses in the atlas."

"In a road atlas of the American states." Alan's tone was carefully neutral.

"Oh. And most of Bill's addresses would be around here, I suppose. Or in the UK, anyway."

"In any case, if there were addresses in the diary, they were copies. Bill kept an address book in his desk. Quite a nice one, leather bound."

"Okay, scratch that idea. Wait! Maybe Walter took them home himself. I don't remember when he said he saw it—before or after Bill disappeared. He might have wanted to try again to figure out who was supposed to be coming to that meeting. And he said he wanted to study the atlas, to get an idea of why it was marked."

"Yes, but you gave him the atlas yesterday. And the paramedics don't think he was attacked this morning—more like yesterday afternoon or evening. That means he never left the museum last night. When would he have taken the things home?"

I shook my head. "Poor Walter. Lying there for all those hours in that cold place—well, at least he wasn't in pain, I suppose. Not if he was unconscious the whole time. Well, so probably he didn't take the things. Anyway, I just remembered—the museum was ransacked, and the calendar and the atlas are the only things missing. So they *must* have been stolen. Which gets us right back where we started. More coffee?"

"Please." He held up his cup. "You're going too fast, my dear. We don't know for certain what's been stolen. We won't until Derek and his crew have made an exhaustive inventory."

"Which," I said, pouring myself another slug, "will be extremely difficult to do with Bill gone and Walter unconscious. Almost impossible, really."

"A nasty job, certainly. There is a catalogue of acquisitions, but it won't list every single paper clip and pencil in the place. The diary and the atlas won't be in there, for example."

I sighed. "I must say I don't envy them the job. Reminds me of cleaning out a gigantic attic, except worse, because nothing can be thrown away. You know, Alan, eventually somebody's going to have to sort through all the piles up there in Bill's storage area. I suppose the job officially belongs to Walter, now that Bill's gone, but the poor boy won't be up to it for a long time. If ever. I *wish* I knew how he was doing. Do you suppose you could call the hospital again?"

"It's only been an hour or so since I called," Alan pointed out.

"Well, I'm going over there. We're not getting anywhere, and I can't stand it, not knowing."

"I'll drive you, then. I confess I'd like to see for myself."

I wasn't at all sure they'd let us in, but once more Alan's influence was a help. With strict instructions not to touch the patient, not to talk, and especially not to disturb any of the tubes and wires, we were allowed five minutes in the ICU.

I wanted desperately to touch Walter's hand, make sure he was still warm. I would never forget the dreadful coldness of Bill's cheek. Walter looked exactly like a crash dummy, plastic and inhuman. He lay unmoving. I couldn't even detect a rise and fall of his chest, but the monitors displayed rhythmic lines that meant, I presumed, that his pulse and respiration and so on were normal.

Yes, and what about his brain?

We asked the nurse when we had tiptoed out of the room. "We won't know for a bit. Perhaps another twenty-four hours, perhaps longer. He's—you're not family, are you, Mr. Nesbitt?"

"No, just friends. Actually my wife and I found him."

"Yes, I know. Do you know anything about his family?"

Alan looked at me. I shook my head. "I'm afraid I know very little about him, other than that he works at the museum and is reading history at the university. You might check with the registrar, or wherever student records are kept."

"Yes, we've done that, and we talked to the woman where he rooms, but we can't seem to reach his parents. I thought you might know if they're away on holiday, or something."

"Is it—I know you're not supposed to talk about patients' conditions, but is it a case of notifying his family because he might—that is, is he really—" My voice was unsteady. I stopped.

The nurse looked at me with sympathy. "I wish I could tell you he'll do splendidly, but honestly there's no telling yet. He's stable, which is a good sign, but he was very badly hurt."

I cleared my throat. "Yes. I see. There was another woman here to see him a little while ago, wasn't there?"

"Yes. I told her she could look in again in an hour. I

think she went downstairs for some tea."

"Thank you. You've been kind. May we come back too, in a little while?"

"You won't see a change, but yes, you can come and at least look in. I do understand how you feel, but we're doing all we can for him, you know."

"We know." Alan nodded his thanks and tucked my hand over his arm. We went to find Jane.

She was in the hospital canteen, drinking tea from a cardboard cup. She had been, anyway. A lot of the tea was left in the cup and after one look at it I could see why. Jane doesn't take milk in her tea, and the fluid in the cup resembled something one might use to pave roads.

We sat down at her table. "Don't get the tea," she said gruffly.

"I hadn't planned on it. Jane, we just saw Walter."

"Looks like nothing on earth, doesn't he?"

"Well . . . I must admit he doesn't look wonderful. They say he's doing all right, but . . ."

" 'Stable.' Could mean anything."

"Did they ask you about his parents?"

"Yes. Don't know anything. Never talked about his family. Don't think they live around here."

"Where does he live, do you know?"

"Boards with someone, up near the university. Cheap place. Not got a penny to bless himself with, that lad."

"Then I don't suppose his landlady would know any more about his parents."

"Not likely. A shrew, from what I hear."

"Well, maybe he has friends at the university who would know something. It's not that big, the university. Surely somebody . . ."

I trailed off miserably. There was Walter, lying unconscious in a hospital bed. His family didn't know, and he had, apparently, nothing better to go home to than a cheerless room with a shrewish landlady.

"Might do some checking myself," said Jane. "Family needs to know."

I sighed. "I wish there was something I could do."

Jane nodded. "Told you helpless is the worst feeling."

I brooded and wished I could have a decent cup of tea. Was there no way I could help?

Well, there might be, come to think of it. "Alan," I said slowly, "a while ago we talked about somebody needing to go through Bill's storage and workroom at the museum. It's a rat's nest of papers and all sorts of junk, but there might be something interesting, something useful in there. Do you suppose Jane and I—?"

Alan shook his head regretfully. "The whole museum's a crime scene for now, Dorothy. Sealed off. You're right, the storage room needs to be searched, but it'll have to be done by evidence technicians. And it may be several days before they get around to it. Derek's shorthanded, as usual, so they might in a pinch allow me to help, but I'm afraid I haven't a prayer of getting you two in there. In any case, we have to face the fact—I'm sorry, Jane—that as Bill's fiancée, you're an interested party. No one thinks you had any hand in anything that's happened, but . . ." He spread his hands.

I sighed. "Well, as long as someone does it. I suppose maybe they can do some organizing while they're at it. Walter won't want to face that mess when he gets back to work." I didn't admit the possibility that Walter might never get back to work. It hung in the air of the room, as real and heavy as the hospital smell.

We invited Jane over for lunch, but she said she had to feed her dogs. It was just an excuse. She wanted to be alone. My heart ached for her, but Jane is not an easy person to comfort, and she's seldom in any doubt about what she wants.

So Alan and I, saying we'd check with her later, went back, alone, to our house with the Christmas tree in the parlor and the Christmas cards on the mantel and two friendly cats dozing on the hearth rug. It ought to have been a comforting scene, but to me it all seemed infinitely dreary.

We lunched on canned soup and cheese sandwiches. It didn't matter. We were eating to live. One flavor of sawdust tastes much the same as another.

"We never got round to talking about the letter," Alan commented when we had finished and were drinking tea.

"Letter? Oh. The letter." I added milk and sugar to my tea.

"Snap out of it, Dorothy!"

I gave such a start I spilled my tea. Alan had never before shouted at me.

"You're feeling sorry for yourself, and blaming yourself, and working yourself into a fine tizz, and I won't have it. You're not God. You're not even Super-woman. You're a perfectly healthy, sensible, intelligent woman, and I love you, and I'm not going to let you sit there and make yourself miserable."

I made an effort. "I'm sorry, Alan. I know I'm getting gloomy over this. It's just that—well, I've been wondering if I'm getting too old for this sort of thing. My brain seems to be turning to mush. I can't seem to pick up on the obvious. Do you suppose I'm getting—" I couldn't bring myself to say the word.

"Alzheimer's? No, I don't suppose any such thing. You're under stress, that's all. In any case, you didn't miss anything that everyone else didn't also overlook. You thought of the tunnel before I did, or Derek. It was too late. Very well. It might have been too late five minutes after Bill went down there. We don't know how he died. But wallowing in guilt isn't going to help anyone, least of all you. Furthermore, don't you realize I'll love you every bit as much if one day you do turn into a drooling idiot?"

"Oh, Alan!" He took me into his arms, and I cried and cried and, finally, got it out of my system.

"All right," I said, dabbing my eyes and blowing my nose, "the letter. You never did tell me what it said, exactly."

Alan looked me over, decided I'd do, and returned

to business. "Well, it wasn't complete, as I think I mentioned. It was the first page only, beginning 'Dear Waffles' and ending with an incomplete sentence. It was a rather pointless letter, really, telling 'Waffles' all about someone, apparently a friend of both writer and addressee, who was planning a trip to America, to Indiana, in fact."

"When did you say this letter was written?"

"I didn't. It had no date. It looked old, but I'm no expert on these matters."

"Hmm. Do you suppose I could see it?"

"No reason why you couldn't see a copy, I'd think. The original will be in an evidence bag by this time, of course."

"And they will have fingerprinted it, I'm sure. There are ways of lifting very old prints from paper, aren't there?"

"There are, but they won't have done that."

"Why not?"

"Because (a) it's expensive, and (b) the letter is only what we call tangential evidence. Bill didn't die violently, Dorothy. He wasn't murdered. We won't know for sure how he did die until they complete the autopsy, but the betting is on either heart attack or stroke, something cardiovascular. The police are keeping the letter only because Walter was attacked. That's a crime. And Bill was in the tunnel. That's an odd thing. When odd things happen in the vicinity of a crime, we tend to think they're connected."

"You're talking like a policeman."

"I am a policeman. Or I was."

"Well, stop being one for a minute. As an ordinary human being with a good brain, tell me what you think the connection might be between that letter and Bill's death and Walter's attack."

"I think," Alan said slowly, "that Bill died because he was under stress. I think he took that letter down to the tunnel for a reason, but the effort was too much for his system, and he collapsed shortly after he got there."

"Why shortly after he got there? Why couldn't he have been there for a while before he died?"

"For one thing, he wasn't very dirty. His clothes and hair were almost free of cobwebs and dirt. You must have noticed that the tunnel was full of both. If he'd spent much time there, he'd have been covered. Cobwebs are sticky and hard to brush off."

I shuddered. "You're telling me!"

"And the other reason I think he'd only been in there a few minutes was that he still had the paper in his hand."

I frowned. "I don't get that one."

"My dear, what would he have been doing down there except trying to hide that letter? But he hadn't done it, so . . ." Alan spread his hands.

"Hide it. Yes. That makes sense. Except that it doesn't. Why would he have wanted to hide a boring letter about someone's travel plans?"

"I have the feeling that when we know that, we'll know a great deal more about his death and whatever's going on at that museum."

TEN

AFTER WE'D CALLED THE HOSPITAL YET ONCE MORE AND heard that there was no change, I went next door to see how Jane was doing. Really, I suppose, I was restless and wanted to do something, anything. Getting no answer to my knock at the back door, I poked my head in. The dogs, for once, only whined instead of setting up a cacophony of barking.

Jane was asleep in the kitchen rocking chair. She looked, suddenly, very old, and somehow defenseless. I felt like a peeping Tom. She would hate my seeing her without her usual stoic armor. I backed away as quietly as I could, hoping the dogs would stay still, and went back to Alan.

"Sleep is the best thing in the world for her," he said when I told him.

"Yes, but I'm antsy. I feel like Don Quixote. I'm itching to run off in all directions at once, tilting at whatever windmills present themselves."

"Well, then, suppose I go get a copy of the letter, and we can worry over that for a while." So he went over to the police station and came home with not one copy, but two.

We sat down in front of the fire with them. "I can't believe Derek is letting me look at this," I said, shaking my head.

"Only tangential evidence, as I said before, love.

And don't forget you have a few special privileges."

"Wife of VIP. Right." I grinned at him and stuck out my tongue.

"Ah, a prophet is not without honor save in his own home. All right, let's see what this can tell us."

"Read it out loud, Alan. I'm still not too good at English handwriting, and this is old and dirty, besides."

He cleared his throat. "No return address. No date. Here is the text:

Dear Waffles, Good to get your last letter. Sounds as though things are fairly quiet there, ha-ha. I heard from an old friend of yours the other day, Sam Smith. He's going on a little trip soon. Do I recall that you used to know some people in the States? He's going to try to get to Indiana, though travel is difficult these days. Plans to visit some pleasant little towns called Donaldson, Tiosa, Spring Grove, Laketon, and Rolling Prairie. I've not heard of any of them, have you? Then it's on to Mount Auburn—he says he may visit there twice— before he sees Orestes and then rests from his travel in Dabney or Manson. Sounds frightfully dull to me, but if you have friends that way, you might warn them that Sam's toddling through. They might want to be ready"

Alan stopped reading.
"Be ready for what?"

"I don't know. The letter ends there."

" 'Be ready to entertain him,' I suppose. Well. That surely isn't very interesting, is it?"

"Dull as ditch water. Which makes one wonder all the more why Bill thought it worth hiding."

"And worth copying onto a map of Indiana. I *wish* that atlas weren't lost."

"I think I brought back the Indiana map we bought when we went to the States for that visit. I'm afraid I haven't the least idea where it might be, however."

"I suppose we could order one from W. H. Smith or somebody. Or I could get my friend Doc Foley to buy one and send it to me." I went back to the letter. " '. . . though travel is difficult these days.' What do you suppose that means?"

"I thought it might refer to the austerity program after the war." He didn't need to say which war. To people of our generation, there is only one war. "Do you know about the currency restrictions and so on?"

"Just from old Agatha Christie novels. You were allowed to take only a few pounds out of the country, right?"

"So few that most people couldn't travel abroad at all, unless they had bank accounts in another country, or wealthy friends."

"Why, in that case, would an Englishman want to go to all that trouble to visit a bunch of boring places in Indiana? Besides, it doesn't sound as though he was planning to go and stay with anybody, so how could he possibly have managed the money angle?"

Alan shrugged. "There was a thriving black market, of course."

"In Europe, probably. But in the wilds of Indiana?" I shook my head. "Anyway, I had another thought. What if the letter means *during* the war? The paper and ink look old and faded enough to date back sixty years or so."

"But your objections would apply tenfold, a hundredfold. Travel to America in those years wasn't merely difficult, it was nearly impossible, and wildly dangerous. The U-boats were attacking commercial shipping as well as warships, you know."

"I was pretty young at the time, but I do read occasionally," I said pointedly. "Maybe we're wrong about the time frame. Maybe it was later, in the late fifties or early sixties, and travel was difficult only because money was tight. Look, I've just had an idea. We've agreed that the letter must be important, somehow, or Bill must have thought it was. Do you suppose Derek and his crew would turn loose of it long enough to have an expert date it?"

Alan ran a hand down the back of his neck. "Dorothy, do try to remember what we're dealing with here. Officially, I mean," he added hastily as I opened my mouth to protest. "We have one man dead of apparently natural causes and one attacked, and a couple of items of no value apparently stolen from a museum. When Walter recovers—"

"*If* he recovers—"

"All right, if he recovers, he may be able to tell us

who his attacker was, and—"

"Alan, I'm sorry to keep interrupting, but you know perfectly well that's not likely. He may have some brain damage, and even if he doesn't, he's almost certain to have amnesia about the events immediately before the blow. Even I know that much about head trauma. And he may not have seen his attacker at all. He was hit on the back of the head, don't forget."

"All right, given all that, what I was about to say was that we have a serious but not major crime here. So long as there's the possibility that Walter may be able to help solve it, the department isn't likely to spend the money to chase this particular wild goose." He tapped the letter. "You and I may think there's funny business going on and this letter's at the heart of it, but the police operate on evidence, not hunches."

I am not easily squelched. I sat and thought about that for a while. "All right. Suppose I came up with a way to have it looked at that wouldn't cost the department anything. Would they allow that?"

"What are you thinking?" he asked, deeply suspicious. "You're not planning to send the thing to America to some friend of yours, are you? They'd never allow—"

"Of course not. I'm thinking of a friend of mine who works at the British Museum. Charles Lambert, you'll remember him, he's been to dinner a time or two. You've probably forgotten that he's an expert on old documents. Really old, I mean, Old Testament and like that. But I'll bet he'd know somebody who's an expert on twentieth-century stuff, and I'll bet he and I between us could get that expert here to look at this. For free."

"Are you, my love, saying that you plan to use your feminine wiles on not one but two men, right under my nose?"

"Well," I said, batting my eyelashes for all they were worth, "the alleged expert might be a woman, in which case you'd have to use your masculine wiles, wouldn't you?"

It took a while to hunt Charles down. A transplanted American like me, he came over to work in the museum for a year and never went home. He hides in the warren of basement rooms in the venerable building, and he doesn't like to be disturbed by the telephone. I had to let my voice quaver quite a little bit to get the museum operator to keep trying, but eventually Charles's irritable voice came over the line.

"Lambert here. What is it?"

"Goodness, Charles, you sound as though you've just traveled through a couple of millennia."

"I have. I *was* working. Who's this?"

"Sorry, it's Dorothy Martin, and I have a mystery for you." For Charles had helped me solve the very first problem I'd encountered in Sherebury, years ago, and had found the matter as intriguing as the academic puzzles he solved for a living. I counted on that.

"Oh, well, then!" There was a sound of a chair scraping and a grunt as Charles sat down. "Got an ancient manuscript for me to look at, have you?"

"No, unfortunately it's quite a modern one. But it's pretty mysterious, all the same. Who do you know at the museum who can reliably date something written within the last—oh, fifty or sixty years, at a guess?"

"Fifty or sixty years, woman! The ink will still be wet! That's so easy, there's no fun to it."

"Easy for you, maybe. The thing is, I'm involved in sort of an ugly problem here, and I have a letter that I think is important. It isn't dated, but Alan and I are betting it was written during or soon after the war."

"*About* the war?"

"I don't think so. The letter is incomplete."

"There's a guy here, worked in MI5 during the war and for quite a while after. Documents were his specialty. If your letter is from that period, he'd know right off the bat."

"I knew you'd know someone. Now, the hitch is, the letter is with the police—"

"Good Lord! Not mixed up in another murder, are you?"

"Not exactly. The thing is, the police aren't inclined to treat the letter as very important evidence, and Alan doesn't think they'll pay to have it dated. I know it's asking a lot, and I've got a nerve, but if I invited you and your friend for dinner one day soon, and we managed to get hold of the original letter—all we have now is copies—do you think he'd be willing to look at it and give an opinion?"

"It wouldn't be definitive, you know. There should be tests on the paper, the ink, all that."

"Yes, I know, and I don't think we'll be allowed to do that. But I'd like a seat-of-the-pants opinion."

"Hmm. Do you still have any of that California wine you served me last time?"

"I think we could dredge up a bottle or two."

"Would you make steak and kidney pie?"

"I would. How about tomorrow night? The pie's better the second day."

"I'm free. I'll have to check with James. It's only two weeks till Christmas, and he might be busy."

Christmas! I'd forgotten again. "Do ask him, and let me know. If we can't do it now, I suppose after Christmas would do, but the sooner the better. And of course we'd love to see you," I added.

Charles's chuckle came through clearly. "You don't have to pretend. You don't want my charming company, you want to pick my brains, and James's. James Wilson, he is. I'll call you back."

I hung up. "He knows someone, and he'll call back to let me know if they can come tomorrow. He wants steak and kidney pie. I'd better get to the grocery."

I made a quick list, got my coat and hat, and headed out the door. I had planned to walk—I only needed a few things—but I changed my mind in a hurry. A wicked wind had come up, sending the last of the dead leaves skittering down the street. The sky was the color of pewter, and a few drops of rain were beginning to fall. I went back inside for my car keys and a sturdier hat, and when I came out again, Jane was just coming out of her door.

"I'm going shopping," I called, shouting against the wind. "Can I drop you someplace?"

She nodded, not bothering to shout back. I backed the car out of the garage and waited while she got in.

"Have you heard—" I began at the same instant that Jane said, "Heard anything from the hospital?"

"Well, I guess that answers that." I put the car in gear and started down the street. "Did you have a nice nap? I stopped in earlier, but I hated to wake you. You looked so peaceful."

"Hmph. What people say when you're in your coffin."

There wasn't really any reply to that, was there? I changed the subject. "Where are you headed?"

"Supermarket, same as you. Dogs out of food."

"I'll bet you are, too. You haven't been thinking about food much, these past few days."

She shrugged.

"Jane, how are you doing, really? I know none of this has been easy for you, and I wish you weren't so stoic about it."

She cleared her throat. "Not as bad as you might think. Bill and I—friends. Nothing more, no matter what the gossips said."

"But you were planning to be married!"

She shrugged again. "Marriage of convenience. He needed a place to live. I was lonely. He was the one insisted on marriage. For form's sake."

I tried to readjust my thinking. "But—you were terribly upset when we realized he was missing."

100

"Thinking about what might have happened to him. My oldest friend. We'd seen a good deal of each other, these past few years. Remembering the old days. He gave me somebody to look after a bit. I bullied him, but I was—fond of him. Thought all kinds of things when he disappeared. Knowing is better, even . . ."

"I think so, too. Reality can be almost unbearable, but it's never quite as bad as what our minds can conjure up."

"But," she went on, "don't think I don't want the bastard who made this happen! You any closer to figuring out who it is?"

"I'm working on it. Do you remember Charles Lambert, at the BM?"

"Mmm."

"Well, he's coming to dinner, probably tomorrow night, and he's bringing an expert who might give us a start. Do you want to come, too?"

"Might as well. Nobody to cook for now."

I drove on to the store in silence, wondering just how close Jane and Bill had actually been, and whether she was taking his death as well as she pretended.

ELEVEN

I COULD HAVE WAITED TO DO THE GROCERY SHOPPING. Charles's friend James, I learned when I got home, wasn't able to come for several days. I put the kidneys in the freezer, cooked the round steak for Alan's and my dinner, and spent the evening discontentedly addressing Christmas cards.

The next morning the world looked brighter, as it often does in the morning. For one thing, I'd slept well and indeed rather late. For another, the sun was shining. Halfhearted, wintry sunshine, true, but it was better than the unrelieved gloom of yesterday. Even the cats were in a better mood. They hate cold, wet days because going out is no fun, and of course they take their disgust out on Alan and me, at whose feet the blame for the weather must clearly be laid.

Alan had hot coffee and news for me when I came downstairs. "Jane rang up," he said, setting a steaming cup in front of me as I sat down.

I took a grateful sip. "Ah-hh! There is nothing in the world I welcome as much as a cup of good coffee first thing in the morning."

"*Nothing?*" said Alan with a meaningful intonation, favoring me with a kiss on the cheek before sitting down beside me.

"First thing in the morning, nothing. Don't get ideas. And don't change the subject. What did Jane want?"

"She was at the hospital, and she had good news. Young Walter is responding to stimulus."

"What does that mean? Is he conscious?"

"Not quite, but he opens his eyes when he's spoken to and moves both his arms and his legs when they're poked and prodded."

"Has he said anything?" That, to me, was the critical

matter. It wasn't so much that I expected him to help the police at all. I doubted he knew much about Bill, and it was virtually certain he wouldn't be able to remember anything about his own attacker. It was just that I passionately wanted him not to be brain-damaged.

"Not yet, but apparently the medical staff are quite pleased with his progress and hopeful for the future."

The coffee tasted even better after that. We had a second cup each and ate our cereal and toast with a good appetite. It was my week to dry, and as I was putting away the cereal bowls I said, "I think I'll go over to the hospital. Walter might be sitting up and taking notice by now."

"Best call first, love. If they move him out of intensive care, they'll want him to rest a bit before he has any visitors."

"Oh. You're probably right. Actually, I suppose once he's fully aware of what's going on, he'll probably hurt a lot and need a good deal of rest anyway."

"You could go and talk to Jane as a next-best thing. She'll be able to give a full report."

"Good idea. I can see how she's doing, besides. I'm really sort of worried about her. Yesterday I thought she was taking it all too calmly. It's not healthy to tamp down your feelings as much as she does, and don't you lecture me about English self-control."

"Actually, my dear, you're the one who has an *idée fixe* about that. I quite agree that Jane may need, as you'd say, to 'vent' a bit."

"I've never said such a thing in my life! You've been watching too many American TV shows. I may go with her if she wants to take the dogs for a run, so expect me when you see me."

It really was a beautiful day, if a little chilly. Not at all Christmassy, but the thought of Christmas raised lots of anxiety right now anyway, and I was glad to pretend it was spring. Jane had just returned from the dogs' walk, so I didn't get my exercise, but I was glad to settle down in her pleasant kitchen.

Jane was looking a lot better. Her cheeks were pink, and her eyes had lost that dead, defeated look. She offered me coffee, which I refused with some regret, and then bustled around putting her kitchen in order and looking almost like the old Jane.

"So tell me how Walter's doing," I demanded. "Alan's report was pretty sketchy. How's he looking?"

"Better. More color. Human."

"Well, that's a major improvement over yesterday. Do you think he knew you?"

"Couldn't tell. Nurses thought perhaps."

"Did they tell you when he might be fully conscious?"

She raised her eyes to the ceiling. "Won't commit themselves. Platitudes."

"What do *you* think, then?" I persisted. Really, trying to get information from Jane was like trying to run through quicksand.

She shrugged.

"Blast it all, Jane, you have some idea, you know perfectly well you do. Alan won't let me go over there, says the boy probably needs rest. I admit he's right, but I want to know how he is!"

She sat down at the table and sighed. "Not a nurse or doctor. Looks better to me. On the mend, I'd say. Think he'll be talking in a day or two. Don't want to build too much on it, in case . . ."

Ah. So that was why she wouldn't talk. "Yes, I see. I'm superstitious about that kind of thing, too. Sort of like not daring to count on good weather tomorrow, because one wants it so much for the picnic. But I'm betting on your diagnosis. Okay, you may not be a nurse or doctor, but you've lived a long time and know a thing or two. I'll take your opinion anytime."

"Don't think he'll remember anything much."

"About his attack, you mean. I don't either."

"What are police doing about it?"

"I haven't really asked Alan this morning. I wanted to talk to you, see if we can come up with some ideas. There must be *something* we could do. I feel very much at a loose end."

Jane nodded. "Found his parents," she said casually. "Or his mother. Father dead."

"Oh, good for you! How did you manage that?"

"Your idea. Friends at university. Warned me about the mother. Said she was—a bit offhand."

"What does that mean? That she's not concerned about him?"

Jane shrugged and shook her head. "Doesn't seem to be. Moaned about bad timing, Christmas coming, off on holiday soon." She said nothing more, but a muscle in

105

her cheek moved as though she was clenching her teeth.

"Some people," I said bitterly, "have no right to be mothers. So I suppose she isn't even coming to see Walter."

"Told her not to bother," said Jane. "I'll see to the boy."

I smiled at her, and sat and watched the play of light on the red geraniums in her kitchen window. Half my mind was taken up with fury at a negligent parent, half struggling to come up with a useful idea.

Something was trying to come to the surface, some vague association . . . flowers . . . red . . . poppies . . . veterans . . .

"Jane, I just thought of something! You remember I thought Bill's disappearance might have something to do with the war? You thought it was a silly idea."

"You didn't know him well. Wasn't the kind to keep a secret. If he knew something from back when, during the war, would have told everybody. Not the cloak and dagger type. Can't imagine him hiding something all these years."

"Okay, but I still think there might be something to it. Darn it all, Bill went down to that awful tunnel for a reason, and he took that letter for a reason."

"Stroke. Out of his head," Jane suggested.

"Maybe, but even when people do crazy things, they're operating on some kind of logic. And certainly Walter was attacked for a reason. You can't say that was just craziness."

She couldn't, so she said nothing at all.

106

"All right. What I'm getting at is this. I know Bill was getting on a bit in years, and so are his contemporaries, but there must still be a few people in this town who knew him during the war. Maybe even men who served with him in the RAF, who knew what went on in the battles. I'd really like to get a picture of Bill's war. You may think it's nonsense, but I've got this bee in my bonnet, and what could it hurt?"

"Couldn't, I suppose." Jane's face took on a contemplative look, and then she shrugged. "Worth a try. No other ideas on tap, are there? Bill's contemporaries. Hmph. Not many left now, but a few. Could introduce you, if you want."

"I do want. I think there's something to be learned." I also thought that talking with Bill's old friends might be therapeutic for Jane. They might be able to get her to open up about him, reminisce a little, as I could not. "Could you call some of them now? I'm pining for action, and I can't think of anything else to do that's at all useful."

"No time like the present." Jane got up from the table and went to the small desk in the corner of the room. There was a telephone on it, and under the phone a small pile of books. She pulled one out, opened it, and ran her finger down a page.

"Ah. Stanley Rutherford. Bit of an old bore. Lives with his granddaughter, nothing to do all day. Be glad to talk to you, I'll warrant. Trouble is shutting him up." She queried me with her eyebrows.

"By all means. He sounds perfect."

She picked up the phone and dialed.

Stanley Rutherford was apparently starving for company. I could hear him on the other end of the phone, his high voice creaking out an invitation for us to come over and see him as soon as we liked. Jane looked at me. I nodded eagerly. "Right. There in a few minutes, then."

She hung up the phone and turned to me. "Talk your arm off. Don't say you weren't warned."

As Jane drove through the maze of narrow, winding streets, I asked her about Stanley and his family.

"A bit older than Bill and me. Eighty-five now, or nearly. Made a difference when we were kids. We weren't close friends. He joined up before Bill, but they landed in the same squadron. Wounded in the Battle of Britain, I think it was, but back in action in a few weeks, for the whole war. Married when he was demobbed, three kids. Wife's been dead for years now. Kids have moved away, all of them, but the granddaughter's still here."

"It's kind of her to look after her grandfather."

"Hah!" Jane made a face, but made no further comment.

"What's her name?"

"Caroline something. Don't recall her surname. Works in one of the shops in the new mall."

"Any children?"

"Three." Jane's expression and tone of voice were grim enough to give me a pretty good idea of the youngest generation.

However, when we pulled into the drive of the almost-new, semidetached house at the edge of town, only Mr. Rutherford was at home. He opened the door before we could get out of the car. I was sure he had been watching for us.

Jane had said he was only a few years older than she, but those years sat heavily upon him. He stood at the open door, one hand braced on a walker, the other clasping a shawl around his shoulders. He could never have been a large man, but now he was stooped and wizened and resembled nothing so much as a garden gnome that had been left out for too many winters.

"Come in, come in," he called in a high, cracked voice. "Too cold to stand here with the door open."

There was an obvious answer to that, but Jane and I simply hurried up the path to the door, avoiding the bicycle, skateboard, and scooter that lay in wait to trip the unwary.

"Stanley, Dorothy Martin. Stanley Rutherford."

"How do you do?" I murmured.

"I know you," he said accusingly. "The American prodnose. Well, I can tell you a thing or two you've never heard before, believe me. Come in, sit down if you can find a place. Caroline's not the best house-keeper in the world."

It was an understatement. The tiny front hall was cluttered with wellies and umbrellas. Hats, scarves, and gloves were piled on a small table atop a stack of newspapers and unopened mail. Through an open door into the kitchen I could see the dishes piled in the sink. Nothing looked actually dirty, but the level of untidiness was more than I could tolerate on even my messiest days.

Stanley led us into a front room that was no better. The three-piece suite of plush furniture was nearly buried in sweaters and jackets and magazines and electronic toys. A platform rocker in front of the television set, obviously set aside for Stanley, was the only unencumbered chair. Jane swept a pile off one end of the sofa and gestured to me to do the same. We waited to sit until Stanley had lowered himself slowly, painfully, into his seat.

"I can't get you tea," he said, panting a little from the exertion. "Caroline won't allow me in the kitchen anymore. Says I might set the place on fire. Pah!" He pulled a handkerchief out of the pocket of his cardigan and blew his nose. I watched his trembling hand and thought to myself that Caroline might have a point.

"So you want to know about Bill, do you?" he went on. "Why?"

I'd thought about that a little on the way over. I'd planned to spin a little yarn about feeling bad I'd never gotten to know Bill better, trying to get a picture of what I'd missed, that sort of sentimental nonsense. I hadn't reckoned on Stanley knowing anything about me and my "prodnose" activities.

"I think," I said slowly, "that there are some things in Bill's war background that might help us to know why he died."

"Died of a heart attack, didn't he? Or is that a load of whitewash?"

"No, you're right. Or it may have been a stroke. They haven't finished the autopsy yet. But natural causes, almost certainly."

"Then what do you mean about 'why he died'? Obvious, isn't it?"

I didn't intend to tell him much about my reasoning. I'd read enough mysteries to know that saying very little is almost always the wisest course. "I can't tell you, really. It's just a feeling I have, that there are some unexplained factors in here somewhere. Indulge me, will you? I promise I'll come back and tell you the whole story if I ever figure it out."

"Not talking, eh? Well, Jane here will tell you I can do enough talking for two." Stanley cackled a laugh that turned into a coughing fit.

"Shall I get you some water?" I asked, alarmed.

"No—no," he gasped out between coughs. "Be all right in a minute." He pulled an inhaler from his pocket and sprayed it into his mouth, and gradually the coughing slowed down and he began to catch his breath.

"Lung cancer?" I asked Jane in an undertone.

"Emphysema, he says."

Stanley blew his nose again, put away his inhaler, and settled his shawl around his shoulders. Then he shifted his gaze from Jane and me to some point in the middle distance and began to talk.

TWELVE

"YOU'LL WANT TO KNOW ABOUT THE WAR. WHAT A TIME that was, what a time! I joined up first thing, you know, September, 1939, the day after Warsaw fell. I was in some of those first raids over Germany. Raids, they called them! I mean to say! Dropping propaganda leaflets! There were some, you see, back then, who thought Jerry didn't mean it, that we could negotiate with him. Negotiate! He was killing Jews and Poles, little children and all. We were sick as mud when we had to fly over there dropping leaflets! The confetti war. Pah!

"But then the Hun started bombing English ships, and we got down to real work. Ran night raids, mostly. Ah, many's the day I set out in the evening not knowing whether I'd be alive by breakfast. I wasn't an officer, you know. Tail gunner in a Typhoon, and oh, she whipped us around like a typhoon when there was a wind up. But I did my job, even if I did have to be sick in a bucket every few minutes. And cold! So ruddy cold up there I thought my fingers would freeze off working that gun. But I did it, all the same. Fifty-seven targets I hit, planes and submarines and all. And the plane was shot down, too, did you know? In the Battle of Britain, that was, long before Bill joined up. We all got out alive, but wounded. Did I ever show you my medals, Jane? I gave the rest of my gear to the museum, but not the medals. Wouldn't part with them. They're here somewhere, if Caroline hasn't lost them, or the ruddy kids—"

He started to organize himself to stand up, and Jane said hastily. "Seen them, Stanley. No need to show Dorothy now. What about Bill? When did he join up?"

She knew, of course, but it got Stanley back on track.

"Not until '43. He was just a youngster then, of course, and green as grass, but he got a commission because he could fly. We needed pilots then. We'd lost a lot of good men. So Bill found himself in the same squadron as me, and I taught him a thing or two." Stanley chuckled. "It wasn't easy, mind you. He was young and thought he knew it all. He soon learned. War'll do that to you. You learn or you die."

The smile was still on his lips, but it had left his voice. The old, rheumy blue eyes focused again on some distant point and I knew he was seeing things and people sixty-odd years ago, young men long dead, beautiful swift airplanes long reduced to splinters. I cleared my throat. "Were you and Bill in the same plane?"

"Sometimes. Not always. Depended on who was fit and ready to fly on any given day. There was a lot of illness, you know, specially in the winter. God, we were cold! Our barracks wasn't heated, nor the officers' quarters, neither. They fed us well, of course, and there was a fire in the mess, but we all had chilblains and colds in the head nearly all the time. The planes weren't pressurized as well as they are nowadays, either. You went up in one of those Typhoons with a cold in the head and you'd think the top of your head would come off, the pain was that bad. We all should have had those Purple Hearts the Yanks gave out. But we were tough, mind you. Took more than a cold in the head to keep us from our duty. I was sick that day, really sick, couldn't hold my head up. Turned out to be the flu coming on. I couldn't go up for three weeks. Flu was a real disease back in those days, not a glorified cold like now."

He paused to blow his nose again, possibly remembering the bout with flu. Slightly confused, I got in another quick question. "So you weren't in the plane the day Bill was shot down?"

"I'd be dead if I was, wouldn't I? The other two men in that plane were killed. Only Bill and the pilot got away. They both bailed out—"

Jane interrupted. "John Merrifield, was it? The pilot?"

Stanley made a disgusted sound. "Him! Those men'd be alive today but for him. He thought he was a hotshot, a real ace pilot, and he took chances."

This time it was I who interrupted. "But surely you have to take chances in wartime."

"Risks, yes. It's always a risk going up against the enemy. Many's the time I was shot at, and caught a few bullets, too. My scars—"

"But tell us about the day when Bill's plane went down," Jane prodded.

"I was telling you, wasn't I? If you'd let me talk!"
He gave both of us a severe look and continued. "So
Merrifield took Bill up—Bill was second pilot—and
they headed out for Berlin. It was the night of
August 24, you see."

He looked at me meaningfully. I shook my head. "I
was a child at the time. I'm afraid I don't know many
of the details of the war, only a broad outline."

"Hmph! You Yanks had it soft. Nobody bombed
your houses."

"We lost a lot of men," I pointed out, slightly net-
tled. It was all right for *me* to acknowledge that American civilians hadn't been subject to the horrors of
war, but it was another matter to hear someone else
say it. "And we helped win the war. If we hadn't been
there for D-day—"

"All right, all right! I thought you wanted to hear
about Bill."

"I do. Sorry."

"August 24 was the night of the Battle of Berlin.
The plan was to do to Berlin what we'd done to Ham-
burg. Jerry was on the run by that time. Too many
fronts to fight on, too many men lost, and the war'd
gone on too long. Hitler'd begun to realize he might
lose, and we wanted him to keep on thinking that. So
we set out for Berlin. Not me, I don't mean," he said
impatiently, as I opened my mouth. "I told you I was
sick. And just about fed up over missing that raid, I
can tell you. But our men went up, and by God, they
did the job. We gave Jerry what for that night! But we

lost a lot of men and a lot of planes ourselves. Bill's plane bought it, because Smartypants Merrifield was flying too low and too slow. He was trying to stay under their radar, I suppose, but he didn't get away fast enough from the antiaircraft fire on the ground. The kite was hit just as they were about to fly back over the Channel. Just blew up in their faces, the way I heard it. He and Bill bailed out, as I said, but they drifted in different directions. Merrifield landed in a field and got lucky. The farmer, who was in the Resistance, got different clothes for the blighter and helped smuggle him to the coast and off for home.

"Bill landed a couple of miles away in the village, straight into a nest of Nazis. He was taken prisoner, and that was that."

"How did you know all of this if Bill was taken prisoner and the rest of the crew died? I don't suppose Lieutenant Merrifield—he was a lieutenant?"

"Wing commander then. Ended his service as air commodore. RAF used naval ranks."

"I see. Wing Commander Merrifield, then. I don't suppose he would have told you he made mistakes."

"Hah! Not he. He never talked to anyone but an officer if he could help it. No, I got it from Bill years later, when he came home. I had to drag it out of him, mind you. He didn't like talking about it. He had a bad war."

And Stanley was away again, seeing the past, the days of excitement and glory and fear and blood and death. But only for a moment. He shook his head and looked sharply at Jane. "He must have told you all this."

Slowly Jane shook her head. "No details. Didn't want to hear. Bad enough that he was captured, crippled, that we . . ." She turned her head away, but not before I saw that her jaw was working.

I was too astounded to hear Stanley as he droned on and on. Was this the Jane I knew, sticking her head in the sand? Jane, the capable, forthright, salt-of-the-earth sort?

Jane hadn't really wanted me to dig into Bill's past. She'd tried to pooh-pooh the idea that anything relevant to the present could be buried in his wartime experiences. Could it possibly be that she was afraid of something I might find?

Had Bill really told her more than she was admitting? And why would she hide it, unless . . .

". . . wasn't all on the up and up on the home front, either." Stanley's voice had dropped to a confidential near-whisper, so conspiratorial that it jerked me back from my uncomfortable thoughts. "There were rumors . . . oh, I could tell you—what was that?"

Stanley jerked upright in his chair, startled by a noise at the door. More than startled? Afraid?

Of course not. Stop imagining things, Dorothy. What could an old man be afraid of in his own home?

Actually it wasn't his own home. It was his granddaughter's home. That fact was brought forcefully home in a moment as the door into the front room was banged open and a harried woman of about forty strode in, a cigarette in one corner of her mouth.

"Entertaining visitors, are we then, Stan?"

"Caroline, my dear, you'll remember my old friend Jane Langland, and this is—"

"Yes, well, it's not exactly the day for a party, is it? Or had you forgotten the kids have a half day off school today? They'll be home any minute, *and* bringing their friends to lunch, and look at this lounge! You *said* you'd spend the day in your room, so I'd have the space to clean."

"I was only—they wanted to talk about the war—"

"I can imagine how much talking they got to do, can't I?" She stooped, glared at me, and picked up the pile of assorted debris I had dumped on the floor, dropping ashes on the floor as she bent over. "Mental, that's what he is," she muttered in a furious undertone. Stanley began to cough.

"I'm sorry if we came at an inconvenient time, Mrs. Rutherford," I began.

"The name's Simmons." She squeezed past me, pointedly, to pick up a few more things.

"Just leaving," said Jane, standing. It might have been accidental that she stood in Mrs. Simmons's way, but I didn't think so. As she moved over to shake Stanley's hand, Jane managed to fill most of the available space in the room. "Good to see you again. I'll ring up soon, take you out to tea." Ignoring Mrs. Simmons completely, Jane took me by the elbow and steered me out of the room. I glanced back at Stanley, who had controlled his coughing and sat looking like a whipped puppy, and winked at him. I don't know if he saw.

"Whew!" I said when we were safely back in the car. "What a shrew! Poor Stanley."

Jane made an eloquent sound of disgust. "Only keeps him for the sake of his pension. Spends most of it on herself and those kids of hers, I shouldn't wonder. Count yourself lucky you didn't get to meet them. Spoiled brats, the lot of them."

"And no wonder, with a mother like that. Is she really his granddaughter, or the wife of his grandson?"

"Really his granddaughter. Doesn't act like it, does she?"

I thought about Alan's grandchildren. They were younger, true. Caroline Simmons must have been about thirty-five or forty, and Alan's oldest granddaughter, Cynthia, was twenty-two, if I remembered correctly. But they adored their grandfather, all of them, and treated him with both respect and affection. They were warm and friendly with me, too, which was nice of them, for they could well have resented me, taking the place of their real grandmother.

Would it be different if we ever had to live with one of them? Suppose we became so feeble we couldn't manage on our own, and had to impose on one of them, or on Elizabeth, his daughter, who still lived in Sherebury. Would they treat us like nuisances, make it quite clear that our room would be preferable to our company? I didn't think so, but then I hoped the situation would never arise. How awful it would be! Sitting there lonely and useless, knowing oneself a burden . . .

"Where are you?" demanded Jane. "Asked you three times if Stanley was any use."

"Sorry. I *was* far away. In a place I didn't like much. Anyway, I liked Stanley. Yes, he does tend to go on and on, but the poor old man doesn't have anybody to talk to. He'd be better off at Heatherwood House, I should think. At least there they'd be nice to him, and look after him properly. I wonder if that woman even gives him enough to eat."

"If he dies, the pension dies. Imagine she feeds him."

"She surely doesn't nourish his soul. And can you imagine her smoking in front of him, when he has emphysema? We've got to follow up on that promise to take him to tea, Jane."

"Want to pick his brains again?" Jane chuckled.

"No," I retorted, "just be nice to him. I don't think he really has much to tell us, though I did get something of a feel for the war. I hate to admit it, but he's right about Americans, at least this American. I'm woefully ignorant about the period. I missed some of what he said, though. I got to thinking about something else just before that awful woman came in. He was making all sorts of dark hints. What was that all about?"

Jane's hands tightened on the steering wheel. She became very busy negotiating a corner where there was no traffic at all. "No idea," she said after an interval. "Likes to think he's important and knows all sorts of things other people don't. Load of rubbish. I've errands to run. Okay to drop you off at the end of the street?"

She took off like a scalded cat the moment she'd let me out, and I stood looking after the car and wondering more than ever what desperate worries could make Jane Langland rude.

THIRTEEN

I WASN'T A GOOD LUNCH COMPANION FOR ALAN. I WAS trying to work something out, and I replied absently if at all to his comments. Finally he gave up, ate his sandwich, and left me to my thoughts.

The fact was, I'd been dabbling in crime for quite a while now. That sounded odd, even in my own mind, but I meant on the side of the angels. Not committing crimes, but trying to help bring to justice those who do. And *that* sounded prissy.

What I was trying to figure out was whether my preoccupation, avocation, call it what you might, was changing the way I dealt with people. There was a time when if I wanted to know what was on someone's mind, I'd ask. In recent years, though, I'd developed the habit of approaching the question from left field somewhere. Devious Dorothy, that was me.

Well, that was probably appropriate when I was nosing around into a case of murder. I don't think it's generally recommended that a detective, especially an amateur, go up to a suspect and say, "I was just wondering if you killed Mr. X." Indirection was more apt to get results, and it was certainly safer.

But this time I wanted to know about a friend. "So why don't I just ask her?" I said aloud.

Alan looked at me quizzically. "I give up. Why don't you?"

"You're right. I will."

I left him shaking his head.

Jane was just finishing her lunch, and didn't look especially pleased to see me. The dogs were extravagantly hospitable, however, and by the time Jane got them quieted down and shooed them away, it was pretty hard for her to stand on ceremony or pretend she was just leaving.

I sat down, unasked, in a comfortable chair in the front room and said, "Okay, Jane, what's up?"

She raised her eyebrows.

"Uh-uh. We've known each other too long. You're acting weird. Something's wrong."

"One man dead, one badly hurt—that enough for you?"

"No. Of course you're grieving for Bill, but you're not acting sad. You're acting scared, or wary, or something. And you're not really eager for me to try to find out what happened to him and Walter. Usually you egg me on, and especially, I would have thought, when one of the victims is someone you loved. Now I could waste a lot of time trying to figure out what's going on, but I'd rather spend it figuring out who attacked Walter and what was going on with Bill. So, like I said, what's up?"

There was silence for quite a while. Jane stood quite still, looking at a point on the carpet some distance in front of her. I didn't mind. Jane isn't chatty at the best of times. I was prepared to wait.

At last she raised her head. "Coffee?" she asked.

"Sure." I followed her into the kitchen.

She said not a word until she had completed the ritual. When the coffee had been measured into the French press pot, the boiling water had been poured in, and sugar and cream and mugs and spoons were on the table, she sat down opposite me and began to talk. Being Jane, she began in the middle.

"Bill was a stranger in some ways. We'd been apart too long. Happened twice. Once when he was in the war and the prison camp. Seeing him when he came home was a shock, because nobody knew he was alive. Missing in action, he'd been listed. And he was odd. Didn't want to talk about the war. That wasn't unexpected. War had been hell for him. A few weeks of training and action, then years of pain and starvation and—well, as I said, he didn't talk much. But he was—different. Quiet, all the time, about everything. A sorrowful man, not the happy boy I'd known years before. Thought it must be what he'd been through, but it wasn't easy. In a way, almost a relief when he moved away."

"But then he came back," I said. "After a lot more

years. I suppose that must have been a shock, too."

Jane pushed down the plunger of the pot and poured us each a cup of steaming, fragrant coffee. "Not as bad as the first time," she went on. "Both of us older, calmed down. Didn't expect anything much of each other, only companionship. Couldn't pick up where we left off. Too much water under the bridge. Not the same people. He was happier than in the bad time. Limped, of course. Never had proper care for his broken leg. In pain a lot of the time. But—content. Settled."

She took a deep breath. "Until the last few weeks. He shut up again. Closed me out. Knew something was troubling him, but he wouldn't talk. Thought it might have to do with the museum, so asked him what he was working on, if something interesting had come in."

"What did he say?" I asked eagerly.

"Wouldn't say. Said routine sorting work, nothing special. Got cross about it, so I left it alone. He relaxed a bit then, said we should go ahead and marry quietly, live in my house—you know about that.

"Then he disappeared, and you started in about the war. I remembered how he'd been when he came home, and I—wondered. Knew much of the collection at the museum had to do with the war. Didn't know what it was about, and—ashamed to say it—didn't want to know."

I took a deep breath. "You're afraid we'll find out something to Bill's discredit."

124

"Don't know what I'm afraid of. Stupid. Not like me."

I sipped my coffee. I had to think carefully about what to say. "I think right now," I said slowly, "maybe you're just afraid that something else terrible will happen. The psychologists call it 'undifferentiated anxiety,' I think. A feeling that the sky's been falling in big chunks and is likely to keep on falling."

I watched her face. She didn't look skeptical, so I went on. "The thing is, from what you've told me about Bill, I wouldn't have said he was likely to be mixed up—recently or long ago—in anything shady. I sort of figured he was a pretty upright sort of guy, or you wouldn't have been attracted to him."

She nodded. "No plaster saint, but a steady, reliable sort."

"Right. So we're unlikely to find out anything awful about him. But what if we do? Wouldn't it be better, in the long run, to *know?* You said yourself you felt a little better knowing what had happened to Bill. Isn't this the same? Because if we don't ever learn what's been happening, you'll always wonder, and you'll always be uncomfortable with his memory. And I don't know about you, but that's sure not the way I want things to be."

After a long pause, she looked me straight in the eye. "Very well. Fire when ready, Gridley."

I laughed, perhaps a trifle hysterically. It had been a long time since I'd seen a spark of humor in Jane. "Where'd you learn that one? That was Admiral

Dewey, as I recall."

"English are taught history. Unlike some nationalities."

"Ouch! You got me, pal. All right. I'd like to go on talking to the people who knew Bill during the war. What about that pilot, Wing Commander What's-His-Name? Is he still around?"

"Merrifield. Still alive, last I knew. Lives at Heatherwood House, but doesn't get about easily. Even older than Stanley, nearly ninety. Don't know how much help he'll be."

"Stanley didn't like him much, did he?"

Jane made a sound that could almost have been a chuckle. "Stanley didn't like officers. Except Bill. Even with him, some resentment. Younger chap, green, with a commission just because he could fly."

"What do you think of Merrifield?"

"Haven't seen him for years, or not to talk to. Bill used to mention him now and again, said he almost never left his room. Pleasant, or used to be, a gentleman. RAF was his career, not just for the war. Retired as an air commodore; Stanley told you that. Probably a better flier than Stanley says."

"Okay, I'd like to see him if it's possible. Do you want to call Heatherwood House to check, or shall I?"

"Know the number," Jane said quietly, and picked up the phone.

Yes, Air Commodore Merrifield was certainly still alive and in quite good health for his age, Jane reported. He rested for a time after lunch every day, but would be up for his walk around three and would welcome visitors. " 'A remarkable gentleman,' " Jane quoted, imitating the condescending tones of the nurse.

"Yes, well, let's hope he really is. At ninety he has a lot of experience to draw on, and he could be some help to us if his memory is still any good."

"Apt to be, that far back," Jane said. "Recent events first to go."

"Don't I know it! I can't remember where I put my glasses two minutes ago, but ask me about my college days and I can go on for as long as Stanley Rutherford."

Jane actually laughed, and then she sobered. "Dorothy," she said, looking at her hands. "Sorry about—didn't want to talk for fear—behaved badly—"

"Don't give it another thought. You've been under stress. Now, you are going to drive me out to Heatherwood House, aren't you? Because there's that roundabout between here and there, and I still can't negotiate it with my eyes open."

Heatherwood House is a very lovely old house on the outskirts of Sherebury. Built in the early 1700s by a family named Delacourt, it's made of red brick accented by stone that was probably once white but has now mellowed to the color of sun-washed sand. The Delacourts, originally wealthy wool merchants, somehow found the money to keep on living there until they died out in 1980 or so. At that point the heir, a cousin far removed in both relationship and distance, put the place on the market, and it was bought by a firm that was just beginning to establish nursing homes in southeastern England. Jane once told me how much had been spent in repairs and remodeling, but the figure was too fantastic to lodge in my brain.

At any rate, they'd made a success of the place. From the outside, except for a discreet wheelchair ramp up to a side door, the house looked exactly as it must have when it was a family home. The gardens had been simplified for easier maintenance, Jane said, but they were still peaceful and beautiful. On a summer day residents could be seen dotted around the grounds in wheelchairs or comfortable lawn chairs. This afternoon, though the sun still shone, the air was chill. An evergreen wreath hung on the massive front door, and electric "candles" shone in each of the front windows, but no human being was in sight as we rolled up the drive and parked in the "Visitor" area.

A reception desk in the magnificent front hall was the first sign that this was no longer a manor house. A pleasant young woman, after asking our names, told us Air Commodore Merrifield was waiting for us in the sun porch, and pointed. "It's just down that corridor. Oh, and he never uses his rank. He's been retired for a long time, and he prefers to be called Mr. Merrifield. Now, shall I show you the way?"

"Know where it is," said Jane a trifle brusquely.

Now that I was back on her wavelength, I thought I could hear the suppressed tears in her voice. The last time she'd visited here, it had undoubtedly been to see Bill. The holly and ivy festooned about the hall, the lighted Christmas tree in the corner would simply serve to deepen her sadness.

"You won't stay too long, will you, or let him walk too far? This is a good day for him, so he may overestimate his stamina. And then, you know, he sees very few people besides his son, and conversation with anyone else takes its toll."

We promised not to exhaust Mr. Merrifield and started down the hall to the back of the house.

The sun porch had obviously been converted from a conservatory in the old house. On a windy, cloudy day it was probably drafty and miserable, with all its windows, but today it was almost too warm. Merrifield, seated on an upright chair near the door, rose somewhat stiffly, with the aid of a cane, and greeted Jane warmly.

"My dear! It's been far too long. You are a welcome sight, indeed. And how is it that you have not changed at all, while I have become an old man?"

"Flatterer," said Jane gruffly, a smile trying to work its way out. "Want you to meet my friend Dorothy Martin."

He extended a courtly hand. "John Merrifield. I'm delighted to meet you. I've heard a great deal about you."

His voice was warm and strong, his handshake firm.

He was a handsome man still, high cheekbones accenting a thin, aristocratic sort of face. David Niven with snow-white hair. Doubtless he had once been a commanding figure. Now his aging body was thin and frail, but I could feel the strength of his character. "I hope the reports of me haven't been too lurid," I said, smiling.

"No, no, quite complimentary. You look exactly as I would have expected." He smiled at my hat. "I must say, though, you don't sound like a Hoosier."

I smiled a little at his pronunciation of the Indiana nickname, something like "Who's your?"

"No, I've lived in England long enough to take the edge off," I said, and found a chair. The three of us, and the inevitable Christmas tree, were not the only occupants of the room, but the two old ladies over by the windows were dozing. I thought we could carry on a reasonably private conversation there, and anyway there was nothing confidential about the questions I wanted to ask. I was mostly looking for Bill's background, more details to light his shadowy past.

I wasn't sure how to begin, so I was relieved when Jane spoke first. "Wanted to talk about Bill. What you remember about him. What happened in the war."

Merrifield nodded, a look of compassion on his face. "I was so sorry for your loss. I seldom saw Bill of latter years, even when he moved to Heatherwood House. I seldom see anyone except nurses, indeed, and my son, of course. They will have told you I've become quite a hermit. I am not suited to the communal life, I fear. After my retirement, my dear wife and I gloried in the privacy one could never achieve in the Air Force. However, I do of course hear the news that circulates, and I was stunned to hear of Bill's death. I thought he was in excellent health."

Jane simply nodded.

Merrifield looked around the room. The two old ladies were still slumbering peacefully, but the old man shook his head. "I was about to go for a little walk. I walk every afternoon, rain or shine. One must keep moving, I find, or the joints cease operating altogether. If you'd care to accompany me, we could talk privately."

My pulse quickened a little. If he desired privacy, did it mean that he had something to tell us that was off the record?

FOURTEEN

A DOOR LED FROM THE SUN PORCH STRAIGHT OUT INTO the grounds. There was a graveled path leading to a rose garden, now sere of leaf and barren of flower, but beautifully tidy. I wondered in passing how much it cost to live at Heatherwood House. They obviously had a complete and hardworking staff, and that doesn't come cheap.

"You've asked about Bill's war experiences," Merrifield began. "I'm afraid I knew him for only a few months. He joined up early in 1943, April if I recall correctly—"

"March," said Jane.

"Ah, yes, you would remember better than I, of course. He had just turned eighteen, I believe."

Jane nodded.

"He was assigned to my squadron. We flew out of Luftwich Airfield, not far from Great Yarmouth in Norfolk. You'll remember that, I expect." He looked at Jane, who nodded again.

"The field is long gone now, of course. It was all a long time ago. A long time ago." He was silent for a moment, then resumed his narrative tone. "Bill was very young, but boys grew up fast back then. They had to. So many of them died or were wounded before they ever saw their twenty-first birthday." He sighed. "At any rate, I was dubious when Bill was assigned to my wing, but I soon learned that he was an excellent flyer, and reliable, as well." He hesitated for a moment. "There were some young officers commissioned at that time who—well, shall we say they never seemed quite to understand the responsibilities of an officer. Bill was quite different. Although his background was perhaps somewhat lacking in polish, he learned quickly, not only the technical aspects of what we were doing, but the social niceties as well."

I stole a glance at Jane behind Merrifield's back, wondering how she was reacting to his comments about Bill's working-class origins. I'm often uncomfortable about England's class structure, which I find a good deal more rigid than what I was used to in America. Apparently, though, Jane was unperturbed. Well, she'd lived with it all her life, after all.

"So he got along well with the other officers?" I asked.

"And with the men as well. He was quite popular in the mess, though he was a quiet chap. Not at all hail-fellow-well-met, but friendly, and with a sense of humor. He had a tendency to fraternize with the lower ranks a bit too much; I had to call him down a time or two about that. It wouldn't do, you know. An officer must be respected. I suppose you find that undemocratic?" he added to me, smiling.

The man was perceptive, wasn't he? "A little, perhaps, but I do understand. When an officer gives orders, they have to be obeyed without question. Especially in wartime."

"Precisely. Well, as I say, Bill was with me for only a few months, but he was a valued member of the wing. I was extremely sorry to lose him—especially because, of course, I thought he had probably been killed."

"Can you tell me what happened, exactly? When the plane went down, I mean."

Merrifield smiled a little. "No, I can't, exactly. I've never been sure myself. I don't imagine you can picture what it was like. We had completed our mission, quite successfully. It was a bombing raid on Berlin, did you know?"

"I know a little about it," I said. "One of Bill's buddies told us the bare details."

"That will have been Rutherford, I expect. How he did hate me, to be sure! His account may have been a trifle skewed, and of course, he wasn't there.

"You realize there were hundreds of planes involved in the operation, many from Luftwich. You have never, probably, been involved in any kind of military operation, but believe me, the level of noise and confusion is like nothing any civilian can conceive. Apart from anything else, the smoke from the bombs and, I'm afraid, from a good many planes that had been hit made it impossible to see anything clearly. It was a night raid—we did most of our bombing at night—and I had to rely quite heavily on my instruments to have any idea of where I was.

"You probably know that the planes were extremely primitive compared to anything we have now. The instruments were limited in number and not terribly sophisticated. We flew by sight whenever we could, relying on landmarks to find our way. That was impossible on that particular night. Once we had dropped our bombs I wanted, of course, to get out of there as fast as I could. The Luftwaffe was out in force, naturally, and there was heavy antiaircraft fire from the ground as well. I put the plane on a compass heading for home, but flying by compass alone can be disastrous, because it doesn't account for wind drift. The wind that night was from the north. I had no desire to find myself pushed southward over France, so I was flying as low as I dared, and just above stall speed, in the hopes of spotting something that would give me my bearings. Of course that kept us below radar range, as well, so it was quite standard procedure.

"Unfortunately, exactly what I had feared was what happened. It was nearly dawn before there was enough light to see anything, and then what I saw was the coast of the Channel—but the wrong coast. I was far off my course, over France, at about Boulogne, I reckoned. I was just making the turn straight north to make for home when all hell let loose. A burst of anti-aircraft fire caught us, and the plane caught fire at once."

A pair of stone benches stood by the path. Merrifield paused. "I'm feeling a little tired. Would you mind if we sit for a little, or will you be too cold?"

"No, of course not," I said with some dismay, "but should we turn back? They told us—I mean, I don't want to wear you out."

"They told you I tire easily, I suppose. It's true, I do. Only to be expected at the incredible age I've achieved. What they don't realize is that a little rest refreshes me quite thoroughly. So if you really don't object . . ." and he lowered himself gingerly to the cold bench.

Jane and I sat on the other. It was freezing. The sun had lost all its warmth and most of its light by now.

"So the plane was on fire," Jane prompted.

"Yes. If hell is meant for punishment, I shall never have to see it in the next world, for I already have done in this. I won't attempt to describe it. I haven't the words, and if I had, they would distress you immeasurably. I could do nothing to save the plane or my crew. I was scarcely able to think at all. The plane was falling to pieces around me, but I managed somehow to get out and inflate my parachute. I hoped the rest of the crew had done the same.

"You probably know the rest. Bill will have told you, or you have Rutherford's version. I was extremely lucky. I passed out shortly after I landed— I'd been rather badly burned and was in a good deal of pain—but when I woke, I was in a barn, tucked up very nicely in the haymow. I'd been fortunate enough to come down on a farm owned by a member of the Resistance. He was an old man, or so I thought then. Perhaps sixty or so. Seems a mere stripling now. At any rate, he was kindness itself. My French isn't bad, so we had no trouble communicating. He dressed my burns, checked me over, and hustled me out of that conspicuous barn to a rather nasty little hole under one of the sheds. The Germans were all over the place almost at once, of course. They'd seen the plane come down and wanted to make quite sure that the crew were all dead. I lay there in my hole trying not to breathe; they came very close to me, but they never knew I was there. I don't speak German, so I didn't know what they were saying, and I doubt the farmer understood much either. At least he pretended he didn't. He played up beautifully, the stupid peasant to the life. Jean Leclerc, his name was. I've never forgotten him. I owe him my life.

"At any rate, once they were gone he nursed me for a few days until I could move more comfortably, and then he gave me clothes and organized transport back to England. It was all very dangerous, probably even more for him than for me. He was a brave man. I've never known whether he survived the war. After it was all over I tried to trace him, but I didn't know exactly where I'd been, and records were in a shambles. I've never known," he repeated, and sighed.

I was turning to an icicle. I struggled to my feet, my knees even stiffer than usual. "Maybe we should go in?" I suggested.

"Yes," said Merrifield, rising with less difficulty than I. "The day and the story have chilled us."

We were nearly back to the house when Jane spoke. "And Bill? When did you hear anything of him?"

"Not for years, actually. He was listed as 'Missing in action,' and his parents were notified. The war dragged on, though we all knew that Hitler was defeated. It was only a matter of time. Then after the smoke cleared and we had won the war, we began to realize we now had to win the peace. I planned to make a career in the Air Force, so I stayed in. I was posted to various locations and kept quite busy, though I found time to marry and start a family. I was in Africa in late 1945 when word sifted through channels that Flying Officer Fanshawe had been found in a prison camp, ill and malnourished, but likely to survive. I was delighted, of course. We'd been given the address of the hospital where he was being treated, so I wrote to him, but he replied only briefly. I thought he was still weak and unable to hold a pen for very long, and dismissed the matter from my mind.

"I didn't return to Sherebury for any length of time until I retired, and by that time Bill was no longer living here. I had lost touch with him completely, so you can imagine my surprise and pleasure when he moved back here and took the job at the museum. My wife had died, of course, and I admit I was rather lonely. We saw a certain amount of each other, although he would never talk very much about his war experiences."

"Didn't you think that was rather odd?" I asked. "So many men like to tell war stories, literally."

"No, I understood. He had suffered terribly in prison, and he felt, I think, that he'd done very little to help his country. He was wrong about that—the Battle of Berlin alone was a tremendous boost for the Allies—but he preferred to talk of other things, and I respected that. And then of course I became unable to keep the house in good condition and had to sell it and move here, and ironically, we lost touch again."

"Donated some of your war memorabilia to the museum, didn't you?" Jane put in.

"Yes. I do feel rather strongly that the history of Sherebury's contribution to the war must not be lost. Bill and I had a few conversations about a special display paying homage to the men—and women, of course—who served in the armed forces during the war. The memorial in the Cathedral honors those who died, but I felt it was important to remember those who served and lived on, as well. Goodness knows what will happen to the materials now that Bill is gone."

We had reached the sun porch, now deserted in the waning light. As we entered the door I studied it thoughtfully.

"I'm a little surprised that they keep this door unlocked. Surely there is an occasional resident who forgets where home is, and might wander off. I would think they'd limit the exits to those with staff nearby to keep an eye on who comes and goes—not to mention the fact that someone undesirable might come in by a rather remote door."

Merrifield pointed to the ceiling. Sure enough, a small camera, nearly hidden in the decorative molding, was pointed at the door. "One has the feeling of being watched all the time," he said with distaste, "except when we're actually in our own rooms. It's one of the reasons I dislike living here. It is for our own protection, I know, but it gives me an unpleasant feeling. And for this particular door, it's unnecessary, in my opinion. The part of the grounds where we walked today is completely enclosed by quite a high wall. No resident could get far, and no outsider could come in."

"Still, I'm glad the security camera is there. It makes me feel better about the whole thing."

"Ah, yes, Mrs. Martin, but then you are not the object of the scrutiny."

"True enough."

Merrifield sat, rather abruptly, in the nearest chair. "Ladies, I have enjoyed this very much, though I doubt I've been much help to you. The people who could answer your questions about Bill's war would be those who shared his prison time, but I have no idea where you'd find them. Most of them are probably dead by now. I'm among the few who have lived so long. Too long." He sighed. "I'm afraid I have become a bit tired. Would you mind very much if I said good-bye? I believe it's time for my nap."

He looked gray and exhausted. My conscience smote me. "We've talked too long, and I promised we wouldn't. Thank you so much, you've been a big help. Shall I send a nurse to you?"

"If you would be so good." He leaned back in his chair, looking suddenly like the very, very old man that he was.

FIFTEEN

"I HOPE HE'LL BE ALL RIGHT," I SAID AS JANE TURNED the car around and headed back to the road. "Nice man."

Jane nodded. "Bill respected him. Fine officer, he always said. Even-handed with the men."

"That matters a lot. I'm glad I got to meet him. He

won't be with us much longer, I expect."

"Didn't look good, there at the end."

"No. And I don't know that what we got was worth the trouble, for him, I mean. He didn't tell us anything new, really."

"Said why he was flying low."

I smiled. "Yes. Stanley's a bit prejudiced, isn't he? I'm inclined to believe Merrifield's version. There was one question I wanted to ask, but I really couldn't keep him any longer. Do you know where Bill was imprisoned? Which camp, I mean?"

"Colditz. Not one of the worst ones, and nothing like the concentration camps. Not a Buchenwald, or an Auschwitz, or a Dachau. But bad enough."

"They were all bad. I saw some photos once, at the Imperial War Museum. Dachau, I think it was, when it was liberated. Thousands of men lying naked, the dead and the near-dead together. They were no more than skeletons with skin. You could count their bones. The captions said most of them died later, despite everything doctors tried to do. I had nightmares for weeks after looking at those pictures. And if Bill had been Jewish . . ."

We drove back to town in silence.

"Tea?" said Jane when she had parked her car in her drive.

"Thanks, but I need some thinking time. Unless you'd like company? Today must have been hard on you, reliving Bill's horrible experiences."

Jane nodded. "Yes. But worth it if we can get at the

truth. Go home and do your thinking."

"Right. I'll let you know if I come up with anything useful."

Alan came to give me a hug as soon as I'd hung up my coat. He knows me so well he seldom needs to ask about my moods. He questioned me only with a look, to which I shook my head. I wasn't ready to talk about it yet.

"What have you been doing with yourself all day?" I said, mostly to avoid any other subject. "I feel like I haven't been home for weeks."

"Addressing Christmas cards."

"You're kidding!"

He pointed to the pile of cards on the hall table, stamped and ready to mail.

"Good heavens! I didn't know men even knew how to do that. I hope you didn't forget to write notes to—"

"Notes to everyone present and correct. I'm a very exceptional man, my dear. I hope your American friends can read my handwriting."

"They probably won't be able to, but they'll think it's charming even so. Just the way they do with a British accent. Well, for that, my dear exceptional man, you deserve an extraspecial tea. Let's see what we can find."

I made a quick batch of scones and opened a carton of clotted cream. We don't usually indulge in such treats, but any husband who takes over the Christmas-card chore deserves to be pampered. I'd worry about his cholesterol level later.

Alan kept up a babble of remarks about this and that during tea. I replied absently, and suddenly interrupted. "Alan, is there any way to trace the men who were held in a particular POW camp in Germany during the war?"

He had been talking, I think, about his grandchildren. He blinked and redirected his train of thought. "Frankly, I doubt it. The Germans destroyed sheafs of records at the end of the war. Sorting things out when the camps were liberated was a nightmare, and after all these years . . ." He sighed and shook his head. "You're thinking of Bill Fanshawe?"

"Of the men who were in there with him, yes. He spent most of the war in Colditz, and I have the feeling that any secrets he might have taken to the grave with him would have dated from there."

Alan nodded slowly. "They were places for secrets, certainly. Escape plans, sabotage plans, assassination plans . . . desperate men will do anything they can to try to improve their lot. There were thousands of heroes in those camps, you know. Men who helped others to escape, often at the cost of their own lives. Men who tried to hide Jews destined for the gas chambers. Men who smuggled German war secrets out to Allied forces. There were even some Germans who were so revolted by the conditions in the camps, the atrocities, that they secretly helped the prisoners. When they were discovered, they were shot at once as traitors, of course."

"And I suppose there were the other kind, too. Turn-coats. Men who traded secrets to the enemy in return for favors."

"Yes, unfortunately. There are always a few. They didn't last long if the other prisoners found out about them."

"But suppose, just suppose, that Bill found out about one of them and didn't do anything about it, for whatever reason." I was warming up to my theory. "Suppose he was too ill to act, or it happened just before the camp was liberated. What would he have done with that knowledge?"

Alan considered. "Do I recall that he was in pretty bad shape when the camp was liberated? Physically, I mean?"

"I got that impression. He'd broken some bones when he bailed out of the plane, and they were never properly set until after the war. Merrifield said he was sent to a hospital. I imagine most of the men were, though, a field hospital at least. There at the end of the war most of the prisoners were starving, weren't they?"

"In some of the camps, not all. Certainly there was greater need for medical attention than the Allies could easily provide, but they did what they could. However, what I was getting at was that Bill was probably in no condition even to remember details from the camp, much less do anything about them. If he knew something about one of the other prisoners, I'd think he would have reported it to the proper

144

authorities as soon as he could."

"Me, too. But just suppose he didn't, for whatever reason."

"If I were you I wouldn't pose that supposition to Jane."

"Why not?"

"Because it sounds a great deal as if you're suggesting blackmail," said Alan, draining his cup. "More tea?"

"But—I wasn't—how could you—" I spluttered. Alan refilled my cup.

"I don't think that's what you were thinking. I said it sounded that way. And you have to admit it's a possibility. Far-fetched, but possible."

I sat back to think about that. "All I meant was that if Bill knew something that might hurt someone else, that someone might have come to get him. And that might explain why he—Bill, I mean—was in that terrible tunnel. He was hiding. And the effort, along with the fear, was too much for him and he collapsed."

"Almost equally far-fetched, I'd say. You're supposing that someone Bill knew in a prison camp nearly sixty years ago was still alive, knew where Bill lived, knew that Bill carried this secret with him, somehow divined that Bill might reveal it, and— what? Threatened Bill with bodily harm? Didn't threaten but merely turned up, and put the wind up poor Bill?"

"Hmm. I haven't thought it out, have I? But, Alan,

145

you're a policeman. You've known stranger things to happen. You said it yourself: desperate men will do anything."

"Indeed. It's only that I doubt that a man of Bill's age, or older, would be all that desperate about anything."

"Reputation?" I said dubiously.

"Perhaps."

I sighed. "Anyway, it doesn't look like anything I could possibly follow up. The police could, maybe, but they're not dealing with Bill's death right now."

"And your theory doesn't explain why the museum and Walter would be involved. That's what the police *are* worried about."

"You're right." I sighed again. "Okay, so it's back to Bill's old friends, I guess. You know, I started this with the idea of helping Jane deal with Bill's death, and I'm not at all sure it's been good for her. It must be pretty devastating to have the wartime stuff raked up over and over again."

"Jane's tough, Dorothy. I think it may be harder on you, in a way. Don't forget that everyone in England had some personal tragedy in that war. I doubt there was a soul who escaped, who didn't lose a husband or a brother or a son or a cousin or at the very least a home. My favorite uncle was killed at Dunkirk, my cousin was badly wounded, and we lost every chicken we owned in a bombing raid. Oh, you may well laugh, but it was serious for us! The point is that we're used to war stories, very personal ones.

They've lost most of their ability to shock. They're new to you."

"New and extremely unpleasant. I think, as Scarlett said, I'll think about that tomorrow. Tonight I'm going to wrap presents."

But of course I couldn't stop thinking about it, couldn't stop gnawing on the possibility that something could be learned from Bill's fellow prisoners, if only we could find them. The fact that finding them was probably impossible was frustrating in the extreme.

The next day, Saturday, the fickle weather changed again. I woke up cold, and when I looked out the window, a few snowflakes caught the light of a street-lamp. The sky was still dark, but the earth was beginning to lighten under a powdered-sugar dusting of snow.

Alan was still asleep, but I was wide awake. Snow! Real snow for Christmas! Maybe I'd get Alan to go with me to London and do some proper shopping, Harrod's and all that. I dressed and went downstairs to make coffee. The kettle hadn't even boiled when the phone rang.

"Saw your light," said Jane. "Had an idea last night."

"Oh."

"Don't sound keen, do you?"

"Oh, I'm sorry, Jane. It's just that the snow has put me in a Christmas mood, and I wasn't thinking about anything else. What's your idea?"

"Been talking to men about Bill's war. How about a woman?"

"What woman? Bill didn't have another girlfriend, did he?"

"Had lots. Good-looking he was in those days. Picked me. Wasn't what I meant, though. There's a WAAF still alive—"

"A waif?"

"WAAF. Women's Auxiliary Air Force."

"Oh, of course. Yes, a WAAF?"

"Who knew Bill. Fancied him. Stationed at Luftwich. Lives in Lowbridge. Feel like a trip over there today?"

I abandoned my vague ideas of Christmas shopping. I had more than a week left, after all. "Sure. Why not? Only—"

"Only I drive. Right."

We arranged to leave about nine, which gave me two hours to finish my Christmas list and a grocery list, feed Alan and the cats, and wonder what a super-annuated WAAF could tell us about Bill and his war that might be of any help.

SIXTEEN

THE SNOW HAD STOPPED BY THE TIME WE SET OUT, BUT the streets were a little slippery. I was profoundly glad that Jane was driving. I've had more experience on wintry roads, true, but she's much more familiar with

English traffic. "Do you think we'll get any more?" I asked, looking out the window at the already melting snow.

"Telly said rain and fog tonight."

"So much for my Christmas snow."

"Might get some yet. Never can tell, this time of year."

"Yes, the only predictable thing about English weather is its unpredictability. Jane, tell me about this woman. What did she do in the war? The WAAFs didn't fly, did they?"

"Good grief, no!" Jane was so startled she veered into the right lane and narrowly escaped being mowed down by a beer truck. (Or "brewer's lorry," but I still tend to think in American.) "Women didn't go into battle. She was in Ops."

I sighed. "Jane, much as I hate to cramp your style, you really are going to have to translate for me. Standard English I can manage okay. Wartime shorthand, no. I presume you're not saying she had something to do with growing hops."

Jane hooted. "That lorry's got beer into your head. Ops, not hops. Not lost my aitches at this stage of my life. Short for Operations Room. Don't know from my own experience exactly what she did. Never was in the military myself. Believe it had to do with those huge maps on tables, with little airplanes to move about showing where real ones were. Always looked in the movies like a children's game."

"I expect she'll tell us. Anyway, what's her name?"

"Barbara Price."

"Miss or Mrs.?"

"Miss, definitely."

"Was she an officer?"

"All women were officers. The respect factor, y'see."

"Oh, come to think of it, all the women in the American military are officers, too, or were back then, anyway. Okay, what's she like?"

"Let you see for yourself."

And not another word would Jane say, from which I deduced that she didn't like the lady.

Jane had evidently telephoned to Miss Price to say we were coming, because she answered the door of her cottage attired, on a Saturday morning in December, in a tight black silk dress, high heels, and lipstick. She had probably been pretty, in a blowsy sort of way, when she was young. Now her once zaftig curves had run to plain fat, and her complexion had faded. Her hair, however, was a defiant red and her earrings large and green.

"Oh," she said with a note of disappointment, looking at the two of us. "I thought you said Mr. Nesbitt would be coming."

"Held up at the last minute," Jane said, not meeting my eye.

"Well, never mind. Come in, Miss Langland, Mrs. Nesbitt."

"It's Mrs. Martin, actually. I kept my name when I married Alan."

Miss Price giggled. Actually giggled, as if she were eighteen instead of eighty-something. "How very American of you. Come in, let me take your coats. I've just put the kettle on, tea won't take a minute."

Nine in the morning was not a time when I usually wanted tea, but Miss Price looked like the sort of woman who could enjoy a nice cuppa at any time of the day or night. I looked around me, trying to learn more about her. The cottage was immaculately clean, but crowded with ornaments, touristy kitsch from all over Europe. I spotted a brass Eiffel Tower, a china Coliseum, and no fewer than three cuckoo clocks before I even sat down. The room was hot, all three bars of the "electric fire" glowing in a corner of the room.

Our hostess came back carrying a heavy tray laden with pot, cups and saucers, milk and sugar, and a large plate of biscuits and mince pies, and then looked around for a place to put it. "Oh, dear. Miss Langland, would you mind moving the aspidistra? The floor will do nicely, thank you so much. I so seldom entertain that I quite forgot I had put that plant on the tea table. Now, milk and sugar, Mrs. Nes—Mrs. Martin?"

"Yes, please, quite a lot of milk and two lumps." I had an idea that tea in this house would be very black and very strong. For the sake of my stomach, I needed it diluted as much as possible. "No, nothing to eat for now, thank you. The mince pies look lovely, but I'm trying to watch my weight."

"Oh, well, if you're sure, but do help yourself to

151

anything you like." She sounded a trifle offended. It was a bad start to the conversation, but I really could not eat cookies and rich tarts at that hour, and she'd have been more upset if I'd taken them and left them on the plate.

"It was such a surprise to hear from you, Miss Langland," said our hostess. "It must have been years since we've talked. I did want to say how sorry I was to hear about Flying Officer Fanshawe. I'd heard you'd got close to him again, and it must have been a shock for you. I took quite a fancy to him when he was first posted to Luftwich, you know. Of course he never so much as looked at any of us WAAFs. He carried your picture in his pocket, and I was told there was one hanging on the wall of his room as well. Of course I wouldn't know about that personally!" She giggled.

Jane said nothing, and Miss Price looked affronted. "I suppose you wanted to talk about him? You weren't very clear when you called."

"It was more that we wanted to get a picture of what Bill's war was like," I said. "He never talked much about it to Jane, or anyone else, it seems. For a start, I wondered just what you did in the RAF. Jane tells me you were in the Operations Room, but I don't know what that implies."

Miss Price relaxed a little, happy, as people almost always are, to talk about herself. "Oh, it was a very responsible job, very. The men weren't actually keen on letting women do it, at first, but of course the men were needed in the planes, weren't they? And at com-

152

mand posts, naturally. So we were taught to control the flights."

"When you say control . . ."

"Air traffic controller, they'd call us today. We tracked the planes on radar—our planes and the enemy—and directed our pilots by radio until they could see the German planes. When we weren't on the radio—that was rather nerve-wracking, and we couldn't do it for terribly long stretches—we'd plot the positions on the map table. We knew at all times where everyone was, unless they got out of radar range. I think I may say that we did as much to keep our boys safe and help them destroy the enemy as any support staff. They couldn't have done without us, really, though of course we were in very junior positions. I do sometimes think the officers at command level took us quite for granted, but the boys knew what we did, and were grateful to us.

"Oh, I well remember how it used to be when they came home from a mission. Dead tired, of course, and cold. Even in the summer it was cold in the planes, because of the altitude. They'd go first to the mess for hot tea and a meal, but quite a number of them would always come in and thank us for what we'd done. Sweet boys, they were, and so many of them never . . ."

She stopped talking and blew her nose. I had been wondering why she'd never married. Perhaps she'd just told me. I thought it was time to change the subject. "How many men were there at—Luftwich, was it? I mean officers and enlisted men, all of them."

"Well, it varied, of course. There weren't as many at the beginning of the war as later on. At the peak height, we had five squadrons, and we were terribly overcrowded. The aerodrome had been built to accommodate two."

"And a squadron would be—"

"Ten to eighteen aircraft," she replied promptly, "each with a crew of at least four. Two pilots, a wireless operator, and a tail gunner."

"So that would be . . . let's see, fifty to ninety planes . . . at least two hundred men, perhaps closer to four hundred."

"You're forgetting the flight lieutenants and the squadron leaders and the wing commanders and the mechanics and cooks and batmen and the rest of the ground staff, and, of course, us WAAFs. Luftwich was a big place."

"I can see that. How many of those people did you know?"

"Well, the flight crews, of course. And the chief controller, our boss. Not the higher-ups. We knew them to speak to, but we weren't on what you'd call friendly terms. A squadron leader or whoever was someone to salute and respect, not someone to get pally with."

"I suppose you knew Wing Commander Merrifield? I gather Bill usually flew in his crew."

"Yes, I knew him." She picked up the pot. "More tea?"

"No, thank you. What was Merrifield like? He was

a career officer, wasn't he?"

"Yes. A stickler for rules, ambitious, not friendly."

"You didn't like him."

She sniffed. "It wasn't my business to like or dislike any of the men, *or* the officers. I worked with them, I got them where they needed to go and home again."

I switched tacks again. "I suppose there were a lot of secrets to be kept around the base—the airfield, I mean."

Miss Price sniffed at the foolish remark. "It was wartime. Everything we did was secret. Of course that didn't keep the men from talking about it when they shouldn't. We WAAFs heard a lot we weren't supposed to, but we were safe, and the men knew it. They had to talk sometimes. It's human nature."

"What sort of things? I can't imagine they're still secret. The war's been over for nearly sixty years."

"Some things might be. Anyway, I swore not to tell, and I'm not going to tell. Most of it doesn't matter anymore, where missions were going and that, but there were other things . . . no, my lips are sealed. And why do you care, anyway?"

I shrugged apologetically. "Just idle curiosity, I suppose. Everyone likes to think they know things other people don't. But what I'm really trying to do is fill out the picture of Bill's war."

"Why?" she demanded. "Are you writing a book or something?"

I laughed. "No, but Bill was planning to do a special exhibit that highlighted what Sherebury men and women did to help win the war. At the museum, you know. Mr. Merrifield contributed some materials to it, I know. I thought perhaps I could help a bit by writing some narrative about Bill." St. Peter chalked up another lie to my account, but I'd piled up so many by now that I didn't think one more mattered much. "So tell me, did the men have much free time? I mean, I suppose they formed close friendships and did things together in their time off."

"Of course. It happens in wartime. But the men learned not to get too close to anyone, because you never knew . . ."

You never knew when your best friend might not come home. "What about romances? Surely some of the WAAFs and some of the male officers fell for each other."

"We were not encouraged to fraternize with the other officers. They were our superiors, you know."

"I'll bet that didn't stop the women."

"Well—no, not entirely. But a lot of hearts got broken, because the women weren't always able to keep the friendships casual. And when the men didn't come back . . . do have a biscuit."

That was the second time she'd warned me off. I put two and two together. She didn't like Merrifield. She had, I was pretty sure, fallen in love with someone who hadn't come back. Could it have been one of the men killed when Merrifield's plane was shot down?

Jane, who had sat silent, now spoke up. "Bill said you'd got engaged. To one of the other pilots."

Miss Price looked at her coldly. "And when did he say this, if I might ask?"

"Letter. Just before he was shot down."

"Well, if he had written to you later he might have told you that my fiancé was in the plane that day, and was killed. James was a pilot himself, and the best pilot in the squadron, but he was flying tail gunner that day because a lot of the men were out sick with the flu, and the mission was important. So he died. Does that satisfy your curiosity?"

The bitter question was directed to me. "I'm sorry, I never—"

"James Little was a wonderful man, wonderful! We would have been happy together. We neither of us ever looked at anyone else once we'd seen each other; it was love at first sight. And he had just as much courage as any of them, and more than most, and more patriotism than the lot of them!"

I tried to calm her vehemence. "I'm sure he did. I didn't mean—"

"And as for that exhibition—if you're not making it up—I hope you're planning to use the things I contributed, memories of James. I can't imagine any exhibit will be worth seeing if it's just some rubbish Merrifield's dug out of his attic. His concern in that war was looking after himself, and they didn't give medals for that."

After that, the room seemed more stiflingly hot than ever.

We left as soon as we decently could. I took my coat

off before I got into the car. "Freeze to death," was Jane's comment.

"Not me. I'm too ashamed and embarrassed. Why didn't you warn me about the hornet's nest I was stirring up?"

"Wanted you to see for yourself. War's been over for longer than most people in this town have lived. Still bitterness." She pulled onto the main road into the traffic, heavy on a Saturday morning close to Christmas.

I'd said that myself, hadn't I? Said it to Alan, who'd replied with something about long memories. The notion had been abstract then. It wasn't any longer.

" 'The sins of the fathers . . .' " I quoted.

" '. . . unto the third and fourth generations,' " Jane finished.

I brooded for a while. "They don't any of them seem to like Merrifield, do they?"

"No. Didn't realize he was so unpopular. Bill never said much about him."

"Of course Bill knew him for only those few months before the plane went down. I wonder if he really was a bad officer, or if it's just the grudge about him flying the plane when two men were killed. It seems—disproportionate, somehow. How many hundreds of thousands of men were lost, after all? And all this bitterness about two."

"Bitterness about most of them. We've happened across two, that's all."

"True enough. But still. I must say I liked Merrifield

quite a lot, and I can't help wondering why Miss Price and dear old Stanley hate him so. It wasn't his fault about the plane, just the fortunes of war." I shook my head and sighed.

"Still want to go on with it? Not getting anywhere that I can see. Upsetting people."

"Is it upsetting you, Jane? Hashing it all over?"

"Not much. Bill survived the war, lived a long time. Our little romance—over a long time ago. Thinking of him when he was young's a bit—refreshing, I suppose. Makes me remember what he was like then. A long time ago." She cleared her throat. "Haven't heard anything to his discredit, have we?"

"No, not that I expected to. In fact, I agree with you, we haven't learned much of anything. It's so hard to ask a direct question, is the trouble. Even if I knew what questions to ask, which I don't. I'm stumbling around in a fog, feeling my way. I hate to give up, but I wish we could get just one fact, just one idea of a direction to go."

"Push on, then. You never know. I'd like to learn the truth."

That declarative sentence, complete with subject and verb, was for Jane an oration, a trumpet call. I responded like the old warhorse I am. "Very well. I'm in favor of truth myself. Let's go for it. Who's next?"

SEVENTEEN

"GETTING DOWN TO THE DREGS," SAID JANE AFTER A little thought. "Two others, but neither likely to know much. One's Mr. Tredgold, chaplain at Luftwich for a time. Lives at Canterbury House."

Canterbury House was a home for retired clergymen. Having spent their working days in big, drafty old rectories owned by the church, the clergy were often hard put to find housing after their retirement, especially when their meager stipends had been eaten up by the demands of the old houses. So unless their wives had independent means, as few did nowadays, they often ended up in places like Canterbury House, which was better than letting them starve on the streets, but still a poor way to treat men who had served God all their lives. It was, I thought, still harder on their wives, who had to give up the accumulated treasures of a lifetime of housekeeping, the heirloom china, the favorite pictures and chairs and ornaments they had looked after so lovingly, and condense their belongings to what would fit into one or two small rooms. "Store not up for yourselves treasures on earth . . ." was an injunction, however wise, that most of us preferred to ignore.

And like clergy wives, most of us might have to get rid of our treasures someday, if we couldn't afford to keep our houses, or if their upkeep became too much for our strength . . . a depressing thought. It was true that you couldn't take it with you, but I wanted to keep it as long as I possibly could. I wrenched my mind back to the chaplain. "Does his wife live with him, or is he widowed?"

"Never married. Very High Church. Oxford Movement type."

Well, the Oxford Movement, an attempt to return the Church of England to Catholic practices, happened in the middle of the nineteenth century, about a hundred years too soon for direct influence on the Reverend Mr. Tredgold. Undoubtedly he had imbibed its principles through a devout mother or grandmother, or a clergyman who touched his imagination. "Hmm. He doesn't sound very likely."

"Said we were scraping the bottom of the barrel. Only other survivor I know of is even less of a starter. Leigh Burton, widow of Bill's best childhood friend George. He was at Luftwich, too, though not in Bill's wing."

"Oh, well, it had better be Mr. Tredgold, then. He is—um—*compos mentis,* I hope?"

Jane permitted herself a grim smile. "As much as he ever was."

Typically, she didn't expand upon that remark.

We went back to Sherebury before heading out to Canterbury House, which was several miles out in the country. I took some bicarbonate of soda to offset the effects of the extremely tannic tea and then asked Alan to call the hospital and check on Walter. I knew he'd get more information out of the nurses than I would.

Alan is one of those irritating people who say little on the phone, so I couldn't tell from his end of the conversation what was going on. A smile crept across his face, however, so I was panting to hear the news as soon as he hung up.

"Good news! He's fully conscious, and they've moved him out of intensive care. He isn't making a great deal of sense when he talks, they say, and he has no idea what's happened. However, he can move all his limbs, is responding properly to stimuli, and wants something to eat. They think he's going to make a full recovery."

"Hallelujah! But you didn't ask when we can go and see him."

"They volunteered the information, love—said not for a day or two. They want him kept quiet until he's talking more or less normally. After that, he can have company."

"I don't suppose he's told them anything about his attacker. Or no, you said he doesn't even know what's happened."

"And we knew he wasn't likely to at first, or perhaps ever."

"Yes, well, I'm going to run over and give Jane the news. I don't suppose you'd care to fix us all some sandwiches?"

Jane, working in the kitchen, was pleased with my report, but declined my offer of lunch. She was pouring a brown batter into square pans. "Gingerbread," she said briefly. "Never knew a youngster who didn't like it."

"Who's it for? I doubt if they'll let Walter have anything that good, not yet."

"One pan's for Nigel and Inga. She'll be too busy with the baby to cook much. Make another batch for Walter when he can eat it."

"Lucky Walter!"

So Alan and I ate our sandwiches, and I did a little halfhearted Christmas decorating. When Jane came back from delivering her gift, the two of us headed out again.

"I'm beginning to feel like a traveling salesman," I complained mildly as Jane negotiated a complicated double roundabout. "I've been living in one car or another for the past few days."

She emerged from the roundabout, shifted gears, and roared down the road. "Hmph! Not making many sales, are you?"

"Not a one. Not even a hint of interest. Am I barking up the wrong tree, do you think, Jane?"

"Turning over the wrong stones? Mixing the wrong metaphors, for certain."

"All right, all right." I sniffed the air. "More gingerbread?"

"The other pan. For Mr. Tredgold. Most men have a sweet tooth, even at his age."

I forbore to comment on her generosity. Jane gets embarrassed easily. "Tell me more about him, Jane."

She raised both hands in the air. "Can't describe

him. Have to see for yourself."

"In that case," I said in a strangled voice, "maybe you should concentrate on driving. This road is awfully narrow."

"Not to worry. Ruts'll keep the car going where it should." She grinned, but put her hands back on the wheel and slowed down a little. I tightened my seat belt and tried to breathe normally. The road, little more than a lane, really, had no ruts, but a lot of curves. The high hedgerows on either side reduced visibility to near zero. I wondered what would happen if we met a car, and then decided not to think about it.

I'd heard about Canterbury House, but had never been there. It was certainly a depressing sight as we approached it that gloomy winter day. The predicted rain had begun, turning the long drive up to the house into a squelchy mass of mud. The gravel with which it had once been paved had given up long ago and sunk into oblivion.

The house itself was a Victorian monstrosity in dark brown brick. I suppose it had once been red before generations of coal fires had embedded their soot in the very pores of the house. There were wings and ells and bays and various other excrescences, giving the whole place a vague resemblance to a rhinoceros or some other ungainly animal. I couldn't imagine any family actually living in such a place. Perhaps it had been built as an institution to begin with, a rather nasty school or an orphanage. Certainly it looked enough like my idea of Lowood. Jane Eyre would have felt right at home.

There were gardens to one side of the house and presumably in back. Those I could see were, like Lowood's, "all wintry blight and brown decay." There had been roses, but the bushes were brown and nearly leafless, the beds spotted with coarse grass and tall weeds.

"What a dreary place!" I exclaimed. "How awful to have to live here."

Jane shrugged. "Not so bad inside. Done their best to brighten it up, paint and wallpaper and so on."

I personally felt that all the paint in the world couldn't bring cheer to that repellent place. I shivered as we left the car and scurried through the rain to the door.

Jane was right. It was a little better inside. Fresh paint and a pleasant striped wallpaper disguised some of the innate ugliness of the entrance hall, and touches of Christmas here and there showed someone's good intentions, but nothing could remove the institutional smell or the atmosphere of resources strained to their limits. The young woman who greeted us, however, was cheerful enough.

"Good afternoon! Actually, it's a wretched afternoon, isn't it? I do loathe rain at Christmastime. I'm new here. Do you know your way about, or can I help you find someone?"

I glanced at Jane, but she had folded her arms and retired into silence. I smiled at the young woman.

"I've never been here before. We wanted to see the Reverend Mr. Tredgold, if it's convenient."

The young face clouded. "Oh. I'm not sure if . . . well, I'll ask. He—um—he has good days and bad days, you know."

"Oh, no, I didn't. I've never met him, you see. I just wanted to ask him some questions about—about a mutual friend." That was less than candid, but I didn't feel I needed to go into a long explanation to the receptionist.

However, she became even more doubtful. "Questions? He may not—I mean, he isn't gaga or anything like that. Not like some of them, poor old dears. But he sort of lives in a world of his own, if you know what I mean. Conversations aren't always—but I'll ask."

She picked up the phone. The call brought another woman, older, with the sort of wrinkles around the eyes and mouth that come from smiling. "You wanted to see Mr. Tredgold?" she asked, looking at Jane and me. "Forgive me for asking, but just what did you want to talk to him about?"

I opened my mouth, but this time Jane forestalled me. "Old friends," she said firmly. "Reminisce a bit."

"I ask only because there are some subjects that worry him a good deal. He's a very dear old man, but he feels himself a failure in many ways. He doesn't like to be reminded of the war, for example."

Well, then, what were we doing there? The war was exactly what we wanted to talk about. I looked at Jane.

"Know about that," said Jane. "Just want to talk about one of the flying officers, not the war as such. We'll be careful."

"Well—if you're sure—we have no rules here really, you know, but we do try to keep the residents happy."

I would have given up then and there, but Jane is made of sterner stuff. "We'll be careful," she repeated. "He still lives on the first floor?"

"No, he's had to move to the ground floor. He can't manage stairs now, and he doesn't like the lift. I don't like it myself, if it comes to that. How long has it been since you've seen him?"

"Going on for two years," said Jane.

"Ah, you'll find him sadly changed, then. Physically, I mean. He's virtually lost the use of his legs, and he's very thin. He's over ninety, of course, and quite ready to meet his Maker for some time now."

"Can he have sweets?" Jane indicated the plate of gingerbread.

"Oh, he loves them, and he can eat nearly anything. Shall I show you to his room? I'm afraid the house is a bit confusing."

She led us through a maze of corridors; I was lost after the first two turns. Eventually we fetched up at the door to a small room at the end of a corridor.

"It's quieter here. He likes quiet. And the view of the garden is lovely in summer. Mr. Tredgold, I've brought you some visitors."

The old man was sitting in a wheelchair by the

window, reading. He was meticulously dressed in a black suit with a gray shirt whose clerical collar, though frayed and much too big for his wrinkled neck, was spotlessly white. His hand, as he extended it to Jane, had once probably been slender and graceful. Now it resembled a claw.

"Miss Langland, isn't it? How very nice to see you. And bless my soul, is that gingerbread you've brought? Oh, that calls for some tea. Mrs. Hart, might we have some tea, please?"

Mrs. Hart smiled and nodded and went away to see to it.

Mr. Tredgold inclined a courteous head to me and then asked Jane, "And your friend is—?"

"Dorothy Martin." I held out my hand. His was as dry as an autumn leaf, but his grip was firm. His voice, reedy and fluting, seemed made for intoning psalms. Perhaps it had developed that quality through decades of practice.

"Have we met, Mrs. Martin? I fear I am a bit forgetful. Were you one of my parishioners in London, perhaps?"

"No, I'm an American. I moved to Sherebury only a few years ago, and I suspect you were already retired."

"Retired. Yes. I still read the offices every day, you know. Now and again someone is kind enough to come and read them with me." He gestured to the book in his lap and I saw that it was the Book of Common Prayer, the old version whose stately language I loved so much.

"Your eyesight must still be very good, sir, if you can read that small type."

"Bless you, my dear, the book is only a symbol. I know it all by heart. Did you come to read Evensong with me? It's a trifle early in the day, but perhaps, as I retire very early . . ."

"I'd love to do that before we leave, but I really came to talk to you about the old days and some of the people you used to know."

"The old days?" His voice sharpened. "How old? Not—not the terrible time?"

"Well, around then, I'm afraid, but I didn't want to talk about the war, only—"

"I won't talk about the war. I can't talk about it. Please don't ask me to. I've given everything away, everything to remind me of the noise, the stench, the death—they all died, you know, all the young men— pain and suffering and death and hell—"

His voice rose higher. His hands shook. Tears gathered in his eyes and rolled down his incredibly wrinkled cheeks.

Alarmed, I looked at Jane. "Should we call a nurse?" I whispered.

She shook her head and moved nearer to the old man. "It's all right, sir," she said soothingly. "Don't talk about anything you don't want to. Only came to ask if you knew my friend, one of the men who survived."

"Survived?" The old eyes looked vague. "One who survived? He didn't die? But they all died, all—"

·"No, Bill didn't. Bill Fanshawe."

"He died." Mr. Tredgold's voice was sharp again, though the tears still coursed down his cheeks. "I read about it. He died just yesterday. I'd given him every-thing, all those terrible things, for the museum. And he died. Perhaps they killed him."

We accepted that and I took over our end of the con-versation again. "Yes, but he died full of years," I said, hoping the biblical turn of phrase would make him feel better. "A full fourscore years."

"By reason of strength," Mr. Tredgold said, nod-ding. "He was a strong man, a good man. Ah, here is our tea."

When tea had been handed round and the maid had left, I took up the conversation again. "You did know him, then?"

"Know whom?"

"Bill Fanshawe," I said, praying for patience.

"Of course I knew him! He ran the museum. It is only the past few weeks that I have been unable to get about. I visited him there."

"But it was earlier that we wanted to know about. When he was a young man. During the—when you were at Luftwich."

His face crumpled again. He put down his tea, and the prayer book slipped from his lap. "Luftwich! A terrible place! Death, and deceit, and treachery! War—I won't talk about the war!"

It was hopeless. We were torturing the poor old man, and there was nothing to be gained. With a sigh, I took another sip or two of tea and then, picking up the prayer book from the floor, turned to the Order for Evening Prayer. " 'I acknowledge my transgressions, and my sin is ever before me,' " I said, choosing at random one of the several suggested opening sentences.

" 'The sacrifices of God are a broken spirit; a broken and a contrite heart, O God, thou wilt not despise.' " Mr. Tredgold responded with another and then proceeded right through the whole service, not missing a word.

He was calm, even serene, by the time we left. "So good of you to come," he said gently. "I will sleep now, but I enjoyed having company in my prayers. Come again."

We left quietly as he repeated to himself the words of the Nunc Dimittis: " 'Lord, now lettest thou thy servant depart in peace, according to thy word . . .' "

"He's forgotten that we ever asked about Bill," I whispered.

"Likely," said Jane, nodding. "A blessing, I suppose."

"Why did he get so upset? Did something particularly terrible happen to him in the war? Is this lingering shell shock, or whatever they call the World War II equivalent?"

"Not unless spiritual disintegration is shell shock." As we drove home, Jane proceeded to explain Mr. Tredgold to me. She'd had the story from the men who came back, the men she talked to in the months while she was waiting for Bill to come home. It was a sad and in many ways a familiar story.

Mr. Tredgold had joined the RAF almost as soon as the war began, full of high ideals about the purity of sacrificing oneself for one's country. "Mixture of High Church and Arthurian legend," was the way Jane put it. One gathered he pictured the men as latter-day knights, mounting their silver steeds to bring truth to the world and save it from Hitler's godless ways. He would be their chaplain, the devoted priest to whom they could make their confessions before going into battle. He would pray with them, offer them the Sacraments, convert those who saw the error of their ways.

The brutal reality of war completely undid him. He found the men to be no nobler than most men. They gambled, they drank, they chased skirts, they quarreled with each other, they tried to avoid dangerous duty. They shocked him. Not all of them, of course, but even one would have been too many, given his rose-colored picture of the way things ought to be. He tried to reform them. They laughed at him and went on boozing and whoring.

And then they started to die, and to kill. He didn't know which was worse. They killed, and gloried in it, or they failed to kill and came back maimed for life, or they didn't come back at all. They caught diseases and died cursing the God who'd let them in for this.

Some few listened to him. Some were comforted. But not enough, never enough to make up for the horror.

He became a pacifist. He urged the men to lay down their arms, to cease the carnage. The men didn't like his attitude, and the military authorities threatened him with court-martial. They probably wouldn't have done anything—imagine court-martialing a chaplain!—but he was then shunned by everyone. In despair he volunteered to go with the men on a particularly dangerous mission, hoping he would be killed. The next-best thing happened. He was so severely wounded that he was invalided out. By the time he recovered from his wounds, the war was over and he was a civilian again.

He asked for and was given a slum parish in London, where he buried himself in unremitting toil and began to recover his sanity.

"Thought himself a failure. Hoped to work himself to death, I suppose," Jane concluded. "Didn't manage it."

"It's amazing that he never lost his faith. Men have lost it over far less."

"Slums saved him, he used to say. Real work, real needs to be met. Saw some real courage and compassion amongst the parishioners. Spent the rest of his working life there, then retired to Canterbury House. Been there for thirty years, more or less."

"Waiting to die, I suppose." I shuddered. "He must wonder why the Lord's taking so long to release him."

Jane looked at me a little oddly, then shook her head. "Kept himself busy for years. Took his turn at the chapel altar, helped the feebler residents, wrote devotional tracts. Even took services at the Cathedral now and again, when the canons were indisposed or away. He's from these parts and knows everyone, and quite clearheaded, even now, except for the one little quirk."

I nodded. "King Charles's head."

Jane took her eyes off the road and gave me a sharp look. "Know your Dickens, do you?"

"I'm pretty good at *David Copperfield*. It's always been one of my favorites. And *Great Expectations* and *A Tale of Two Cities*."

And we quoted Dickens to each other the rest of the way into town, but the back of my mind was thinking about the great sorrow this world could dole out to its idealists.

EIGHTEEN

"MAKING ANY PROGRESS?" ASKED ALAN CHEERFULLY when I returned home. I set a plate of gingerbread on the kitchen table. Jane had managed yet another batch before we'd taken off for the afternoon, and had, typically, refused any thanks for it.

Alan was in his study, trying to work on his memoirs. I say "trying" because one cat was lying on the desk on top of a stack of papers he needed for reference, and the other was in his lap, meowing crossly whenever his typing happened to disturb her slumber.

I looked over his shoulder at the screen. "I'd say

I've made just about as much progress as you have. Emmy isn't much help, is she?"

He grinned. "I typed nearly a page before I looked up to check my work and discovered my right hand had been one key over. It looked like comic-book swearing, with quotation marks and semicolons all over the place. So you didn't learn very much from the good padre?"

I dropped into Alan's comfortable, squashy old chair and sighed. "He's a sweet old man, but he can't talk about the war years without breaking down." I related our conversation, such as it was. "And he wouldn't say a word about Bill, or Luftwich, or any of the people there. He nearly went into hysterics. I had to stop asking, out of pity."

"Poor chap."

"Yes, there must be some terrible memories buried in his mind." I fell silent.

"This business is depressing you, isn't it?"

"Well, it is, a little. Oh, a lot, actually. Jane and I have been talking to so many old people. And, Alan, I call them old, but some of them aren't all that much older than we are. Ten, fifteen years. I keep wondering what's going to happen to us."

Alan got up from his desk and came to sit on the arm of my chair. "It's something to think about, isn't it?"

"Do you think we'll age gracefully? Or will our minds turn to mush and our bodies to a collection of painful, nonfunctional parts? Because if that's what lies ahead, I don't think I want to live much longer."

He took my hand. "Well, it isn't our decision to make, is it? And of course we don't know what lies ahead. We can make some guesses, though. For example, I have no Alzheimer's disease in my family. Do you?"

"Two of my cousins, but they inherited it, I think, through their mother who was my aunt by marriage, not by birth. My own parents lived into their nineties, and though their minds failed at the end, they were fairly sharp until the last few months. My grandparents all died rather young, though, so I don't know what would have happened to them."

"What did they die of, your grandparents?"

"One was killed in an automobile accident before I was born. The others followed the typical pattern: a fall, a broken hip, pneumonia, and that was it. A couple of weeks of distress and then it was over."

"That was how my mother died. My father was drowned in a boating accident off the coast of Newlyn. He was eighty-seven and still going out fishing every day. I suspect he'd have lived to a hundred if a storm hadn't come up. So we both come from good, sturdy stock. I'd say there was every chance of our keeping fit for a good many years yet."

"But if we don't?" I couldn't rid myself of the nightmare visions.

"If we don't," said Alan, pressing my hand again, "we'll cope with whatever comes, when it comes. We have enough money, if we're reasonably prudent, to see us through. We have our house, and we can afford to hire help if we begin not to be able to do all the work ourselves. National Health will see to our physical problems, after a fashion."

"Oh, Alan, I know all that, and when I'm rational I know you're right. But it could all go sour, somehow. We don't *know* what will happen. You said it yourself. I can just see us, our minds slipping away . . ."

"Love, if your mind slips away, after a while you won't care. You won't know."

"And what if mine doesn't, but yours does? And I have to watch you deteriorate?"

He stood and pulled me to my feet. "My dear woman, anything could happen. We could both be struck by a lorry tomorrow, crossing the High Street. Right now we're well and happy, and there's no point in letting what might or might not happen tomorrow poison today. I promise we'll deal with whatever comes along." He enfolded me in one of his bear hugs.

"I'm not sure I'm convinced," I said when I could speak again, "but I'm glad you're willing to talk about it. I hate it when people say things like 'Don't worry' or 'It'll be all right.' Because it might not be."

"It might not," he agreed. "But it is not a bridge that needs to be crossed this instant. In fact, what you need to do this instant is decide what your plans are for supper. Because Elizabeth has invited us over to see their Christmas tree and spend the evening. I said I'd ring her back, but it's my opinion you need the company of the young for a bit."

"You're right about that. If all the people I've talked to lately were laid end to end—"

". . . they'd lead to the *Guinness Book of World Records*. Or something. Elizabeth said about six, if that'll do."

"Wonderful. It'll give me a chance to put my feet up."

Most days I can nap without difficulty. Today, when I'd risen so early, I expected to be snoring two minutes after my head hit the pillow. But there was too much on my mind. I lay trying not to fret about advancing age, but the more I tried not to think about it, of course the more I thought about it. Have you ever tried strenuously *not* to think about a large pink rhinoceros?

The only solution, since my mind refused to relax, was to occupy it with other thoughts, and the ones that immediately popped up all had to do with Bill.

I'd talked with four people now who had known him well during the war. What, if anything, had I learned?

From Stanley Rutherford and John Merrifield I'd had slightly different accounts of the accident that had cost Bill his freedom and most of the crew their lives. Stanley was sure it was Merrifield's fault, but then Stanley didn't care for officers. Stanley had wanted to brag about his own war. I wondered if I should have let him. I might have learned more from meanderings. Maybe I'd have to go back.

Merrifield had given me a bit of a picture of what life at the airfield was like. So had the WAAF—what was her name—oh, yes, Price. Barbara Price. She hated Merrifield even more than Stanley did, but that was, I supposed, understandable. Her fiancé had perished in the plane crash, and of course she blamed the pilot. She'd presented the most vivid picture of life at Luftwich, the cold, the segregation by rank, the temptation to talk more than one ought about military secrets. I probably ought to visit her again and just let her ramble.

And then there was poor old Mr. Tredgold. What a dear he was, but how utterly useless as a source of information. Yes, I'd go and visit him again sometime. I'd take some knitting or a piece of needlepoint and sit and talk about theology, or his work in London, or whatever subject seemed neutral and safe. I wouldn't ask him about Bill or Luftwich or, in fact, anything at all that happened between 1939 and 1945.

I may be a busybody, but I do draw the line at torturing harmless old priests.

Then there was the last contact that Jane had mentioned. Somebody's widow, whose husband had been a friend of Bill's and stationed at Luftwich. She didn't sound very likely, but she might be able to tell me something about Bill. I resolved, this time, to be collecting anecdotes for a book about the war. That way I didn't have to ask direct questions. If I simply let her tell what she remembered, there might be some wheat among the chaff.

There might be. More likely there wouldn't be. More likely I was chasing wild geese. I began to watch them as they flew overhead in formation, one in front, then two by two, hard to count because they kept changing position . . .

"It's after five, love. Did you want to change clothes before we go?"

I'd slept a little, after all.

The evening was pleasant. We admired the tree Elizabeth and her family had decorated, had a little light supper, and when the teenagers had retired to the den to watch television, we sat and talked about nothing in particular.

"I suppose you're mixed up in this business in the Town Hall, Dad," Elizabeth said eventually.

"And why do you suppose your poor old dad would be getting himself involved in crime at my age, poppet?"

"First, because you always were intrigued by anything the least bit out of the ordinary, and second, because you married someone exactly like you!" She smiled broadly across the room at me, and I felt a sudden stab of gratitude for my adopted family. Elizabeth didn't treat me like her stepmother; she treated me like a trusted friend. Idiotically, my eyes were wet. I faked a sneeze to give me an excuse to blow my nose.

If my worst fears were realized, it might not be so terrible to have to live with Elizabeth and her family.

Sunday morning dawned foggy and chilly, as predicted. Even the sound of the church bells nearly overhead was muffled. I had no desire whatsoever to get out of bed, but I felt I needed the consolation that church might provide. So I pulled myself out from under the covers, showered and dressed, and had time for a quick cup of coffee.

Alan, who had been up early, had waited for me, and together we rushed across the Close, too late for the early Eucharist, but almost on time for Matins.

I brooded through the service. The beauty of the words usually drew me in, but this time I muttered the General Confession without really paying attention to what I was saying. The lessons weren't inspiring, I hated the ultra-modern choral setting for the Te Deum, and I didn't even hear the sermon.

I made an effort to pull myself together after the service. Our young friends Nigel and Inga Evans were there, with their new baby, a tiny mite not even a month old who had slept peacefully through prayers, music, and all. After we had exchanged comments about Jane's wonderful gingerbread, I duly praised young Nigel Peter to his adoring parents and grandparents, though really I don't think babies are very interesting until they get a bit older and start to turn into people. Maybe it's just as well I never had any.

Margaret Allenby, the dean's wife, caught up with Alan and me as we were about to leave the Cathedral.

"Morning, you two. Looking a bit gloomy today, Dorothy. Has poor Walter taken a turn for the worse?"

Margaret always knows everything, including most of what upsets me. I've come to accept and welcome her insight, but today she was missing the point. "No, I believe he's doing quite well. I hope to be able to visit him in a day or two. It's the rest of the problem that's getting me down."

"Not getting anywhere?"

"Not an inch. I think I must be taking the wrong tack. I was so sure that Bill's war experiences were somehow at the bottom of all that's happened, but I've talked with several people who knew him back then, and nobody seems to think there was anything out of the ordinary going on with him. Of course, I don't know what happened in Colditz, and I probably never will. I suspect that information died with Bill, and just as well, maybe."

"I suppose you've talked to poor Mr. Tredgold." Margaret smiled sadly.

"Tried to. Of course I didn't make any headway at all. How long has he been that way, Margaret?"

"Oh, for as long as I've known him. He talks quite rationally about everything except the war, but that subject is absolutely forbidden."

"It's such a shame. He seems like a sweet old man. And then there's John Merrifield, his mind sound, but his body deteriorating. And Stanley Rutherford—he's a Nonconformist, I expect, do you know him?"

"Oh, yes, indeed. A stalwart Baptist, but he comes to jumble sales and that sort of thing here from time to time, especially when they're in aid of war veterans or their families. It doesn't seem to matter which war, so long as he has a chance to buttonhole people and tell them about *his* war." She laughed gently.

I chuckled, too, but then I remembered how miserable Stanley seemed to be, living with his granddaughter. It wasn't really very funny, was it? "He's lonely. So is Miss Price. So are they all, lonely and weary and unhappy. It's pathetic. I tell you, Margaret, I'm terrified of getting old. Really old, I mean, outliving my usefulness and all my contemporaries and having to live in some sort of ghastly home. I get really angry at God, just thinking about it. Why doesn't he let people die when they're ready, instead of making them hang on and on until they're fed up with life, and everybody else is fed up with them?"

Alan put his arm around my shoulders and started to say something, but Margaret forestalled him. "I rather think that's a question for my husband—and here he is. Kenneth, my dear, Dorothy wants to know why God permits the ravages of old age."

Some clergymen might have dodged the awkward question, but the dean was no coward. "Do you know, I've often thought about that very point, particularly as my own age advances and my aches and pains multiply. One can never know for certain why God does anything, of course, but I wonder if perhaps he allows aging as a way of easing us from this world? We don't belong here, you know, not permanently. He's made us for his world, for Paradise, but we become attached to our lives here and loath to give them up. I will never believe that God *causes* any distress of any kind, but he obviously *permits* a great deal of suffering. I've toyed with the idea that he uses it, as he can use any evil in the cause of good, to make us a little less sorry to leave our earthly home."

He smiled. "Just my own idea, you know. Don't try to find Scripture to prove it. And I quite realize it's of very little help when one is coping with the agony of watching a parent or friend or spouse slip into the mists of senility. But perhaps the notion might make one's own aging a little more tolerable."

One of the canons demanded his attention then, and he shook our hands and bustled away, leaving me with something new to think about.

The weather that dreary afternoon grew colder and colder. The fog and rain began to freeze, loading the trees with a heavy coat of ice. The Sunday afternoon quiet was punctuated with explosive cracks as over-burdened limbs broke under the weight. Some lovely old trees were going to die in this storm, I thought, and once again pondered the mysteries of aging.

NINETEEN

ALAN GOT A CALL FROM DEREK AS WE WERE SITTING IN front of the fire that evening, trying to ignore the storm outside. He took the call in his office, but came padding back into the parlor with the phone. "Derek wonders if I could run over to the museum tomorrow. They're ready to begin sorting out the storeroom and would like my help. Will that upset any of your plans?"

"Not a bit, since I have no plans. And I'm dying to know what you find, besides. Still no chance I could help, I suppose?"

He shook his head, as I'd expected he would, and told Derek he'd meet him at nine o'clock.

"What will you be looking for?" I asked when he'd snapped off the phone.

"Your guess is as good as mine. First we'll have to figure out what Bill's system was, assuming he had one."

"Oh, I know a little about that. Walter told me. Bill was sorting things by families, and within families by date. There are other piles for big-deal events, local and national, and of course those overlap with the family ones. It's all fairly complicated and needs to be catalogued and cross-referenced, and as far as I could tell when I worked up there that one day, Bill hadn't got around to doing much of that for the newer stuff."

Alan groaned. "I was never meant for a librarian."

"That's why you need me. I'm good at that kind of thing."

"Well, you needn't be smug about it, my dear. Much as I'd appreciate your help, it can't be allowed, and that's that. So you can get on with Christmas preparations. There isn't a mince pie in the house," he added reproachfully.

"I know, I know. I like them, too. But we still have over a week. I might make a batch of cookies tomorrow. They're easier than mince pies and all that fiddling around with tart pans. But then I think I'll ask Jane if we can talk to one more person about Bill. There's some woman, a widow of one of Bill's friends from way back when. She might just know something."

"You never know," was Alan's tepid comment as he got up to poke the fire and add another log.

Privately I was of the same opinion. In fact, I had decided that if I didn't learn something of importance, some hint that I was looking in the right direction, I was going to give up the whole thing. Maybe Bill's death had been the purest accident. Maybe he'd gone down in the cellar to deal with the rats. Maybe Walter was attacked by some kid in search of drug money, who trashed the museum out of pique when he didn't find what he needed.

So it was in no very hopeful mood that I plodded across the back lawn on Monday morning. I was bringing a package of freshly baked butter cookies to share with Jane over coffee, but I nearly dropped them several times. The back garden was a bumpy, irregular mass of ice, almost impossible to walk on, and made worse by the twigs and small branches that littered the ground. I looked around and then decided not to. The place was a mess, and cleanup would take forever, but there was nothing to be done until the ice melted, and I might as well ignore what couldn't be fixed right then.

Jane's dogs greeted me eagerly as I walked through her back doorway.

"All right, kids, be good, now. These cookies aren't for you."

"Isn't the cookies," Jane said, appearing in the kitchen doorway. "Haven't had their w-a-l-k today."

The dogs recognized that particular word, even

spelled out. Their whines and tail waggings became even more frantic.

"Not today," said Jane firmly. "You've been out. That's enough. SIT!"

Reluctantly, every sense a-quiver, they sat, reproach writ large in their eyes. I followed Jane into the kitchen and shut the door behind me. "I wouldn't think even they could keep their equilibrium on that ice," I said, sitting down at her kitchen table.

"They can't. Coffee?"

"Please."

"Legs splayed out like newborn colts," she went on, chuckling. "Could barely stand up long enough to do what they went out for."

"I'm not sure I can stand up long enough to do what I intended today, either. I'd thought about going to see that last woman on your list, the widow?"

"Leigh Burton. Yes." Jane considered. "Bit of an iceberg, but she'll talk, if you can get her going."

"Another Stanley?"

"No. He wants to talk about himself. She wants to talk about George."

"That'd be her late husband."

"And Bill's best friend at Luftwich, though they had little enough in common. George's parents were well off, had a country estate, all that. But the estate was near here. Suppose there were common roots, something of that sort."

"Was Leigh from around here?"

"No. George met Leigh at Hurstpierpoint."

"Hurstpierpoint? Isn't that the public school near here? I thought it was a boys' school."

"Is. Always was. Leigh lived in the village, worked at her father's tobacconists' shop. Pretty girl."

Jane said no more, but her tone of voice said it all. I could see Leigh Burton, or whatever her name had been before she married. A sweet, pretty girl, working where the boys would come for sweets and the occasional forbidden cigarette. Chocolate-box prettiness, probably, all pink and white complexion and blond curls, irresistible to an impressionable young man just beginning to appreciate the charms of the opposite sex.

I wondered what would have happened if their marriage had lasted beyond George's youth.

"Was George—um—of an intellectual bent?"

"Smarter than she was, do you mean? Don't need to pussyfoot with me, you know. Yes, he was. Wanted to go in for engineering. One reason he became a pilot. Got into the war earlier than Bill, talked him into asking for assignment to Luftwich."

"They stayed close, then?"

"Like brothers."

"Did they get in touch with each other after the war? After Bill came back home, I mean?"

"George never came back. Plane shot down during Normandy invasion. No survivors."

I closed my eyes, reminded once more of how horrifically England had suffered in what was, to me, mostly a history lesson. "Bill must have been devastated when he found out."

"Yes. Here's your coffee."

All right, so Jane didn't want to talk about that part. The terrible shock of George's death might have been the reason Bill refused to talk, ever, about his war experiences. He must have told Jane just enough for her to understand his pain, but she wasn't willing to share it. Fair enough, unless it was relevant to our problem.

Probably it wasn't, though. For now I'd let it go and concentrate on Mrs. Burton.

"So do you think the roads are too bad to try to see her today?" I pursued, after we'd each had more cookies than were good for us.

"Warming up," Jane said, glancing out the window. "Hear the dripping? Streets probably clear by afternoon."

"Where does she live, at Heatherwood House?"

"Not she. Inherited some money, bought herself a nice house. Stone's throw away, just off the High Street."

"Well, I don't intend to go around throwing any stones today, or walking anywhere, either. Can you drive us, or give me directions?"

"Give you directions. Easy enough. Get on better by yourself. Leigh doesn't like me."

"Why not, for heaven's sake?" Jane liked, and was liked by, almost everybody. She was that kind of person.

"George died. Bill lived."

Sometimes Jane's terse style hides a depth of insight into the human heart that is almost epic.

So Jane gave me directions and a phone number, and that afternoon, after a hasty lunch (Alan decided not to come home) and a call to make sure Mrs. Burton was home and would see me, I went off in search of information I had little hope of finding.

Her house, I discovered, deserved a better adjective than "nice." It had probably been the home of a wealthy wool merchant, built perhaps a hundred years before mine, which would put it early in the 1500s sometime. It was a museum piece, lovingly restored and maintained in its half-timbered glory. I had passed it and admired it a hundred times without ever bothering to find out who lived inside. That inheritance must have been a handsome one, I mused as I rang the bell with something like awe.

I waited long enough, before the bell was answered, for my imagination to conjure up an anachronistic picture of a maid in cap and apron. Calling on memories of my favorite Agatha Christie books, I decided she would be wearing a neat flowered-print dress for daytime; black was for evening. Her name would be something like Florence—"faithful Florence." She would drop me a small curtsy when she answered the door and would go off to see if the mistress was "at home." Or perhaps she would have been told I was coming and would put me in the parlor to wait . . .

The door was opened by a tall, slender woman with steel-gray hair, wearing a blue wool dress and pearls.

The pearls looked very expensive indeed, and the dress certainly had not come off the peg. It was cut with a high neck, perhaps to hide the wrinkles of age, but the face above the soft blue wool had the taut firmness that comes only from youth or excellent cosmetic surgery. She held a walking stick, with a finely wrought silver handle and ivory inlays in the ebony shaft.

"Mrs. Martin? I'm Leigh Burton. Do come in."

I blinked away images of the maid and tried to adjust my other ideas as well. This woman had never in her life possessed chocolate-box prettiness. She would have been truly beautiful when she was young, perhaps a Diana Rigg type, with high cheekbones and an aristocratic bearing. She was still striking, even at eighty-whatever, and her accent was impeccable.

What in the world had she been doing in a tobacconist's shop in the village of Hurstpierpoint sixty years or so ago? I was consumed with curiosity, but there was really no tactful way to ask.

I collected my scattered thoughts as she showed me into a drawing room—it was the only possible term for the room—that would have made any antique collector go weak at the knees. I'm no expert about fine furniture, never in my life having been able to afford it, but I've visited enough museums to know that some of these pieces belonged in one.

Curiouser and curiouser.

"May I offer you some sherry?" My hostess seated herself, somewhat stiffly, on a fragile chair I wouldn't have dared touch, let alone sit in. The piecrust table next to it held a silver tray with a crystal decanter that was definitely not of recent manufacture, and two small, exquisite glasses. I was certain that they, unlike my sherry glasses, had not come from Marks and Spencer's at five pounds the set.

"No, thank you. It's a trifle early for me. But please . . ." I gestured at the tray.

Mrs. Burton gave me a wintry smile and folded her hands in her lap. I perceived that the offer had been a pro forma gesture, and also that she was not going to help me get started with my interview. Well, she hadn't been all that cordial on the phone, either, but Jane had said that talking about George was one of Mrs. Burton's favorite pastimes. So I'd let her talk about George.

"I do apologize for intruding on your time," I began, "but as I said on the phone, I'm trying to write a book about the war, for Americans but from an English point of view. I've always felt that people of my generation didn't really understand what it was like for you folks over here, even though we lived through it back in the States. And of course for the younger people it's all something they read about in the history books."

I stopped to draw breath. I was explaining too much. The more one tries to prop up a story, the more it sounds like the fabrication it is. Well, I was stuck with it now.

"So I thought I'd begin with some of the people in

Sherebury and their stories. And Jane Langland told me of your personal tragedy, and I wondered if you might be willing to tell me about it. If it's not too painful, of course."

Another chilly smile. "It happened many, many years ago, Mrs. Martin. I am not so thin-skinned as all that. What do you want to know?"

"Well, really, anything you can tell me about Mr. Burton and Luftwich. I'm trying to get a feeling for the period, you see. Did you two meet at the base?"

Well, she wouldn't know I knew better, would she? And it probably had nothing to do with my inquiry, but I couldn't restrain my curiosity about her.

"Yes. Well. You'll understand that some of my memories are apt to be rather vague. Don't rely on me for exact details. But if it's atmosphere you want . . ." She paused for a moment and then went on, and her voice took on a different quality, less brisk, warmer.

TWENTY

"WE MET WHEN GEORGE—MR. BURTON—WAS AT Hurstpierpoint. He was only seventeen, and I a little younger. I lived in the village. We encountered each other now and again when he came in to shop or buy a treat. Boys that age have hollow legs, of course, and he could put away any amount of sweets. We took a fancy to one another from the first. He began buying me candy, taking me out for ices, that sort of thing. It was all very boy-girl and innocent, but my parents didn't approve."

"Why not?"

"He was a public-school boy. My parents were working-class with very little money. They kept a shop, and thought it better not to mix with the toffs. I was bright enough, but there'd been no money to give me an education. I'd left school when I was fourteen and gone to work in the shop. This was in the late thirties, you understand. Times were hard, and my father used to say it would do no good, me getting used to treats and a soft life, because there was none of that in my future."

Her accent had altered subtly with her reminiscence. Just a trace of the old vowels had crept in, a slight change of cadence. I was hearing a bit of Leigh at age sixteen or so.

"George and I had other ideas, of course. He was going in for engineering. He was going to build bridges and dams, go all over the world, make pots of money, not to mention his family's money. Oh, he was full of dreams, and I dreamt right along with him.

"Then the war came. As soon as he left Hurstpierpoint, George enlisted in the RAF. He had learnt to fly while he was still in school, and he thought he'd meet important people, make contacts that could help him when the war was over. He was commissioned, of course, and entered as a flight lieutenant."

"And went to Luftwich," I put in.

"Not at first, no. He was sent to a few other places

first, but after about a year he was posted to Luftwich. They had suffered some heavy losses of men there and needed experienced flyers badly. And by that time I had turned eighteen, so over my parents' objections, we were married."

"How did *his* parents feel about it?" That was really pushing it, so I backtracked a bit. "Of course it's none of my business, really, but wartime marriages are always interesting . . . the strains on a relationship that parental objections can add, and that sort of thing." I hope that didn't sound as lame to her as it did to me.

She answered readily enough. "They were not best pleased, as you might imagine. They had hoped for a far 'better' marriage for their only son. Not that they were extremely wealthy, not then. They had the estate, of course, Deepings, but they'd suffered losses after the First War, like everybody else. Then they had nearly recovered from those when along came another war, even worse. But they knew the right people and had enough capital that they felt they could recoup their losses after the war, when things began to look up again."

"But they didn't like you at first," I pursued.

"They had nothing against me personally. It was my background to which they objected. However, they were besotted with George, and when they saw that I was, too, they softened toward me. We're straying rather far from the story of the war, aren't we?"

"Perhaps, but it's the human interest I'm really trying for." I had a sudden inspiration. "History books focus on events, on battles and dates and treaties and that sort of thing. This book is to be about people, ordinary people, military and civilian, and what the war did to them. So anything I can garner about the interactions of people is useful.

"However, I do have some questions about Luftwich, about the life there. I gather they had quarters for married officers."

"For some of the very senior officers, yes. Not for us. I took rooms in Alder's Green, the village near Luftwich, and saw George when I could. He flew a lot of nights, of course, but not every night, so we did have some time together."

"Ah, yes, tell me about that. I need to get a feel for the schedule of operations at Luftwich. Most of the flights were at night, then?"

"Most of the RAF flights, from all of England, not just Luftwich. It was more difficult for the crews, but safer. The Hun couldn't spot them as easily. Of course, our boys couldn't see their targets as well, either, so it evened out a bit. Actually, I sometimes wondered if the whole concept might be a mistake. I asked George about it once, I remember."

"Asked about the night flights? Surely he couldn't have done anything about the schedule."

"Oh, no, of course not, he was far too junior. But I wondered if he could just mention to his superiors . . . well, it did seem as though the raids were far less productive than they should have been. It seemed that so few German targets were hit, and so many of our planes destroyed. I think I said that they lost far too many men, and to little purpose."

"Hmm. I had the impression that the RAF contributed a great deal to the eventual Allied victory."

"That's the way the history books have it," she said, and there was an odd note of bitterness in her voice. "Myself, I've always thought that either the historians were being patriotic and exaggerating, or else Luftwich was rather the odd man out. Casualty figures were secret, of course, but I knew who was being lost at Luftwich, because they were George's friends. And one would read in the papers about so and so many German planes shot down, so and so many factories destroyed, and I used to wonder by whom. Certainly not by flights from Luftwich. And given the caliber of men stationed there, that seemed peculiar."

"They were good men on the whole, then?"

"They were excellent men. Excellent flyers, excellent fighters. I got to know a good many of them quite well, of course. George and I had so many friends, and such good times . . ." Her voice had softened still more, but there was pain in it, too. "Parties, dancing . . . we were young, and there was a feeling . . . I can't describe it, a feeling of belonging, I suppose. We were united against a diabolical enemy, and our differences didn't matter."

"The camaraderie of wartime," I suggested.

"Yes, but more than that. It wasn't just mindless patriotism. The menace was real and terrifyingly close by. France was in German hands, and France is twenty-one miles from England."

I gulped. "I suppose I knew that, as an abstract fact, but when I think about it . . . that's closer than we are to London."

"On a clear day one can see the coast of France from the cliffs of Dover. George and I did that once when he had a few days of leave. Luftwich is in Norfolk, of course, and travel wasn't easy. We had planned to drive—George had a car—but we couldn't get the petrol, so we had to take the train. It was crowded and stuffy, I remember, and we had to take the long way 'round because part of the line had been bombed. But when we got there it was wonderful. The air was clean and fresh and the sun was shining, and we went out on the cliffs. And George pointed and said, 'He's over there, Leigh. He's over there hating us and wanting to destroy us. And I'm not going to let him.' "

"He sounds like a fine man, your George."

"He was. Most of them were." The bitterness was back in her voice, and I thought that despite her claim to sangfroid, there were still raw nerves not too far from the surface.

I changed the subject slightly. "Tell me about the men. I suppose George had some particular friends."

"He was friendly with everyone. He was like that. He was one of those people who made life seem brighter every time he walked into a room. He had some special friends at first, but one learned, in wartime, to try not to get too close to anyone, because one never knew . . ."

We were at a dangerous point again. "Was George under Air Commodore Merrifield's command?"

"Wing commander then. Yes, and George thought highly of him. Some of the airmen didn't care for him, and I confess I never did, myself. A trifle too smooth for my taste, although"—the wintry smile again—"he was the best dancer I've ever met. He made rather a point of dancing with his officers' wives when there were gala affairs in the mess. I do believe I was his favorite partner."

"Even though—forgive me, but even though you came from a somewhat humble background?"

"As I said, those differences began to be quite unimportant. And less obvious, as well, at least for me. It was there, at Luftwich, mixing with the other officers and their wives or girlfriends, that I began to learn to speak properly, dress properly, talk about the right things. You'd wondered about that, hadn't you?"

"Well . . . yes, to tell the truth. That is, when you told me about your background . . ." I gestured vaguely around the room. It was an awkward subject, especially for an American who wasn't used to talking about class differences, but she had, after all, raised it herself.

"The class structure in England has never been as rigid as foreigners suppose. It has always been possible to transcend it, and times of war help, oddly enough. The great leveler. Oh, yes, I would have made a proper wife for George after the war. But of course I never got the chance."

This time I couldn't think of anything to say to head her off the painful subject.

"It was near the end of the war, you know. We all thought it was only a matter of months, and in fact it was all over less than a year later, at least in Europe. But meanwhile . . . it was over Normandy somewhere. I never knew where exactly. That battle was . . . well, you've read reports. You know what a scene of mass confusion it was."

"I do know a little about D-day, yes. Many, many Americans were killed."

"Yes, of course. But the RAF provided valuable air support, and lost many men, too. George . . . well, we all waited and waited for word about our men. When it came . . . his body was never recovered. Lost at sea somewhere off the coast, it was assumed. None of them, none of that crew, survived."

"What did the wives do? What did you do?" Without meaning to, I glanced at the luxurious appointments surrounding me.

"And how did I acquire all this?" She laughed, a brittle sort of laugh with no amusement in it. All her defenses were up again. "It's quite simple to explain, really. After George was killed, his parents invited me to come to stay with them." She hesitated and then went on. "I was expecting a baby, you see. I couldn't very well go on living in two rooms in Alder's Green, and they had a room to spare."

"But—I must be confused. I thought they had a big house, a country manor."

Impatiently, she said, "Yes, of course. I told you. Deepings, just on the Kent border. It has twenty bedrooms, I believe, but most of them were occupied by the children who were billeted there. You know about the evacuation of children from London?"

I nodded. Many parents who lived in London had, during the worst of the Blitz, sent their children to the country where they might be safer from enemy action. One of the many tragedies of the war was that so often the parents were killed in bombing raids, and the children orphaned. Even those who weren't were often treated badly by their foster parents, sometimes beaten and starved. I had often wondered if the evacuation had been entirely a good thing.

"So the Burtons made room for me, and little by little we grew closer. I had become far more sophisticated by that time, and they weren't ashamed to let me meet their friends."

"Eliza Doolittle," I suggested.

"Something like that. And of course they were solicitous of me, because of the baby. George's baby."

She stopped. I waited. Jane had said nothing about a child. I had the feeling I wasn't going to like this story.

"There was an air raid, very near the end of the war. The night was foggy, and they said later that the planes had probably lost their way and bombed the wrong target. Looking back, I suspect the German pilots simply didn't care. They knew their cause was lost, and they only wanted to drop their bombs and get back safely as soon as they could. At the time I couldn't see that it mattered much, one way or the other. For whatever reason, one wing of the Burtons' house was destroyed. Three evacuee children were killed, and I lost the baby."

Her voice was steady, her eyes dry. She had come to terms with this second tragedy in her life, perhaps better than with the first. I couldn't quite match her aplomb when I said, "I'm so very sorry."

"It was long ago. At the time I wanted to die, but one doesn't die of wishing. The Burtons were very kind, though quite dreadfully disappointed. They had wanted that grandchild almost as much as I had wanted George's son. For some reason I was sure it was going to be a boy. But there were some compensations. You see, I was now the only link George's parents had to him. They began to draw me more and more into their lives, treat me more and more like their daughter. I'm a quick study, and they completed my social education. I learned how to dress, how to carry on a genteel conversation, how to behave in their world. After a while it became my own."

"Yes, I see. Did you ever—that is, you were young and now single, and mixing with eligible young men. Did you ever consider remarrying?"

"No. Oh, no. That wouldn't have done. I had grown fond of Grace and Andrew, and they of me, but theirs was a possessive sort of love. I was of value to them only as George's widow. If I had remarried they would have lost interest." She spoke about it dispassionately. Apparently the passage of years had taken the sting out of that possessiveness as well. That or the acquisition of wealth. Money may not buy happiness, but it surely can soften the blows life deals us.

"So you went on living with the Burtons."

"For about a year after the war ended, yes. Then one of their friends, Sir Robert Lesley, offered me a position as his confidential secretary. He was a widower with a big country house in East Sussex. He needed someone to oversee the running of it and deal with his business affairs. Well, of course I had no money of my own and couldn't keep on sponging off Grace and Andrew forever. I leapt at the offer.

"It worked out very well. I had exactly the qualifications he needed: tact, a presentable appearance, that sort of thing, and I'd learnt enough from Grace about the operation of an important house that I could manage very well. He didn't require a stenographer, and I learnt typing very quickly. Sir Robert was getting on in years and was not in the best of health. He came quite to rely on me, and when he died he left me a nice little bequest and a glowing letter of recommendation. The contacts I'd made while working with him made it easy for me to find another position, this time for a cabinet minister's wife at their country house in Kent. Living there, I had no expenses to speak of and was able to save nearly all my salary. So what with one thing and another I had acquired quite a pleasant nest egg, and I decided to buy this house. It was near enough to Deepings that I could keep in close touch with the Burtons. Frankly, I had thought they would probably remember me in their will, but I had no idea they would leave me as much as they did. Of course, if George had lived, or even if his son had lived, there would have been Deepings . . . but they both died. I was left with enough, however, to furnish this house rather nicely."

Her glance strayed around the room, caressing the Adam fireplace, the Persian rugs, the Wedgwood sconces. Her austere face softened into a half smile that wasn't entirely pleasant and I got a sudden jolt. There was a wolfish look about that smile, a revelation of avarice that sent my thoughts off on an entirely new tack.

Perhaps it was true that she hadn't known about the Burtons' will. Perhaps she hadn't known about Sir Robert's will, either. Perhaps she hadn't exercised any of what lawyers call "undue influence" on any of them. But if what I thought I'd just seen of her character was accurate, I was willing to bet she'd been happy enough to take the money and run, and had shed few tears about the demise of her benefactors.

I wondered what she'd gotten out of the cabinet minister?

"You must have been devastated by the death of George's parents," I said sweetly, testing her.

She didn't bat an eyelash. "Of course," she said, and glanced at her watch.

I was jolted into remembering why I'd come. "Oh, dear, your story is fascinating, but I'm taking too much of your time, and I did want to ask a bit about

Bill Fanshawe."

"Fanshawe? Why?" Her voice sharpened; her disturbing smile disappeared.

"Only because I know most about him. I thought I'd make his story the focus of the book, relating everything else to him, you see."

"No, I don't. He was at Luftwich for a matter of months. George was there for years. I know George had some sort of attachment to Fanshawe, but really he was a complete bore. Oh, I know he just died, and *de mortuis* and all that, but really! He flew a few raids, never accomplished much of anything, never hit a single plane or ship or any target of any importance whatever, at least to my knowledge. He was a nonentity. I should think he'd be worthy of a footnote, at best. He wasn't even an effective curator for our museum. He was extremely casual about some memorabilia I donated, very casual, indeed. Of course you've been talking to Jane Langland, who thought the sun rose and set on her precious Bill. For whatever good it did her."

This time her look at her watch was long enough that she could be sure I noticed, and furthermore she rose, leaning heavily on her cane, from her chair. Clearly our interview was at an end.

I stood. "Yes. Well, thank you so much. It's been most interesting to meet you, and your house is simply beautiful. I wish I'd had time to see it properly."

"Yes, a pity." Her tone made it quite clear that I would never be invited for a tour. I shook her hand and walked to the door with hypocritical expressions of gratitude, and made my escape.

What a shame she hadn't the strength to have assaulted Walter. That cane would have made a marvelous weapon, and I wouldn't have bet a nickel that any milk of human kindness would have stayed her hand.

I wondered just how long ago Sir Robert Lesley had died, and if it would be possible to find out exactly what he'd died of?

TWENTY-ONE

THAT WAS THE FIRST THING I ASKED ALAN WHEN HE came home. I accosted him before he'd finished hanging up his coat.

"If somebody died quite a while ago, is there any way I could find out how he died?"

"I'm delighted to see you, too, my dear," he said, dropping his hat on the hall table. He plodded into the parlor and sank into his favorite chair. Grunting, he pushed his shoulders back, rotated his neck. "Out of condition," he complained. "I haven't pushed papers about for years. And what's this about somebody dying?"

"Never mind. I'll ask you later. I might have come across something useful today, that's all. I forgot about your project. How did it go? And would you like a drink, or some tea?"

206

"Tea, thanks, love. The museum was frightfully cold."

I put the kettle on and came back to the parlor, sitting on the arm of Alan's chair and massaging his shoulders while he made blissful sounds. When the kettle shrieked, I gave him a final pat. "There. My hands are giving out. That'll have to do."

I laced the tea with a little Jack Daniel's to complete the relaxation routine, added some goodies to the tray, and came back to find Alan had recovered enough to build a fire. It blazed up almost immediately and felt lovely.

"Mince pies!" said Alan. "Isn't it a little early to eat them?"

"Men! You cry for mince pies, I give them to you, and you complain that it isn't Boxing Day yet. Fie upon thee, thou black-hearted foosh! Pretend it's ten days from now and eat them. I'll make more if we run out. But tell me about today at the museum."

In between sips of tea and bites of the flaky little tarts, he told me. There wasn't much to tell, actually. He and two other policemen had spent the day trying to organize Bill's files.

"There's an incredible amount of material in that room, and if it has ever been organized in any fashion whatsoever, we could find no evidence of the fact."

"Alan, that's odd! Because there certainly was some rudimentary organization when Jane and I left it the other day. I won't say the room was a model of neatness, but the papers were in stacks and the other artifacts were in piles, and if you could figure out Bill's system, it was easy enough to assign categories to the groups. Names, events, whatever."

"This morning it was chaos."

"Then the intruder, whoever he was—or she—searched up there, too."

"And, of course, may have found whatever he or she was looking for. Which might make our search fruitless. It has to be done, nevertheless. Is there more tea?"

There was. I poured it out. "I don't suppose you found Bill's calendar. Diary. Whatever you want to call it."

"No, nor much of anything else. The three of us got through quite a lot of, frankly, extremely boring memorabilia of various prominent Sherebury families. We were able to sort it by family and date, not much more. We'll leave the historical aspect of it to whoever takes charge of the museum. Our concern is with anomalies, and if we found any today, we didn't recognize them. But you said you might have a line on something."

"Oh, probably not. I went to see a woman named Leigh Burton. She's the widow of one of Bill Fanshawe's war buddies. I told you."

"You didn't mention the name. So you went to see the Ice Princess, did you?"

I snickered. "I see you know the lady."

"We've met. I can't say I was ever on friendly terms with her, but then I haven't enough money to be of interest."

"So she really is as fond of money as she seems to be. I think she's also something of a social snob. Funny, given her background. She was the daughter of a tobacconist, you know."

"Hard as she's tried to keep that titbit hidden, yes, it's well known. But you know, my dear, there's no snob quite like the nouveau riche."

"And that's what I was wondering about. She must have a *lot* of money to have a house like that."

"Pots of it, I understand. The story is she inherited it from a grateful employer and her late husband's family."

"Oh, well, if you know the whole story there's no point in me telling you." I checked the teapot. It was empty.

"I suppose you were wondering if she did them in."

"Oh, for heaven's sake! Why am I going around wasting my breath when you know everything anyway!"

Alan laughed. "Not everything, but I do happen to know about the fair Mrs. Burton. There was an inquiry, as a matter of fact, when her employer died. He had no close family, but there was a third cousin or something who thought he was coming in for the boodle, and was livid when darling Leigh scooped the lot."

"All of it? She gave me the impression—well, in fact she *said,* 'A nice little bequest.'"

"Every penny the old man had, and there were quite a number of them."

"This was around here?"

"In Kent, but we heard about it. There was quite a to-do, but it was absolutely proven that the old man had died quite legitimately of whatever he had been expected to die of, and about when he had been expected to die. And his will made it quite clear that he left Mrs. Burton the money because she'd been kind to him and the cousin had ignored him for years. Of course the cousin tried to prove undue influence, but the courts made short work of him."

"Oh, dear. And she would have been such a lovely villain. I'd thought maybe Bill had found out something about her and she'd come to the museum to talk to him . . . although I doubt she could have struck down Walter, and come to think of it, Bill wasn't even there when Walter was injured. Well, I mean he was there, but he was dead. Oh, well. I don't suppose she did in her in-laws, either?"

"If she did, it was the perfect murder. They died in an automobile accident near their home in Hampshire. It was in the seventies, sometime, and Mrs. Burton was in hospital at the time, appendicitis, I believe. In Surrey," he added before I could ask.

I sighed. "If I'd known you could tell me all that, I could have saved a good deal of time."

"But you went there to talk to her about the war, didn't you?"

"I confess, I got interested in her background. Jane had told me enough about her that I was thoroughly taken aback when I saw that house. So I got a bit side-tracked. She did tell me a little about the war, though, from her husband's point of view, of course. She seemed to think the Luftwich operation was pretty much a washout. She said their missions weren't often successful, and so on. And she had no opinion at all of Bill, called him a 'nonentity.' Which put the final stamp on my opinion of her."

"Not a congenial sort of person," Alan agreed, "but almost certainly not a murderer."

"Pity. I liked her in the role."

"Have you heard anything about Walter today? I intended to ring up the hospital, but the time got away from me."

"Yes, as a matter of fact. When I got home from visiting the Ice Princess, I went over to see Jane, and she'd been to the hospital. They let her see him for a few minutes. She said he was much better, still somewhat confused, and chafing because he couldn't remember, but he knew her, and was able to say a few sensible things and move his arms and legs. So that's good news."

Alan shook his head slightly. "Good news for Walter, of course. But now that there's no risk of his death, the investigation steps down a notch or two. Assault is a serious crime, but not as serious as murder. And when there are never enough men—"

"I know, I know. It's your theme song. Never enough men on the force to do it all. The more fools they, then, for not using woman power when it volunteers itself. But I know your answer to that, too. Now, do you want some more of those waistline-destroying tarts, or shall we start thinking about some real food?"

We ended up going to the Rose and Crown for dinner, and had a pleasant time talking with the Endicotts, when they could spare a moment from serving the pre-Christmas crowd, about the newest exploits of their grandson, Inga and Nigel's son. It seemed he had slept through the night for the first time, and produced an absolutely unmistakable smile, and such remarkable accomplishments had to receive their due praise.

Next morning Alan headed back to the museum, leaving me at a loose end. I needed to go to London to finish my Christmas shopping, but first I needed to organize my mind. I sat down to make lists.

The Christmas shopping list was soon finished. I added a few trinkets for the Evans baby, some videos for Alan's younger grandchildren, and a really nice sweater for Alan.

Then I pulled a fresh spiral notebook from my desk drawer, fended off Emmy, who dearly loves to sit on paper, and began to put down my few ideas about what I was beginning to think of as The Museum Mess.

I found, as I sat and chewed on my pen, that my ideas were sorely in need of organization. I had nothing, really, that seemed to add up to any satisfactory whole or even reasonable-looking pieces. I'd talked to a lot of people, but their stories were so diverse, so lacking in focus, I wasn't sure that I'd learned anything at all.

Well, I'd better do something chronological, then. It had started—yes, a little over a week ago, when Jane and I had entered the museum looking for Bill. I remembered I'd been fretting about having done so little about Christmas.

Bill had presumably been dead then, but we hadn't found him until—no, take it in order. I began to write:

1. *December 8, Monday. Go to museum. Bill missing. Search for him, call in his assistant, Walter Tubbs.*
2. *Tuesday. Bill still missing. Go back to museum, search through Bill's workroom. Find nothing interesting except Bill's atlas of the United States. Discover markings on the Indiana page.*
3. *Wednesday. Take the atlas to Walter to see if he can make anything of it.*
4. *Thursday. Find Bill, dead, in a tunnel under the museum. Walter has been attacked and seriously injured, apparently the night before. The atlas and Bill's engagement calendar are both missing; the museum has been ransacked. Bill is clutching a letter in his hands, but it doesn't make much sense.*

That reminded me that Charles Lambert and his friend were coming to dinner tomorrow to take a look at Bill's letter. I should get that meat mixture made for the steak and kidney pie. Like most stews, it was much better the second day. I made a note on another page of the book and turned back to my uninspiring task.

5. *Friday. Go to see Stanley Rutherford and John Merrifield. Stanley wants to talk mostly about Stanley and how heroic he was. Hints there might have been something funny going on on the home front. Merrifield fills us in on the day his plane went down, killing everyone except Bill and himself.*

6. *Saturday. Go to see Barbara Price and the Rev'd Mr. Tredgold. Price gives me some details about life at Luftwich, not much. Hates Merrifield at least as much as Stanley does. Tredgold a washout. Falls apart whenever the war is so much as mentioned.*

7. *Sunday. Do nothing except brood about old age.*

I made a face at that. If I wasn't careful, I could talk myself into a real depression about growing older. And really, when one considered the only alternative . . . I went on with my list.

8. *Monday, yesterday. Talk to Mrs. Burton. Learn a lot about her background, not much about the war in general or Luftwich in particular, except that she thought Luftwich men didn't accomplish much.*

I looked at that entry again. Put in contrast with

Stanley's bragging, it was suddenly a bit startling. Stanley had bragged about how many planes he'd shot down, had sounded as though he'd won the war practically single-handedly. I marked that down as an oddity and then looked back once more at my chronology and sighed. If there was anything enlightening in that disjointed set of impressions, it certainly wasn't casting any bright light on my mind. And Jane had run out of people for me to interview.

It had all happened so long ago. Almost everyone who might have remembered anything was dead. And did any of it matter, anyway? The idea that Bill's death was somehow connected with his war experiences was my own obsession. Nobody seemed to share it.

Well, maybe Alan would come up with something today at the museum. If not, the document expert who was coming to dinner might discover something interesting. For now, I washed my hands of the whole mess. If I got moving, I could get that stew made and still have time for a little shopping today.

I pushed Emmy off my lap and headed for the kitchen.

TWENTY-TWO

I WAS LATE LEAVING SHEREBURY'S SHOPPING MALL, OUT at the edge of town, and the rain that had begun when I was driving out there had started to freeze. By the time I got home and staggered into the house with all my parcels, it was well past the supper hour and Alan, bless his heart, had started preparing a meal. It was only some leftover curry he'd found in the freezer, but it smelled wonderful.

"Alan, you are a jewel. I'm sorry I'm so late, but you found my note, right?"

"I did. The shops must have been a nightmare this time of year."

"They were, even in our little mall. You wouldn't believe the crowds! But I managed to do quite a lot. I still have to make the trip to London, though, if for no other reason than to buy chestnuts from the street vendors. I love them. So Dickensian."

"Yes, indeed. Did I mention that I encountered them in New York the last time I had to venture over there?"

"Killjoy. No, no beer for me, thanks. I love it with curry, but I'm so cold all I want is pots and pots of absolutely boiling tea."

We ate as if we hadn't seen food for weeks, and when we'd finished the last grain of rice and crumb of flat bread, we settled down in front of a lovely hot fire.

"So how did your day go at the museum?"

"Much like yesterday. A great deal of work to no apparent end. The storeroom is looking far tidier than it did, but I can't say we learned anything of interest. However, I do have one small piece of news for you. The ME finally completed the autopsy on Bill, and there were no surprises. He died of a massive cerebral hemorrhage. The ME said it must have been instantaneous. He would have had no pain, probably not even any sense of disorientation. He simply died."

"Well, that'll be a relief to Jane, probably. When are they releasing the body for burial?"

"Anytime. As there's no family to notify, I suppose Jane will be the one to make the arrangements."

"She may have already talked to the dean. She's very efficient. Let's see, today's Tuesday. The funeral will probably be Thursday; that'll give time to let everybody in Sherebury know. Alan, I'm glad that part of it is over. There's something about the permanency of a funeral that helps people get on with life. Not that Jane's been falling apart or anything, but I think she'll feel better when the funeral's over."

"What the psychologists call 'closure'?"

"Well, if they do, they're wrong. A chapter of one's life, an important one, is never closed. But it can be set aside, and it must be, eventually."

"Yes. And speaking of setting things aside, have you abandoned your sleuthing for the pleasures of commerce?"

"Only temporarily. I sat down this morning to try to figure out what, if anything, I'd learned, and there was so little of substance I decided to wait until we talk to Charles and his friend tomorrow."

"Ah, yes, the letter. I've managed to get permission for your expert to look at the actual document, although he'll have to operate under a few restrictions. We're no nearer solving the assault case, and the letter is being considered as a piece of evidence. He won't be able to touch it, for example."

"I don't expect he'll like that, but I'm eager to see what he'll make of it. To me it might as well have been written by Lewis Carroll."

"A piece of jabberwocky, you think? But it isn't funny."

"No. Well, we'll see."

On Wednesday I suffered no temptation to go anywhere. A slow, steady rain had set in, which was perhaps just as well, since I had plenty to do at home, with guests coming. I got down to some serious housecleaning, a task I'd been neglecting for days, and made a trifle for dessert. The total cholesterol count of our dinner would be enough to clog all the arteries in town, but it was the holiday season, a time when overeating seems almost a duty. We'd return to healthful habits in the New Year.

I was busy polishing silver spoons when Alan came home from another day of slaving at the museum. This time, however, he had something to show me.

"Look at this, my dear." Still in his coat and hat, he pulled out of his inside pocket two plastic envelopes and handed them to me.

The first was the letter we were to examine tonight, the letter found clasped in Bill's dead hand. "What?" I said.

"Look at the other one."

I did as he bade me, and gasped. It was, without a doubt, the missing second page.

"Where did you find this?" I demanded. "Was it in a family stack?"

"Unfortunately not. It was buried at the bottom of a box of old financial records, bank statements and that sort of thing, for the museum itself."

I looked at the paper more closely. The signature was "Pickles," as nearly as I could make out. The text was brief and no more informative than the first page had been. It simply finished the sentence from the preceding page with "to greet them" and went on with routine wishes for good health and prosperity and then that infuriating signature.

"Well, if Charles's expert can make anything of this, I take my hat off to him."

"Considering some of your hats, my dear, that's a handsome offer."

Anyway the waiting was almost over. I barely had time to tidy away the mess in the kitchen and get the pie in the oven before the doorbell rang and there were Charles and a desiccated little man whom he introduced as James Wilson. Alan poured drinks while I made the salad and put the potatoes on to boil, and then I went back to the parlor to sip a little bourbon and enjoy Mr. Wilson.

If I had been inventing an MI5 expert on documents, I couldn't have come up with anyone more perfect than James Wilson. He was shorter than I and weighed a whole lot less. His hair was gray and somewhat sparse in front, but very neatly combed. His toothbrush mustache was gray, too, and his tweeds were oh-so-correct. His speech was dry and precise, and I somehow got the impression that Charles had taken him out of a cupboard and dusted him off before bringing him to dinner.

It was a relief to find some amusement, but I didn't dare catch Alan's eye, or I would have giggled and disgraced myself.

Jane arrived in a few minutes. We introduced Wilson and then, in proper English fashion, discussed through drinks and dinner everything under the sun except what was on all our minds. James Wilson grew drier and more precise with every word he uttered, though he displayed an unexpected sense of humor. His nutty little jests were in character, though, so deadpan and British that they went right over my American head. If Alan hadn't chuckled, I wouldn't have known they were meant to be funny.

Jane, who has little time for niceties, grew more and more restive, and finally, over trifle and coffee, Alan took pity on her and cleared his throat.

"Mr. Wilson, we've very much enjoyed your company, but I imagine Charles told you he was bringing you here for a purpose."

"Er—yes. A questionable document, I believe he said."

"Questionable in several ways, but our immediate concern is to fix an approximate date to it. Before I show it to you, I should tell you something of the circumstances in which it was found."

He sketched them out, baldly, with detachment, studiously avoiding any mention of Jane's connection with the dead man. "Some particulars, which I won't go into, lead us to believe there might be something slightly odd about the man's death. That is why the police took possession of the letter. As a former chief constable, I was able to borrow the letter, but I promised I would keep it in the plastic envelope. I happened to find the second page today, but I fear I must treat it in the same way."

Mr. Wilson's face crumpled in distress. "Oh, I'm afraid that won't do at all. I must touch it, smell it, look at it closely. I can't give you even an educated guess otherwise, oh, dear, dear, no. In order to be definitive, I really should have a sample of the paper and ink for analysis."

Alan considered, then compromised. "Very well. I will take it out of the envelope, with tweezers. You may smell it, and certainly you may have all the light you wish to examine it. I can't allow you to touch it."

"My dear man, you're putting blinkers on me! However, needs must, I suppose. Lead me to it, and I'll do what I can."

"Then shall we adjourn to my study? At least, you don't all need to come if—"

Of course we all wanted to come, and though it was a tight fit, we squeezed in. Mr. Wilson was given the place of honor at Alan's desk, the bright reading light focused on the letter.

"Mmm, yes." Wilson whipped a jeweler's loupe out of his pocket and peered at the letter through it. He held the paper up to the light, using Alan's tweezers and a pair of his own that he had dredged from the same pocket. He put his face close to the paper and sniffed delicately. He looked up at Alan. "Fingernail?" he asked.

Alan looked dubious, but nodded.

Mr. Wilson turned the letter over and scratched, very carefully, at the paper, and then studied his fingernail under the loupe. Finally he sat back and very deliberately read the letter, moving his lips in and out rather like a goldfish.

When he had finished, he turned to me. "I believe you are an American, Mrs. Martin. Can you tell me anything about these places mentioned in the letter?"

"Only that they are very small and of little interest to any visitor. I was born in Indiana, and even I hadn't heard of most of them before seeing this." I pointed to the letter. "But when Alan and I consulted an atlas, we discovered the fact that each of them is near a place with an English or a European place name."

"Ah. Tell me those names."

I tried to think. "New Carlisle, I remember. Versailles." I didn't shock his sensibilities by pronouncing it the way Hoosiers do. "Um—Rochester, I think, and Richmond. There were others, but I've forgotten. Oh, Edinburgh, I know. Frankfurt, only we spell it with an *o*."

On a less wooden face, Mr. Wilson's expression would have been a beam of satisfaction. He pushed the letter away, put down his tweezers, and rubbed his hands together with a dry little rustle. "Yes. Well. Not much trouble there. The paper, the ink, the handwriting, all consistent, what?"

Jane opened her mouth, but Alan shook his head slightly. We waited.

"My dear Mr. Nesbitt!" Mr. Wilson looked pained. "Do you mean to tell me you really could not put a date to this letter?"

I bit back the remark I wanted to make. Alan said mildly, "My wife and I had some very tentative ideas, but we thought it best to consult an expert."

"But—oh, very well. I can't give you a precise month or day, but this letter was certainly written in 1944, probably toward the end of the year. Who wrote it, and to whom?"

Alan shook his head. "Those are things we don't know. We were hoping that a date would help us pin it down."

"I'd think you'd want to find whoever they are, then, because there's not a doubt in my mind that this letter is written in code."

"In code!" I burst out. I couldn't help it. "But it makes perfect sense! I mean, if it were some sort of letter substitution, even a very sophisticated one, wouldn't it at least sound peculiar? It's just boring."

"Ah, my dear lady, you are making the common mistake of confusing 'code' with 'cipher.' A cipher substitutes letters, numbers, or symbols for the plain text. It is relatively simple to break if one has an adequate sample. Ciphers are often so simpleminded that any child with a rudimentary knowledge of the alphabet can solve them. Even with more sophisticated attempts, the consultation of a frequency table—a list of which letters appear most frequently in the English, or indeed in other languages—"

"Right," said Jane, her patience at an end. "So this is a code, not a cipher. Substitution of words, not letters. Grasped that. Why d'you think so?"

"I do not think so, madam," said Mr. Wilson, a hint of frost in his voice, "I know. Given the age of the paper and ink, and the general tenor of the letter, combined with the decisive particulars, there can be no question."

"What 'decisive particulars'?" Jane's voice was dangerously near a roar.

"Oh, dear me, didn't I say? This. And this."

He pointed to the salutation of the letter and then a little farther down. "Charles, here, will have told you that I worked with MI5 during the war. I may be old, now, but I have forgotten nothing from that terrible time, nothing. I believe that I am revealing no closely held secrets when I say that 'Waffles' was a code name given to a number of fifth columnists in this country. And 'Sam Smith' was used for the Luftwaffe. Of course, what you have told me, Mrs. Martin, about the place names makes it perfectly clear. This letter is a piece of information about bombing raids."

TWENTY-THREE

IF HE HAD DROPPED A BOMB RIGHT THERE IN ALAN'S study, we wouldn't have been much more shocked. For a moment I thought I actually heard the rumble of a distant mortar, but it was only the sullen growl of some halfhearted thunder.

Jane was the first to recover. "Don't believe it," she said flatly. "Bill Fanshawe was not a traitor."

"My dear woman," began little Mr. Wilson, but I interrupted. I had recovered at least a part of my wits.

"You're quite certain this was written in 1944?" I asked him.

"Quite certain."

"Then don't you see, Jane? This couldn't have been written *to* Bill, because he was in prison at Colditz from the autumn of 1943. And—does it look like his handwriting to you?"

"No." She was still angry and terse.

"Well, then, it isn't *from* him either. So it must be something he found at the museum, just as Alan found the second page today."

"But—"

"That doesn't take into account—"

"You're forgetting—"

There were protests from all sides except Jane, who remained stubbornly silent. The rest apologized, deferred to one another, and finally spoke one at a time.

225

"Handwriting can be disguised, you know," said Mr. Wilson, with a nervous glance at Jane, who outweighed him by a good fifty pounds.

"Mr. Fanshawe might well have hidden the two pages of the letter himself, perhaps in separate places." That was Charles, who had no official qualifications as a sleuth, but who had done enough esoteric research to be an old hand at educated guesses. "Then when something, or someone, threatened his secret, he made off with only the first page, the critical one."

"I'm afraid your theory does have a few other holes, as well, love," said Alan, looking at me regretfully. "For one thing, if he was a collaborator, there's no reason to suppose he couldn't have received communications in the prison camp. For all we know, that's why he was taken there—to make the lines of communication easier."

"All right. I accept that nothing is proven. But I'm with Jane in this. She, after all, knew him very well, and none of us did. And she has a habit of being right about people. She's one of the best judges of human nature that I know. If she says Bill wasn't a traitor, then he wasn't. And I think all *your* theories have a few holes as well. For one thing, if this was a document from Bill to someone else, why would he have gotten it back? Letters generally stay with the recipient, don't they? And if he had received it from someone, under whatever unlikely circumstances back in 1944, surely he would have destroyed it immediately. Colditz would hardly have been a safe place to keep this sort of thing. I thought spies ate letters, or flushed them down the toilet, or burned them, or *something!*"

I was getting heated.

"Simmer down, darling," said my loving husband, laughing. "This isn't a court of inquiry. No one is trying to pillory Bill's memory."

I was not appeased. "Well, it certainly sounds that way! And how convenient to make Bill the villain of the piece. He's dead and can't defend himself. And if it was Bill trying to hide his wicked past all along, will you please explain to me how he managed to cosh Walter over the head when he, Bill, had been dead for two days?"

"Obviously someone else assaulted Walter. It could still be related to this letter." Alan's voice was becoming elaborately patient.

"Of course it has to do with the letter! Now that we know what the letter *is,* it's perfectly obvious why someone was extremely eager that it not be found. A Nazi collaborator could still be tried for war crimes, even now. At least I think he could. And even if I'm wrong, he would certainly be tried in the court of public opinion, and—what's the old expression?— 'sent to Coventry.'

"Now suppose Bill came across this letter when he was sorting through the stuff in the storeroom. What would he do?"

My dubious listeners shrugged shoulders, or shook

heads, or both. Except for Jane. She took the question as a question. "Work out what it meant," she said without hesitation. "Loved a puzzle. Did the *Times* crossword puzzle every day. Best time twenty minutes."

I was impressed. I have never been able to finish even one of the crossword puzzles in the London *Times*. They rely on word plays, anagrams, puns, and virtually every other sort of fiendish clue. I feel a surge of triumph when I work out a single word.

"Knew history," Jane went on. "Knew the war from experience. Looked up the places on the map, worked it out."

"Or at least," I said slowly, "worked out enough of it to be very suspicious. If he'd been sure of what he'd found, I would have thought he'd go to the authorities. The police or the Home Office or someone."

Jane nodded. "If he was sure. But if not—wanted to see fair play. Probably ask whoever gave it to him to explain."

"And of course they couldn't, because there was no explanation that wouldn't condemn them. So—let's see. They'd say they wanted to come and talk to him, because there was a perfectly simple explanation, but they didn't want to talk about it on the phone. At least that's what I would do, if I had written or received that letter, I mean."

I paused to think myself into the skin of a traitor, someone who'd thought himself safe for fifty or sixty years. He would be shocked beyond measure that this piece of damning evidence had come to light. He would be desperate.

"And then—well, then I'd try to figure out a way not to get caught. I could leave the country, maybe. Except the person involved in this is old, perhaps frail. And there aren't many places in the world where one can't be found nowadays, at least not places where a person eighty years old or more would be comfortable. So what are my other options? I could try to steal the letter, of course, or get someone to steal it for me. But Bill still knows, or has suspicions. If the letter goes missing, he'll be even more suspicious, even if I've managed to spin some convincing tale. Was Bill gullible at all, Jane?"

"Most men are," she said with the experience of eighty years. "Most good men. Bill no more than most. Less than some. Some hard times behind him."

"So if he wasn't satisfied with the explanation of—whoever, the villain of the piece—he'd—well, what, do you think?"

"Mull it over," said Jane instantly. "Great one for mulling over. 'Better safe than sorry,' he'd say. 'Less haste, more speed.' Drove one mad."

"But he was an historian," I went on. "He wouldn't want anything to happen to that very important piece of paper. And no matter how gullible he might have been, he certainly wasn't stupid. I could see that for myself. He would have known that keeping such a thing lying around was asking for trouble. So he would hide it, and knowing the museum better than anyone else, he'd know about the one hiding place that no one would think of looking, that most people wouldn't even know existed. He would take the letter down to the tunnel. And it wasn't an easy place to reach, and he was upset about the whole thing, and so he had a stroke. And because Bill had the letter with him down there, whoever was so anxious to get it had to search the museum, and had to hit Walter over the head so he could do it. Search, I mean."

I finished on a note of satisfaction. I had wrapped everything up in a neat little package, and was very satisfied with myself. Only one trifling detail was missing: the actual identity of the malefactor. And surely that could be discovered easily enough, now that we knew what had happened and why.

Alan frowned. "My dear, I'm sorry, but I can't buy it. There are too many holes, too many loose ends. You said yourself that anyone who received such a letter would certainly destroy it, if it were in any way incriminating. Therefore the very existence of the document would seem to argue that it is not incriminating. Therefore why should it be the focus of the trouble?"

"Oh." I thought about that one. It was annoying to have my own argument used against me. I tried again to put myself in the place of a spy, a turncoat, a quisling who would sell out his own country. "Well. It's in a kind of code. Unless the person who received it knew Indiana well, better than I do after living there for sixty-odd years, he would have to keep the letter long enough to look up the references. And then— then I suppose something must have come up, someone came into the room or whatever, so he had to hide the letter quickly and for some reason never got back to dispose of it. It was wartime, after all. Maybe there was a bombing raid or something, and he— she—whoever it was couldn't get back to the hiding place for a while."

"Still," said my loving husband in a maddeningly logical tone, "you'd think he'd have disposed of it as soon as he could. No matter what emergencies befall, one doesn't easily forget that one has a lighted stick of dynamite hidden about the house."

"No, you're right. I have to admit that. It had to have been something quite desperate that kept him from destroying the letter. I just can't think what, at the moment."

Alan looked at me, and then at Jane, and there was pity in his eyes. "There is, I'm sorry to say, one quite obvious explanation. If the recipient of the letter had been taken prisoner by the Germans . . ."

"But the letter was written in 1944! By that time Bill was already at Colditz."

"Mr. Wilson here says it was written in 1944. I'm sure one could find another expert who would testify that it was certainly written in 1943."

Mr. Wilson cleared his throat. "You are forgetting, sir, that the history of the war is involved here. Raids on certain places are mentioned. I know the history of the war rather well, and this particular combination of raids took place in 1944. It is a matter of record. You are welcome to look it up."

He and Alan exchanged polite smiles, the sort the English specialize in, that can freeze you solid at forty paces. Charles, who is of a peacemaking disposition, stepped in hastily. "What I don't understand is why the Germans would part with this information to anyone. Surely this kind of thing is top-secret stuff. If the Brits knew where the raids were going to be, they could muster their forces there and wipe out the German ones."

"Not necessarily," said Mr. Wilson, still frostily. "Look at the Blitz. We knew to a virtual certainty that there would be bombing over London nearly every night, for months, in 1940. We did our best to protect our people, but our best, at that point, was not good enough."

"Well, but by '44 the RAF was in far better shape, more planes, more men. Did they, in fact, defend those places?" Charles gestured to the letter.

"No more than any other places. Our forces were rather heavily engaged just then, as you recall, following up on Operation Overlord."

I must have looked puzzled, because Mr. Wilson said, "The invasion of Normandy. D-day?" He sounded like a kindergarten teacher.

I nodded with some dignity. "Yes, I am familiar with D-day. I had forgotten the code name."

Jane spoke for the first time in quite a while. "Point is, Germans did supply information. What did they get in return? *Quid pro quo.*"

It was then that I remembered Mrs. Burton's remarks about how ineffectual the RAF had been in the war. Or at least—I paused to consider—how ineffectual the raids from Luftwich had seemed to be. "I think," I said slowly, "that I may have an answer to that. I think what they got was a deliberate neglect of duty on the part of someone at Luftwich." I explained what Mrs. Burton had said. "I think it was no accident that the planes from Luftwich so often missed their targets. I think someone there engineered it. I think that letter we found was only one of many, a steady stream coming into Luftwich in return for preferential treatment. And I can think of only one person who is in any way connected with this business and who had a high enough position in the RAF to see to that."

"Merrifield." Jane's voice was flat.

I nodded. "He'd made recent donations of artifacts to the museum, too. That letter could certainly have lain unnoticed at the bottom of some pile until Bill found it. Oh, and he'd been to Indiana, too!"

"How d'you work that out?"

"When we talked to him that day. I just remembered! He said I didn't sound like a Hoosier. Now the only way he'd know that—the only way he'd probably even know the word—is if he'd been to Indiana sometime. Or maybe known someone from Indiana—but anyway, he knew something about the state."

"Hmm."

Jane sounded unconvinced, but I didn't bother to

follow up the point. I was pursuing my own thoughts. "The thing is, I don't know why Merrifield would have betrayed his country that way, though. He seems like a man of integrity, and this—this is the last word in treachery."

"He has property." Jane again, still in a dead sort of voice. "And family. Here in Belleshire, in Kent, Sussex, all over southern England. If he knew in advance where the raids were going to be, he could take steps to protect anything of his that was threatened."

I nodded thoughtfully. "Well, he couldn't do much about the property. You can't shield a house from bombs, or not very effectively. But the people—yes, he could arrange to have the people elsewhere if he knew the bombers were coming. Oh!"

Everyone looked at me.

"I just thought of something else. You know we've always been so grateful that Sherebury was spared any major bombing during the war? No damage to the Cathedral, that sort of thing? And it was a little surprising, because we're not that far from the coast. And even though there weren't any military or industrial targets here, the Germans liked bombing cathedrals, because of the damage to morale."

Their stares changed to looks of dawning comprehension.

"Yes. Part of the deal, do you think?"

"All right," said Charles, still not convinced, "suppose it's true, all this elaborate James Bond kind of stuff—"

234

"Oh, no," I said, interrupting. "Much too low-tech for Bond. More Richard Hannay. *The Thirty-Nine Steps*, and—"

Charles waved away Richard Hannay. "Whatever. What I started to say was, even given your scenario, which I don't yet accept, he must be very old, this Merrifield character. How could he have attacked anyone at the museum?"

"He told me he has a son, Charles. Merrifield's not very mobile himself anymore, true, but the son could have done everything. Attacked Walter, searched the place . . . and I'll bet he would have, too, if he knew what was at stake. Family honor still means something in these parts."

A silence fell. At last Alan said, "Well, it's just possible, I suppose. Far-fetched, but stranger things have happened. It's all the merest speculation at this point, of course, but it'll have to be looked into. I confess I don't know quite who would be responsible for an inquiry like that. International espionage and war crimes are a little out of my line."

"And by the time all the ponderous machinery creaks into motion and anything is determined for sure, everyone concerned will be dead anyway," I said with some bitterness. "I'm sorry I ever brought it up. The whole thing is futile. The war's been over for nearly sixty years. Why not let the dead bury their dead?"

"But Walter is alive," said Jane. "And he deserves justice."

"Oh, I suppose, but—"

The phone rang on Alan's desk, startling us all. He answered, listened for a moment, said "Thank you, Derek," and hung up.

"Well, Dorothy, I think your theory just went up in smoke."

"What do you mean? Did Derek find something that makes more sense?"

"No. He was calling me from Heatherwood House. John Merrifield is dead, and—this information must not be spread about—it looks like murder."

TWENTY-FOUR

It was the next day, Thursday, before any details filtered through, and then not until afternoon. In the morning, Alan and I went with Jane to Bill's funeral. It was only a graveside service, kept brief out of deference to Bill's nebulous religious beliefs. "Wouldn't have wanted a Eucharist," Jane said in an undertone as we walked through the Close to the old churchyard. Very few are buried there anymore—there's no room—but Bill, as a veteran of the war, had earned a place.

"Didn't you want one?"

She shrugged. "Bill was a good man. God doesn't need a lot of words to tell him so."

But funerals are for the living, I wanted to say. For comfort, and support . . . but Jane had decided what she wanted.

Yesterday's rain had diminished to a fine drizzle, against which an umbrella did very little good. We stood and shivered while one of the canons read the service. Besides the three of us, there were only a handful of mourners. Two of the Heatherwood House staff had come, and a couple of elderly men Jane identified in a whisper as friends of Bill's from the home. That was all. Jane showed little emotion, but she's so good at hiding her feelings that I had no idea what was going on under the gruff exterior.

"Would you like some lunch?" I asked after we had trudged back across the Close. "I can whip up some potato soup in no time."

"No, thanks. Want to see Walter." She plodded on. We were through the gate into our street before she turned and said, "Thanks. For coming. A help." She gripped both our hands for a moment before squaring her shoulders and marching sturdily to her front door.

Well, for Jane that was the equivalent of a bear hug. Alan and I smiled a little and shook our heads, and went in to dry off and get started on that soup.

We had just finished lunch when Derek called with a report. Alan repeated it to me almost word for word when he had hung up.

Mr. Merrifield—or Air Commodore Merrifield, to give him the military title under which he would undoubtedly be buried—had been found dead in his room about six by the aide who brought up his supper. He was in his bed, and had been dead for some time. The aide, who was rather new to Heatherwood House, had nevertheless been there long enough to know that death was not unexpected among the residents, so she simply walked out of the room with the tray and told the nurse in charge.

The nurse, who knew Merrifield well, *was* startled. Her patient was strong for his age, with no history of cardiac or vascular problems, and had been perfectly well that afternoon when he took his walk. So she checked carefully when she went into the room. It was she who discovered the rumpled pillow, somewhat damp and with small holes that might have made by teeth. She closed the room then, leaving Merrifield's body exactly as it was, and told her superiors that the police should be called.

"She had quite a job convincing them," said Alan, telling me the story. "Murder is not featured in the prospectus of Heatherwood House. Fortunately, Nurse Ames is a stubborn woman who reads crime fiction and has a lively imagination. She insisted, and threatened to go to the press if the police were not called. Well, publicity of that kind would be absolutely ruinous, so the powers-that-be gave in. Of course, Nurse Ames was quite right. Merrifield had been smothered while he was napping. Poor chap, he'd tried to struggle, but his heart was ninety-two, after all. It gave out quite soon, the ME thinks. Of course nothing is certain until the autopsy."

"And if the nurse hadn't been vigilant, it would have gone down as natural death."

"Probably, given Merrifield's age. In fact, so far as

the general public is concerned, that's what it was."

"I suppose they've checked the surveillance tapes?"

Alan sighed heavily. "There are no surveillance tapes. It turns out that the cameras are used only at night, mostly as a measure against burglary. They feed into a monitor in the security guard's room, and are taped then, but not during the daytime."

"But that's ridiculous! A resident could wander off—"

"The superintendent was emphatic that they have no residents who are at all likely to do such a thing. He refused even to say the word 'Alzheimer's' and acted as though senility were a loathsome disease."

"Fine man to be in charge of an old people's home!"

"My opinion precisely. He's a self-important cretin, but the fact remains that the security arrangements at Heatherwood House are far from ideal."

"Visitors have to check in at the front desk, though."

"And genuine, well-meaning visitors do just that. I have found, my love, over a long and I may say somewhat distinguished police career, that criminals don't always obey all the rules."

"You don't say!" I forgave him the sarcasm. He was tired and upset. "How do you think whoever it was got past the checkpoint, then?"

"We don't know that he or she did get past. There were a number of visitors that afternoon. No one asked to see Merrifield, but then they wouldn't, would they? Visitors who act as if they know where they're going are not escorted to the resident's rooms. And the receptionist doesn't make a record of the names of visitors—who might not give their right names, anyway."

"No. It isn't the sort of place where they check passports. So you really have no idea who was there that afternoon?"

He sighed again, rather elaborately this time. "They're checking, Dorothy. Some of the visitors were regulars, family members who visit every day. The receptionists know them. We're talking to them, hoping they may provide other names or at least descriptions. And of course there's the staff, and the other residents. We haven't much hope. Most people aren't particularly observant. And why should they be, when they're going about their business and nothing unusual is happening?"

"Nothing unusual except the little matter of a man being smothered to death. Wouldn't he have made noise? Cried out, or at least made noises thrashing around?"

"You forget that he was almost certainly napping when the attack came. He would have had only a few seconds of awareness that anything was wrong, and one can't make much noise through a pillow. In any case, the killer would have closed the door, and those doors are good sturdy oak. No one we've talked to so far heard a thing besides the routine sounds."

"It comes down to routine slogging, then. Poor Derek. Dozens of people to talk to with almost no hope of getting anything out of them. And all sorts of other work to carry on with in the meantime. Oh! Alan, do you think they've put a guard on young Walter, in the hospital?"

"Not yet." Alan looked unhappy. "I did suggest it, but there's no obvious connection between Merrifield's death and the attack on Walter. I know, there's your theory that this all has something to do with the war, and I think you're right. But there's no proof, and the force is too shorthanded to send a man off to guard a theory."

I wasn't pleased about that, but there was nothing to be done about it. Nothing the police would do, anyway.

"I'm going over to talk to Jane, if she's back from the hospital," I said with determination. "If she hasn't already figured out that Walter might be in danger, she needs to know."

But Jane hadn't returned. Her house was locked up, and when I knocked at the back door, I was greeted only by a mournful chorus of lonely dogs. They did their best to convince me that they had been permanently abandoned and required rescue, but I ignored them. Stopping only to tell Alan where I was going, I drove to the hospital.

I had to stop to find out Walter's new room number, and the functionary at the desk was inclined to be starchy. "He is in a private room," she informed me, "but he has a visitor. He mustn't see too many people, he still needs quiet recovery time—here! Where are you going?"

I didn't know I could still trot at that speed. I didn't know exactly where I was going, but the hospital wasn't large, and I found the right room before the indignant doorkeeper could stop me. I burst in, my heart pounding, ready to do battle with anyone who was trying to smother Walter.

Jane looked up from the chair by his bedside. "Been doing your morning jog?"

There was no other chair in the room. I leaned against the wall, panting and feeling a fool. "Thank God it's just you!"

I didn't need to explain myself. She could read my mind. But Walter was another matter. He was wide awake, looking pink and healthy despite the bandage on the back of his head, and his face was full of questions.

"I was escaping the nurse, or whoever, who didn't want me to come up. Said you shouldn't have too many visitors. Am I too many, do you think? I'll leave if you're tired."

"Tired of being treated like an invalid, is all. I want to get out of here. I'm perfectly fit, and God knows what's happening at the museum, with Bill still missing."

So they hadn't told him yet. Well, one step at a time. "I think it's in good hands, actually. The police want to find out who attacked you, and they're keeping a close watch on the place. Have they told you when they're going to let you go home?"

"Well, that's the problem, you see." He shifted restlessly. "They don't want me to be alone, and of course Mrs. Gibbs gives her boarders their privacy."

I exchanged a glance with Jane. From what I'd heard of Walter's landlady, the word wasn't so much privacy as neglect. That would be a fine place for a murderer to get at the boy.

Jane cleared her throat. "No need to be alone," she said in her gruffest voice, sounding exactly like Winston Churchill. "Plenty of room at my house. Was just going to tell you."

Walter's face lit up. "Would you really? That would be super! Oh, but . . ." His voice lost its color. "I forgot, though. When they find Bill—I mean, you won't want a stranger around—"

"Changed plans," said Jane with a warning look at me. Well, heavens, I wasn't about to break the news of Bill's death to the boy! Let her handle it her own way. "Could use the company. Some things to do about the house, as well, when you're fit."

I could almost see words of gratitude hovering on Walter's lips. Gratitude embarrasses Jane mightily. I broke in before he could get a word out. "That sounds like an ideal plan, then. You can earn your keep as general factotum, and Jane's a marvelous cook. You'll be close to the museum, too, and there's a bus to the university that stops at the end of our street."

A nurse bustled in. She was cross. It was a pity she wasn't wearing the starched uniform of yore; they crackled so nicely to express irritation.

"I'm sorry, but one of you will have to leave. My

patient is absolutely not to have more than one visitor at a time, and not for more than five minutes. Actually, you should both go. I'm sure you"—she looked severely at Jane—"have been here far longer than five minutes."

"I was just leaving," I said. "Jane, do you want me to talk to someone about discharge arrangements?"

"Discharge?" said the nurse. "There can be no question of discharge until suitable housing—"

"That's what we're talking about." I let a bit of schoolteacher creep into my voice. Not the full she-who-must-be-obeyed intonation, but enough to let the nurse know that I, too, was irritated. "I take it Walter is ready to leave as soon as he can receive reasonable care at home?"

"I can discuss that only with his family or some other responsible person."

"Good. Fine. Discuss it with Miss Langland. She's prepared to make herself responsible. Unless of course you really want to keep him here, taking up a bed when he's well enough to leave." Now I sounded as if I were addressing a roomful of fourth-graders.

"Well, of course we always need beds, but that isn't the question."

"I'd have thought it was. Jane, I'm going to round up the social worker, or whoever handles these things in an English hospital. You'll stay here for now." I didn't make it a question, and the nurse, accepting a lost battle but not final defeat, glared equally at both of us and huffed away.

It took me a while to find the proper authority, and then she wouldn't take my word for anything but had to check innumerable files and make several phone calls and talk to Jane and have her sign papers, and so on. I called Alan in the meantime to assure him I hadn't encountered anything worse than medical red tape. But finally all the releases were approved and all the discharge instructions given, and Walter was wheeled (much against his will; he wanted to walk) to Jane's waiting car. I followed in my own, helped Jane install Walter on a capacious couch to wait for his lunch, and went home through the drizzle with the sense of a large burden removed from my shoulders.

Not that Walter had ever been my problem, really, but I'm one of those women with a regrettable tendency to take on the responsibilities of the world. Regrettable, because it leads to meddling in what's really none of my business and endless fretting that wears me out without accomplishing anything. I suppose I like to feel I'm indispensable, which nobody is. It's a form of egotism, a superiority complex, perhaps. I'd like to mend my ways, but I think I'm too old. And darn it all, sometimes my meddling has been useful.

I prepared an absentminded lunch for Alan and me and sat down, notebook in hand, to meddle some more.

TWENTY-FIVE

THE FIRST THING I DID WAS LOOK OVER MY EARLIER notes. Alas, they hadn't acquired any brilliant flashes of insight since I had written them.

If there was a likely suspect for the murder of John Merrifield lurking in all that verbiage, I couldn't find him—or her. Stanley Rutherford, under the thumb of his granddaughter? Barbara Price, fussy old maid? They'd both hated Merrifield, but very few murders are committed only out of hatred. Anyway, if they'd hated him for years, decades, it wasn't likely that something had suddenly moved them to action.

Poor old Mr. Tredgold? Impossible. He had neither the strength nor the mobility, nor, I was convinced, the moral blindness to commit murder.

And Mrs. Burton? I paused the longest over her name. She seemed a ruthless woman, and she, too, had hated Merrifield. Too fastidious, probably, to kill with her own hands. But she had the money to hire it done. Even in this peaceful English backwater it would, I supposed, be possible to hire a killer. And Leigh Burton was just the sort to eliminate someone without a second thought if it were to her benefit.

But that was the problem. How could Merrifield's death possibly benefit the wealthy Mrs. Burton?

If he knew something to her discredit . . . but what? She might have clawed her way out of poverty and a despised class, but there was nothing illegal about that. It was, in fact, rather admirable in a way, as long as she'd done nothing criminal along the way. Alan didn't think she had, and Alan was seldom wrong about things like that. He had, after all, over forty years of experience with crime.

And then there was the fact that it was Leigh Burton who'd thought there was something funny going on at Luftwich, that their planes weren't succeeding in as many missions as they ought to.

Could that have been an elaborate double bluff? Don't tell the nosy American woman anything helpful, but hint at part of the truth, so if she finds out the rest she'll think I must be blameless?

I didn't think so. Mrs. Burton struck me as the kind of shrewd, grasping woman who was more direct in her methods. Somehow I couldn't see her thinking in such a convoluted way. She could, I supposed, have learned the ploy from detective novels, as I had, but I couldn't remember seeing books of any kind among the valuable ornaments in her expensive house.

Of course Stanley, come to think of it, had hinted about funny business, too. And I suddenly remembered that he had acted frightened when he heard his granddaughter come in. I'd thought at the time that he was afraid of her, domineering woman that she was, but perhaps . . .

I sat and thought for a long time, my notebook abandoned in my lap. Emmy and Sam jumped up on the couch and settled down to purr, one on each side of me, delighted to find me sitting still for a change. Settled comfortably into feline middle age, they were apt these days to prefer a nap to a game, and a nap with their preferred human was pure bliss.

Finally I picked up my notebook again and began slowly, hesitantly, to write a few words:

Medals
"Deceit and treachery"
Bats, or?
Ops
Tea tray

Alan came in just as I made the last entry and looked over my shoulder. "Christmas list, darling? It's hops, not ops. And surely not bats?"

"I—oh, yes. Um—for little Nigel Peter. A crib toy, one of those musical mobiles, you know?"

Alan looked at me thoughtfully. "And I suppose *Deceit and Treachery* is a newly discovered work by Jane Austen?"

"Certainly not. It's the latest mystery by Barbara D'Amato. About Chicago politics."

"Uh-huh."

Of course he didn't believe a word of it, but still less would he have believed the real meaning of my list. I didn't believe it myself. "It's Christmastime, my love. Stop peeking and asking awkward questions."

I wasn't going to confide my ideas to my loving husband until I was a lot surer they weren't so much hogwash. And I was certainly glad I hadn't yet written down "blackmail."

"By the way," I said, happily changing the subject, "you'll be delighted to know that Walter Tubbs has been released from the hospital. Jane, bless her heart, has taken him in." I stood up, to the dismay of both cats (Samantha's expressed by loud Siamese swearing). "I think I'll take them some mince pies. Boys that age are always hungry. I expect I'll be back for tea, but Jane might be boiling up just about now, so if you get hungry . . ."

"I'll look after myself. Don't fuss. And watch your footing. I don't imagine you've noticed, but it's been sleeting for the last hour. And I suppose I shouldn't waste my breath saying it, but you will be careful, won't you?"

We both knew he wasn't referring to slippery sidewalks. I groaned, gave him a peck on the cheek, and went to find a jacket and my warmest hat.

The back door was locked, but Jane was home, of course. She would stay home, or take Walter with her when she left, for the foreseeable future. I didn't know how she was going to keep him tied to her apron strings, unless she told him the truth, but I had great faith in Jane. She'd manage somehow.

She shushed the dogs before she answered the door. "Asleep," she said in answer to my raised eyebrows. "I told him. Knocked him for six. Put him to bed to sleep it off."

I put my bag of mince pies on the table. "Told him

249

about Bill? Or about Merrifield, too?"

"Bill. Enough for now."

I nodded. "Actually I'm just as glad he's not down-stairs. I wanted to talk to you."

"Idea?"

"Well, I do have an idea, but it's so fantastic I don't . . ."

"Tea or coffee?"

Caffeine puts everything, even fantastic ideas, into perspective. Jane does have an instinct for the prac-tical.

"Tea, I think, but something bracing. Not a delicate tea."

She nodded and got out the tin of Prince of Wales. I organized my thoughts while she made some cin-namon toast and we waited for the tea to brew. When it was ready and we sat down I had decided on my first question.

"Jane, when we went to see Stanley Rutherford, he wanted to show us his medals, but you said you'd seen them. Have you, actually, or were you just trying to get me out of having to admire them?"

"Seen them," she said, pouring out.

"Were there any special ones, or just the sort they give out to everyone in service?"

"Don't remember. Some for gallantry, I think. Toast?"

"Thanks. Mmm, good. Would you know the differ-ence, just by looking at the medals?"

"No."

"Neither would I, even with American ones, let alone British. But, Jane, what I'm getting at is this: You remember I told you that when I talked to Leigh Burton, she thought it was odd that air crews from Luftwich didn't ever seem to reach their targets or do much to hamper the enemy. Now I can't quite square that idea with Stanley's bragging about his medals and how many German planes he shot down and all that. You see the problem. Who's got the story straight, Leigh or Stanley?"

Jane sipped her tea with deliberation before she answered. "Don't know. Could find out, about the medals, anyway. Easy research."

"I suppose there are records of that kind of thing, who got what."

Jane snorted. "Miles of them. I meant, research what the medals look like and then go see Stanley again."

"Oh, of course. And I imagine our library would have books about British military decorations. Though"—I glanced at my watch—"it's probably closed by now."

Jane shook her head pityingly. "Twenty-first century, Dorothy. Find it on the Web."

It's downright embarrassing to be made to feel an old fogy by someone who's more than ten years older than I. I slapped my forehead. "You're right, of course. There'll be nice big pictures and descriptions, I'm sure. Why don't you come over after supper and we'll look at them together? You might recognize some of Stanley's."

But Jane shook her head. "Better stay here."

"Oh, yes, of course. I forgot for a minute. How is he, really? You said he was upset about Bill, but is that all?"

"Didn't tell him much," said Jane obliquely. "Just that Bill had a stroke, died in the tunnel. Didn't want to worry him just now. Enough time for that later. Meanwhile, he's safe here with me."

I wondered about that. Jane was sturdy and active, but she was at least eighty. How much protection could she provide against a determined murderer?

Then one of the bulldogs nuzzled my hand and whined for some cinnamon toast and I had my answer. Anyone who went for Jane or for someone under her roof would be set upon by a pack of furious dogs. Yes, Walter was safe enough as long as he stayed here.

"You do the searching," Jane went on. "Ring up Stanley tomorrow and say you want to see his medals."

"Oh—well—yes, I could do that. I *will* do that, if you'll give me his phone number and remind me how to get there."

I could have sworn my tone of voice hadn't changed, but Jane knows me very well.

"Wouldn't ask if it weren't for the boy," she said. Her embarrassment lowered her deep voice so far as to be almost inaudible.

"I know. It's all right. I don't really think Stanley has murdered anybody. His granddaughter wouldn't let him."

"Hmph," was Jane's only answer to that. And indeed, what answer was there?

There was a performance of *The Nutcracker* on television that night, and Alan wanted to watch. Well, I wouldn't have minded seeing the Royal Ballet myself, but I had work to do. As soon as Alan was settled and engrossed, I excused myself, went to his study, and turned on the computer.

It didn't take long. There were a good many Web sites devoted to British military medals, and I soon figured out most of the important ones for World War II. There were, of course, all the routine ones handed out broadcast to all who served, but I found a couple of special ones, too, the Conspicuous Gallantry Medal for fliers, and the Distinguished Flying Cross for officers. I wondered if that distinction, officers versus enlisted men, was made with American medals. I rather thought not, but what did I know? I'd never had much to do with military personnel in America.

At any rate, armed with information, and taking my courage in both hands, I called Stanley the next morning and expressed an ardent desire to see his medals. He was thrilled, as I'd expected. I only hoped it wasn't the thrill of a spider sensing vibrations along its net.

As I finished clearing away the breakfast dishes, I glanced at the calendar next to the back door. Good grief, December 19! Less than a week till Christmas, and I had yet to make that trip to London. The shelves would be half empty by now; some of the stores would be starting their after-Christmas sales. America may begin its Christmas celebrations before Halloween, but England truncates the season at the other end, as if the sole purpose of the holiday were commerce. As, perhaps, for most people nowadays it is.

Well, the day would come and we would celebrate, and somehow I felt I could celebrate more devoutly if I had helped to catch a murderer. Presents could be bought later.

TWENTY-SIX

ALAN, A LARGE MAN WHO EXCELS AT BEAR HUGS, GAVE me a particularly lingering one as I was ready to leave the house. I had told him where I was going, of course, and he didn't care for it much, but he has long since stopped trying to protect me from my whims. He knows I hate to be cosseted. But he can't help his instincts, any more than I can help mine. I was grateful for his concern, and grateful, also, that he chose to express it silently. I was actually a little scared and didn't care to be reminded that I might be doing something dangerous.

I had thought briefly about taking some sort of weapon, just in case. But what? I was terrified of guns, even if I had been able to obtain one, a much harder thing to do in England than in America. A knife, a candlestick, a lead pipe? No. No one my age has any business thinking in the silly terms of a board game. I didn't even know where I could buy a can of Mace. I'd take my wits and the police whistle Alan gave me, and my cell phone, which has a preset button for 999. That would have to do.

I concentrated fiercely on finding my way through Shaftesbury's narrow medieval streets. The sleet had changed back to rain, but it was an especially wet rain that kept my windshield wipers flapping furiously and limited both my visibility and my traction. I was grateful for it. Driving with extra care kept me from thinking too much about what might happen when I reached my destination.

Stanley's granddaughter wasn't home. I hadn't expected her to be on a weekday, and on the whole I was glad she wasn't. I wanted Stanley to be free to say whatever he wanted.

On the other hand, she might have stopped him from *doing* what he wanted, and just in case he wanted to do something murderous . . . no, I wouldn't think about that.

He greeted me as he had before, door open, impatient for me to get inside, an odd mixture of eagerness and rudeness. This time, however, he made no apologies and no preliminary remarks, but simply led me into the crowded lounge and pointed to a small table he had cleared of its load of newspapers and assorted rubbish.

"Look! You've never seen anything quite like that, have you, now?"

He pointed to the display that lay on the table. Inside

a frame of about nine by twelve inches, covered with glass and resting on silk that had probably once been scarlet, lay his collection of medals. There were all the ones I had expected, the 1939–1945 Medal with its Battle of Britain bar, the Air Crew Europe Medal with a France and Germany bar, the Air Force Medal with the France and Germany bar, the Defence Medal—all the medals routinely issued in World War II to British enlisted men, or "other ranks" as the Web pages had delicately put it.

And there were two set off by themselves, not fastened together with the others.

"Know what that is?" Stanley asked eagerly in his cracked voice, pointing to one.

I did, but I let him tell me.

"That's the Medal for Conspicuous Gallantry, that is. The one for fliers. That's the highest award a man could get in that war."

"Unless he was an officer, right?"

Stanley snorted. "Give out stars left and right to officers, they did. And what did they do? Sit on their behinds and give orders that got the rest of us killed."

"You survived," I pointed out.

"Only just!" he said indignantly. "Know how I got that there?" He pointed a shaking finger at the medal with its frayed, faded ribbon. "Hung out in midair, I did, to rescue the other gunner when the kite took a bad hit. Holding on with a rope, and no parachute, mind you, and freezing cold so I nearly lost my hold, too. The way it happened, y'see, was we were on a mission over France . . ."

He went on and on with great gusto. I listened, but I knew what was coming. The story sounded familiar. Very familiar, indeed. Virtually identical with one I had read the night before on the Web, about one Flight Sergeant Crabe.

". . . and he spent five months in hospital, but he ended up right as rain, and all on account of me! And what do you think of that, eh?"

"Remarkable," I said fervently. "A wonderful story." And it was. Apart from the last detail (in Crabe's citation the other gunner had been dead when Crabe reached him), Stanley had reproduced the heroic story almost word for word. "You must have been very proud."

"Ah, weren't nothin'. Wartime, y'know. Did for each other when we could. He'd have done the same for me."

I was tempted to probe a little, ask for details, but on second thought I left well enough alone. Stanley had proved, to my satisfaction at least, that he was a liar about his war record. I wondered where he'd got the medal. From a dead companion, perhaps? I nearly shuddered. Or maybe it was a replica, purchased years later. One could buy such things, sometimes even the real ones. There were sites for collectors all over the Web.

The point was, if Stanley was a liar, was he also, conceivably, a murderer?

I paid little attention as he went on to describe how

he earned the other, the Distinguished Flying Medal, until he began listing the targets he had hit and destroyed, the German factories, the aerodromes, the U-boats. I couldn't very well make notes, but I tried hard to remember a few place names. The account again sounded familiar; I wanted to look it up when I got home.

"Those must have been very dangerous missions," I said with what I hoped was the proper awe.

"Solid walls of flak we had to go through, nearly every time. Didn't bother us. We got them more often than they got us. Wasn't only me, all of them. Good men, they were."

"Well, I must say I'm impressed. It sounds as though Luftwich was a real force in winning the war." Was I laying it on too thick?

Apparently not. Stanley held forth for another half hour, until he had to go to the loo and I could make my escape.

When he had tottered out of the room, I took a moment to pick up the framed collection. If the frame was loose, I might be able to slide the medals out and see the backs. If they were engraved, they might tell me something about their origin.

But the frame was properly sealed, so I shouted a cheery good-bye to the back of the house and got out of there.

I had a good deal to think about, so the tricky drive home was not the blessing the drive out had been. I was happy to pull into my tiny garage and devote my attention to my problem.

It was, I decided in the few steps to my front door, time to consult with Alan. I had a little proof now.

Alan, however, wasn't home. He had left a note. "Derek asked for some advice. Back soon."

I smiled a little over that. There was a time when Alan had felt he was, in retirement, out of the loop. He was punctilious about not interfering in police investigations without an invitation, but he certainly did like it when Derek asked.

Well, I'd have to do my thinking alone. Maybe when Alan returned I'd have some better-organized ideas for his consideration.

Stanley. I heated up the last cup of the morning's pot of coffee and took it to the kitchen table, hoping the caffeine would stimulate my little gray cells.

Stanley. What was I to make of him?

On the face of it, he was a pathetic man, living in the past. Given the nature of his present life, that was perhaps understandable. Was he so eager to be a hero in the eyes of the world—or perhaps the eyes of his granddaughter—that he had bought or stolen medals and adopted other people's war stories as his own? Or was there some more sinister explanation?

There seemed to me to be only one way to answer that question, and that was to ask some more. Of course, my best source of information, John Merrifield, had been silenced forever. Of the remaining possibilities, Mr. Tredgold was out. He wouldn't, or perhaps couldn't, tell me anything, and I would upset him dreadfully. I couldn't do it.

The other two, Barbara Price and Leigh Burton, didn't like me. Leigh most particularly didn't like me, I wasn't sure why. However, they were sane and competent, and if I could think of a way to frame my questions tactfully, they might possibly answer. If not, well . . . there was always Merrifield's son, I supposed, though this was a bad time to approach him, just after his father had been cruelly murdered.

Perhaps the police had asked him some of the questions I'd like to raise, and I could get some answers from Alan. Or perhaps I was being a coward, hiding behind that possibility because I didn't want to face the others involved—the two women.

Many English people I know have commented that Americans have a noticeable need to be liked, that we are almost embarrassingly friendly and outgoing. I confess that I want to be liked. I want people to think well of me, and I don't enjoy spending time with those who obviously prefer my absence to my company. If that's a character flaw, surely it's harmless enough.

When one is investigating a crime, however, it is likely that many of the people one encounters won't be pleasant. The police, of course, have the authority to question witnesses and suspects, and although that authority can't coerce cooperation, it does intimidate, and most people cave in eventually.

My case is different. No one has to talk to me. When I first moved to Shanebury, I could often encourage conversation because I was a foreigner, not a member of the community, and I "didn't count." Now that I've lived here for years and married a prominent policeman, that ploy won't work anymore. I have found that losing my temper sometimes prompts a response, but that's dangerous. I prefer to stay in control, at least of myself.

Well, perhaps it was time for me to develop some backbone, acknowledge that some of my sources of information were unwilling, and act accordingly. It didn't, after all, matter in the end whether I made new friends. What mattered was the truth.

With that noble sentiment to bolster my confidence, I picked up the phone and called Barbara Price. She wasn't thrilled to hear from me, but when I said I had a few more questions about Luftwich, especially her work there, she thawed a little and invited me to come for tea. I made a mental note to tuck some Tums into my purse, and splashed my way next door to get explicit driving directions from Jane.

I had planned to tell her what I had learned about Stanley's medals, but Walter was awake and downstairs, and I didn't want to bring it up in front of him.

"How are you feeling?" I asked him after writing down the directions to Barbara Price's house. "You're looking fine, I must say. You were pretty pale for a while there."

"Much better, thanks. Still a bit of a headache now and again, but I'm not dizzy anymore. I only wish I could *remember!* It's maddening to know someone bashed my head and I don't even know who it was, or why, or anything about it."

"I think they say it's better not to force it. The memory may return in time. Or it may not, you know. Head injuries are odd. You're just lucky it wasn't much, much worse."

He looked me squarely in the eye. "It would have been worse if you hadn't found me. No one told me that, but I could guess from the way they talked behind my back. I think you saved my life, Mrs. Martin. I don't suppose I need tell you how grateful I am."

"Not at all. I just hope you don't take the Oriental attitude that I'm now responsible for you. From the looks of you, there's a good deal of mischief you plan to get into yet, and I don't think I care to make looking after you my life's work."

He chuckled. "No, I think Miss Langland plans to take that on. She's a fine mother hen."

Jane turned brick red and changed the subject. "Need to move your things here. This afternoon?"

"Yes, I've rung my landlady. She's not best pleased."

Jane and I both made indignant sounds. "No, I don't imagine she is," I said. "She's losing a boarder who never gave her a moment's trouble, or cost her a moment's work. You're far better off here. And Jane will enjoy the company. If you're doing the moving early this afternoon, I can help, if you like."

"Thanks, but there's not all that much to move. I haven't many clothes. There are a few books, though."

"I can imagine. And books are the heaviest things on earth. Are you up to that yet?"

"I'll pack them in small boxes. Most of them are at the museum, anyway. I did a lot of studying there." A cloud passed over his face. "I don't know what will happen now."

"Don't worry," said Jane. "Know the trustees. Fix it up. You'll keep your job."

And he would, too, if the money had to come out of Jane's own pocket. She's unstoppable when it comes to the welfare of the young.

"Well, there's no need to ask if Jane's feeding you properly. Lunch smells wonderful."

"Join us," said Jane.

"Can't. I expect Alan home, so I have to feed him something. And I'd better get at it. I'll see you later." I tried to telegraph a message to Jane that I wanted to talk to her alone, but she seemed oblivious. Ah, well. I'd phone her if nothing else worked.

Alan came home a few minutes after I did, and while I put together a quick lunch out of the freezer I told him about Stanley's medals. He wasn't overly impressed.

"It's a bit off, of course, him passing them off as his own, but it's not unheard of. Not the 'done' thing, but Stanley isn't likely to care much about that."

"Not 'an officer and a gentleman'?" I said, bristling a little.

"No. And you needn't go all democratic and American about it. Whether you like it or not, the class

263

system exists. And don't pretend you don't have one in America, either. Your system is based on money rather than birth, but it's a fact of life."

"I suppose. Then there's race, and location. Those who live in the really big cities, especially New York, view themselves as superior to us hicks from the sticks."

"And don't forget the stigma of age."

"Yes, and of all the unfair distinctions—"

"Yes, love. Life is unfair. Eat your stew."

I took a bite. "And speaking of age, what has Derek learned about Merrifield's murder? And what did he want from you?"

"He's stuck. He's taken statements from everyone he could think of, including some of the residents at Heatherwood House. No one saw anything or anyone peculiar. No one acted in any way out of the ordinary. He made a list of all known visitors. No surprises. He asked me to look over the statements in case I might spot something he'd missed. Flattering of him, but I wasn't any help at all. It all looked straightforward and exactly what one would expect."

"Didn't anybody get suspicious? I mean, wonder why the police were asking questions about the death of a very old man in a place where death is almost an everyday occurrence?"

"Derek was clever about that. He claimed to be conducting an inquiry for Merrifield's insurance company, looking into any possible dereliction of duty on the part of the staff. If anyone thought there was more to it, no sign appeared in the reports."

"Hmm. I wonder. Official reports often leave out nuances."

"Not in this county, they don't! My people knew I'd have their heads if they left out a blinking thing, even the slightest hint of a suspicion of a hunch. Derek's carrying on the tradition. It makes for long reports and tedious reading, but one knows everything's there. No, I think the fact of murder is still our secret."

"Good. That means the murderer thinks he's safe. It's a small advantage, but a valuable one."

"God knows we can use any advantage we can get. This one's getting away from us."

So we talked about that and Stanley was forgotten, at least for the moment, but I filed him away. Something was odd, there, and I hoped Barbara Price could help me learn what it was.

TWENTY-SEVEN

MISS PRICE, IN A PLAID WOOL SKIRT AND RATHER elderly sweater, was dressed much more casually than when I had last seen her. She'd been expecting Alan last time. I, a mere woman, and an American at that, wasn't worth dressing up for. I was apparently worth cooking for, though. I smelled fresh-baked scones as I walked in the door, and lovely little sandwiches sat ready on a tray.

The food was good, too, though the tea was as

strong and tannic as before. We made small talk through our meal: Christmas, the depressing weather. When we had finished the tea in the pot and I had declined more as tactfully as I could, my hostess sat back in expectant silence.

"I'm so glad you could find time to talk to me a bit more," I began. "You see, I've hit a snag in my work. I can't seem to find anyone who can actually document the part Luftwich played in the war. I mean the number of missions run, some of the outstanding successes, that sort of thing. Mr. Merrifield might have helped, but of course he's gone now, poor man."

I didn't mention the manner of his departure. It wasn't a matter of public knowledge, and if she knew—but she reacted perfectly normally.

"Yes, well, I wasn't fond of him, but he was a link to the old days. Soon we'll all be gone, and no one will remember."

"Yes, you're right, and of course the point of the museum exhibition is to help people remember. So I wondered if you could give me any of the facts and figures I'm looking for."

"Well, I hardly—that is, surely the RAF would have records. Unless they were destroyed in the Blitz, of course."

"I thought of that, but my heart quails at the idea of trying to get information from a government agency. At least in America, red tape can tie you up for ages. And of course I haven't a shred of authority to ask for anything; I'm just trying to help out. And I know so little. Is there anything at all you can tell me?"

"It was all confidential information."

"Of course, but surely after all these years it wouldn't matter. I mean, the men involved in those missions would have told their stories, to their families at least, after the war was over. There must be thousands of people who know pieces of the story. The thing is, I don't know any of them except you few who live in Sherebury. Any help you can give me would be greatly appreciated, I assure you, and of course acknowledged in the exhibit."

Indecision chased across her face, but at last she stood. "Oh, very well, but I'll have to get my diaries. I can't remember the details after sixty years."

I got out the notebook I had stuck in my purse, and waited.

She was away for some little time, and came back breathless and apologetic. "I'm sorry, it took me a while to find the old diaries. I haven't looked at them for years. Now then, what was it you wanted to know?"

"Well, for a start, can you tell me how many missions were run out of Luftwich?"

"Oh, I never knew that. I only knew about my own shifts, and what I picked up occasionally from the men. They didn't talk much, though. They weren't supposed to talk at all, of course. But as to a number—oh, no, I'd have no idea."

"Well, perhaps I can get that from the RAF if somebody can tell me how to approach them."

"Well, there, again, I'm afraid I'd be no help. You may be right about the difficulties. The military can be so very—military, can't it? Ordinary people like us have no chance dealing with them, do we?"

"Probably not. So what about some of the more notable success stories? Important targets destroyed, or large numbers of planes shot down—that sort of thing. I thought you might remember those."

"Well, you understand that anything I knew, I knew from the men, and of course they didn't always know just how things turned out. They might be quite sure they'd hit a factory, but they couldn't see much through the smoke and the flak. Not to mention the fact that they got out as fast as they could. And then most of our raids were made at night. So I never had anything like a complete record. But I did just note down some of the more exciting missions, the ones I knew about. Just let me find—ah, here. I made a list. I thought I remembered doing that, near the end of the war. This is as of November 27, 1944."

She cleared her throat and began to read. "31 August, 1941: Ruhr valley, fires started near factories. 8 September, hit machine factory. 28 December, Nine SBC x 30-pound incendiaries, bullseye. 26 January 1942, bombed Rotterdam—"

"Hold on a minute, I've fallen behind." I scribbled furiously. "I don't suppose you would let me borrow your diary? I could make photocopies and use them in the—"

She hugged the book to her breast. "Oh, no, no, I

couldn't let you do that! No, this is precious to me. I never let it out of my hands. No, I'm sorry, but I really couldn't do that! It would do you no good, in any case. It's written in code, of course. My own code, you understand. I couldn't make a record of that sort of thing that just anyone could pick up and read."

She sounded quite alarmed. I hastened to reassure her. "Yes, I understand. I'll be happy to copy down what you tell me, then, but you'll have to read more slowly, and explain some of the terms to me. Go ahead."

The list was endless. It was also extremely interesting. She explained what "SBC x 30-pound" meant, although the explanation left me no wiser. She amplified with details of what she remembered of the missions, as she had seen them from the Ops Room. She told me little stories about the men involved, including the ones who didn't come home from this or that mission.

And all the time, as she was talking and I was taking rapid notes, I knew I'd heard it before. From Stanley.

And from the Web. She was reproducing still more of the information I'd found about entirely different men from entirely different bases.

Why were Stanley and Barbara Price telling me almost identical lies?

At last Miss Price closed her diary. It was one of those leather affairs with the little locking flap, and she was careful to make sure the lock clicked. She wanted her secrets kept safe. Such a lock could be picked with any respectable nail file, of course, or easier still, the soft old leather flap could be cut. The lock was symbolic. I only wished I knew for certain what it symbolized.

I was sincere in my expression of thanks before I left. I had, indeed, learned some very interesting things, even if they weren't quite what Miss Price thought she was telling me. This time, I thought as I climbed into my car and headed home through the early December twilight, Alan might pay attention to what I had to say.

I had completely forgotten we'd been asked out to dinner that night. My oldest friends in England, a pair of American expats living in London, had invited us to be their guests at one of their favorite restaurants, The Old Bakehouse out near Maidstone, a good hour away. By the time I got home I had barely enough time to bathe and dress. I did take a minute to put my notebook in a good safe place. I wanted that evidence to present to Alan.

The rain was still pelting down. Alan, driving on roads crowded with traffic, had his hands full. It was not only Friday night, but the beginning of a holiday as well. Most English businesses give their employees the whole week off for Christmas; some give two weeks. I was reminded yet again of my sad neglect of Christmas chores, and spent the ride making to-do lists. Alan had no attention to spare for my theories.

We had a lovely dinner, and a lovely time. Tom and

Lynn Anderson are two of the nicest people I know. They have enough money that they never have to give it a thought, but they're not the way I always imagined the rich to be. They're funny, and kind, and altogether delightful company. They reminded me about the first time I'd ever visited The Old Bakehouse, also at Christmastime, when I was in the middle of another murder, and just getting to know Alan. Lynn recounted all the details, and I nearly disgraced us all by laughing myself into hiccups, as I had on that earlier occasion.

Sated, content, and full of goodwill, we parted with mutual wishes for a happy Christmas. I'd had a fair amount of champagne and fell asleep on the way home, so it wasn't until breakfast the next morning that I got around to telling Alan about Barbara Price.

"The *same* stories? You're sure?"

"Well, I didn't make notes at Stanley's house. But the details sound the same, and I did check my Price notes first thing this morning against what I'd printed out from the Web. I'd wanted to print one story about one medal, and ended up doing forty-odd pages because I wasn't paying attention. Anyway, some of the material in those pages is identical to what Barbara was quoting to me. *Identical,* Alan. Dates, places, events, even the names of the men involved. The only thing is, those men weren't from Luftwich. The reports list their squadrons, and none of them are right. Here, look. I've marked the items."

I handed him my notebook, with a sheaf of printouts

tucked inside. He studied them, frowned, and handed them back to me.

"All right, exactly what is it that you're thinking?"

I took a deep breath. "I think they're in it together, Stanley and Barbara. I think they're cooking up a false history of Luftwich. Stanley's medals are part of it, and Barbara's pretty little war stories."

"Why?"

"I don't know, but it must be because the real history is dangerous. It must have to do with that letter, Alan. It has to!"

He ran a hand down the back of his neck and finished his cup of coffee. "Any more?" he said, holding up the cup.

"No, I just made two cups this morning, in the French press. Shall I put on the coffeemaker?"

"Please."

When I got back to the table his fingers were tented in front of him. I recognized the pose. He was about to hold forth.

"All right. Let's be logical about this. You believe that there was deliberate sabotage of missions from Luftwich, that they failed to achieve their goals because someone made sure they wouldn't."

I nodded.

"And you believe that Stanley Rutherford and Barbara Price knew about it and are now covering up the facts."

"Yes. I know the evidence is thin, but—"

He waved away thin evidence and continued.

"When you first propounded your sabotage theory, you were quite certain Merrifield must have been the saboteur, by reason of his position of superiority in the organization."

"Also because he had the most to lose from German air raids over here. That's if the information someone was providing from the other side was in payment for those sabotaged missions, and it makes sense to me."

"We're not evaluating at the moment, merely formulating. Are you still of the opinion that Merrifield was involved?"

I hesitated. "Well, it would be a big coincidence if he suddenly got murdered when all this other stuff was going on and his murder didn't have anything to do with it, wouldn't it?"

"That's a trifle muddled, my dear. Try again."

I thought a moment. "All right. How's this? Merrifield was the big cheese, but the other two knew about it. At the time, I mean. The sabotage would have been easier with more than one person involved, even though the more people knew about it, the riskier it was. Now suppose Merrifield had some sort of attack of conscience or something in the past week or so. Suppose he was about to tell what he knew. Maybe Bill's death triggered some memories. For whatever reason, suppose he told the others he was going to spill the beans. If they didn't want them spilled, they'd have to do something about Merrifield, wouldn't they?"

"I've not met either of these charming people, but

obviously they're not young. Would either of them have the strength, physically, to get out to Heatherwood House and smother Merrifield?"

"Not Stanley. He can barely walk, and his granddaughter is a tyrant. She wouldn't let him go off on his own, let alone drive him way out there—if in fact he still drives. And I doubt he, Stanley, I mean, would have the strength to do the murder even if he could have got to Heatherwood House somehow. But Barbara—yes, Barbara could. She's fussy and somewhat silly and tries to look much younger than she is. She doesn't manage it, by the way. But she's fit enough, even if overweight. She walks easily and carries heavy tea trays. She could have done it, easily, and she could have attacked Walter, too."

"Why?"

"Obviously because she didn't want—oh, I see. You're saying it takes more than just fear of the exposure of a very old secret to make a motive for murder."

"Murder has been committed for sixpence, or a pair of shoes. That wasn't exactly what I meant. I meant, why now, in particular? If your theory has any basis in fact, either Stanley or Barbara could have simply said that Merrifield was senile, that he was imagining things, or denied that they were ever involved. That's if they couldn't talk him out of his purported confession. Why resort to murder?"

And I had no answer to that.

TWENTY-EIGHT

I HAD TO PUT SPECULATION ASIDE FOR A WHILE. IT WAS Saturday, the Saturday before Christmas, and positively my last chance to do any big-city Christmas shopping. I asked Alan if he wanted to come to London with me. He shuddered. "The Christmas sales? Thank you, but no. Unless of course I'm required as a parcel carrier."

"I won't ask that martyrdom of you this time. I'll take the big rolling suitcase. It should hold everything."

"Mind you get someone to lift it into the train for you. Your back, you know."

"Yes, well, if I can find a porter, I'll do that. There's leftover soup for lunch, and I'll be back in time for dinner."

"We'll go out. You'll be too tired to cook."

I'd be too tired to enjoy going out, too, but maybe I could talk him into take-out Italian or Chinese. That was for later consideration. He drove me to the train, wished me luck, put the empty suitcase in the storage area for me, and jumped off just in time.

And I settled down for the hour's ride to Victoria Station and, getting out my notebook, thought again about murder and assorted acts of violence.

Let's suppose I was right about the sabotage plot at Luftwich and the people involved. Merrifield simply had to have been at the heart of it. He had something to gain, something big, and he had the power. Means, motive, opportunity. The three big questions in any crime, and treason was one of the worst crimes of all. I made a note to ask his son if any of the family holdings had been damaged in the war. I didn't know how I would frame such an intrusive question, but I'd worry about that later.

Yes, Merrifield had to be the boss. Only he was in a position to give orders. Barbara Price could have helped a lot, of course, deliberately guiding the pilots a little off course. A degree or two would make a huge difference. And Stanley, the gunner, could obviously make sure his fire came close to enemy aircraft but didn't hit them.

How would Merrifield have gotten Barbara and Stanley to help, though? They had no self-interest in the matter, or not the same kind as Merrifield. Why would they turn traitor, providing aid and comfort to the enemy?

Well, there again, Merrifield, as a relatively senior officer, had a certain control over them. I thought about that word "blackmail" that I hadn't written in my notes. I wrote it now. Suppose Stanley had been caught in some breach of discipline, or some moderately criminal act? I could easily imagine Stanley being a little light-fingered. He was born to be a snapper-up of unconsidered trifles. And if Merrifield knew, Stanley would certainly consent to a little blackmail, especially if it entailed nothing more than inaction, or misdirected action, on Stanley's part.

Barbara? Oh, for Barbara the impetus would have come from her fiancé. He could have convinced her the sun set in the east if he'd wanted to. I had realized that the moment she began to talk about him. And what hold would Merrifield have had, in turn, over *him?*

I couldn't answer that. I knew nothing about him. Barbara had said he was brave, and a patriot, but of course she would have. If it was true, though, a patriot who wasn't too bright might have been persuaded, by a smooth, clever operator like Merrifield, that England was better served by protecting some of its civilian towns and buildings, even at the cost of failure to destroy some German targets. Merrifield might have talked about revenge bombings if certain German targets were hit. Or he might have persuaded—what was his name?—James, that was it—might have persuaded James that the information coming from Germany was going to be used against them, that it would enable more defenses to be mounted at the sites where the attacks were to take place.

Might have. Supposing. Could have. I pushed the notebook away from me with an angry shove, causing the woman in the next seat to eye me warily. It was all utterly unsatisfactory. My ideas hung together, I thought, as a piece of reasoning. But there wasn't one single fact in there, or nothing that couldn't be explained some other way. Stanley was a delusional collector of war memorabilia. Barbara was concerned with keeping the memory of her fiancé green, and borrowed other people's stories to bolster her contention that Luftwich's missions had produced stellar results.

But Walter had certainly been attacked, and Merrifield had certainly been murdered, and Bill, I at least was certain, had been driven to his death. Those facts were irrefutable and had to be explained. And how, how, how was I or anyone to explain them?

Victoria was just as crowded and hectic as I had expected, and the London shops even more so. I enjoyed myself, even so, at least at first. The day was pleasant, for a change, cloudy but with the sun peeking through now and then, and amazingly no precipitation of any kind. The chestnut sellers were out in force, crying their fragrant wares. I bought some, burning my fingers as I tried to peel and eat them.

There was a long queue for taxis at the station, so I was forced to wedge myself and my suitcase onto a crowded Tube train. Then Harrod's was so crowded and noisy that I left without buying anything, somehow managed to get back on the Tube, and headed for the shops in Piccadilly, which were nearly as bad. After three hours I was exhausted, cross, and starved, and not at all pleased when my favorite restaurant in the area refused to admit me with my suitcase. Thoroughly annoyed, I stole a taxi out from under the lordly doorman at the Ritz, settled for a stale sandwich in Victoria Station, and just made it to my train, fed up with the whole notion of Christmas and profoundly grateful that it comes but once a year.

The journey home gave me a chance for a nap and restored my temper. By the time I met Alan at the door of the train, I was in a mood to be pleased with my purchases and excited again about Christmas. He lifted down the suitcase, raised one eyebrow by way of comment on its weight, and heaved it into the boot. "A successful foray, one assumes," he said rather dryly.

"Entirely, but I'm wiped out, physically and financially. And starved. Lunch proved undoable. Do you suppose we could substitute a really sizable tea for dinner? I don't think I can wait till dinnertime."

Alan grinned. "I'll drop you at Alderney's. You can get us a table while I take the car and your bag home. I'll join you in a tick."

Afternoon tea is, sadly, a dying institution in England. The business world, to which almost everyone belongs at one level or another, has time for no more than a quickly brewed cuppa in midafternoon. The meal is a relic of the Victorian days when ladies with nothing else to do called on one another in the afternoons and made polite chitchat, severely restricted as to subject matter, over tea and minuscule sandwiches. The ceremony became more opulent in the Edwardian era, perhaps because the rotund Prince of Wales himself often joined the tea tables of the rich and required substantial nourishment. When the big hotels took up afternoon tea and turned it into a finely tuned ritual, it was already on its way out elsewhere and well embarked on the transformation into a tourist attraction.

So now it is principally in tourist destinations, like cathedral cities, that afternoon tea is still preserved and hallowed. Sherebury Cathedral draws impressive numbers of tourists in the summer and a good many at other seasons, and so Alderney's, with its picturesque half-timbered setting actually in the Cathedral Close, prospers and thrives. And I, along with many of the other aging residents of Sherebury, express our gratitude by patronizing the tea shop regularly.

I ordered a fine collection of carbohydrates, and Alan, when he came back, helped me do full justice to every sinful and delectable calorie.

"Why is it," I mused as I pushed my plate away at last, "that all the things that are so good to the taste are so bad for the body? It seems unfair."

"Ah, the devil has always been an attractive chap. Temptations would hardly be tempting if they weren't delightful, now would they? You love things that are good for you, too, fish and broccoli and grapefruit and that lot."

"I do, you're right, but they can't compare with clotted cream and buttered crumpets and lemon curd and currant buns with cinnamon. Although one can eat too much of them," I added. My waistband felt miserably tight. "I think maybe I'd better go home and get out of my London clothes before the stitches start to give."

The Close was nearly deserted at this time of day. Evensong was long past and the choir and clergy had gone home to their warm firesides, but one or two vergers kept the Cathedral open for the last few visitors of the day. We cut through, leaving by the south choir door (which is very close to our house) and as we walked through the thickening twilight to the gate into our street, I told Alan all I had surmised, the whole story of the Luftwich plot as I had worked it out.

My husband, bless his heart, heard me out without interruption or quibble, and continued his silence until we were inside the house and had settled in front of the fire, a cat in each lap.

"Yes, Sam, there's a good cat. No claws, now." He stroked the little Siamese for a moment, and then said, "What about Leigh Burton? Where does she fit into this scheme or yours?"

"She doesn't. I thought for a while she might be pulling some kind of double bluff, raising the issue of irregular activities at Luftwich so it would make me think she's innocent, but I don't think she has that kind of mind."

"Hmm. And the Reverend Mr. Tredgold?"

"I'm worried about him. He's such a sweet, harmless man. I think he must have felt there was something wrong at the base, because he keeps talking about deceit and treachery. I wondered at first if he'd gone round the bend—"

"Ah, yes. 'Bats.'"

I ignored that. "Anyway, now I think he was just abnormally sensitive to atmosphere and realized something was wrong, and it got to him. If Barbara

Price killed Merrifield to keep him silent, then I hope she doesn't decide Mr. Tredgold ought to be the next victim. It would be such a waste. Nobody takes him seriously, and he really is a dear."

Alan fell silent again. Samantha's purrs filled the room with peace and contentment. The lights glowed on the Christmas tree; the fire crackled.

"This room is a drug," I said. "Sitting here, I find it hard to believe that anyone could do any of the things I'm supposing they've done."

"Yes, peace can be an opiate. Though mind you, I'm all for it. Peace, that is. However, it's more satisfactory if it's the real thing."

"Yes, and it won't be real until we get to the bottom of all this. Alan, what should I do? Tell Derek my ideas and let him take it from there?"

He stopped petting Sam and ran his hand down the back of his head. "I don't know. The police can't act on suppositions. If there were any hard evidence, or any hope of finding some . . ."

"I know. By the way, have they given up on the museum? You haven't been there for a while, and I haven't heard any reports."

"For now they have. The troubles at the museum don't seem to have a direct connection to Merrifield's murder, and that's what must take Derek's time and attention now."

"Of course. Well, tomorrow after church I think I'm going to try to tackle Leigh Burton again. Maybe I can get her to give me more than hints this time, if she'll let me in the door."

"Take her some mince pies. I take it you baked plenty?"

"Dozens."

"Unless she's positively subhuman, she'll thaw at one bite of your mince pies. If you can get any solid fact out of her, Derek will have something to work with. And he could use it, believe me. He's terribly worried about all this."

"Poor man. It does seem unfair that he has so much on his plate, and with Christmas just around the corner, too. And that reminds me. I must wrap the things I bought today. Out, love. Some of them are for you. And for goodness' sake take the cats with you. The mess they can make with paper and ribbon isn't to be believed."

So I wrapped my presents and put them under the tree, hoping the cats would leave them alone, and Alan and I ended the day quietly with some biscuits and cheese and a little bourbon. Before I fell asleep, though, I planned out a strategy for tomorrow's conversation with the Ice Princess.

TWENTY-NINE

I FEAR MY ATTENTION THE NEXT MORNING IN CHURCH was not entirely on the service. For the second Sunday in a row, too. Doubtless the music was flawless. Doubtless the dean preached a good sermon. He almost always does. But try though I might to concentrate, my mind kept slipping away to Leigh Burton and her beautiful house and her cold, wolfish face.

I had decided not to phone in advance. It is harder to turn away a person standing at the door, mince pies in hand. So as soon as Alan and I had finished lunch, I pulled a dozen of the pastries out of the freezer and slipped them in the oven to get crisp. When they were hot and fragrant, I put them on one of my nicest plates, complete with paper doily, covered them with a napkin, and took off for the Burton mansion.

She might not have been at home. Even if she was, she might have decided not to answer the door. But she was, and she did, and the moment I saw her I launched into my prepared speech.

"Do forgive me for calling unannounced, Mrs. Burton, but I felt we somehow got off on the wrong foot the other day. I've baked a peace offering, and I do hope you'll accept it and my apologies if I have somehow offended you."

Well, after that, she'd have had to be downright rude to turn me away, and downright rudeness was not a part of Leigh Burton's normal repertoire. Chilly politeness that could freeze you out, yes. That's the proper English way. The only really rude English people I'd ever encountered had been at one extreme or the other of the social scale: one peer of the realm who, when introduced to me by a friend, had nodded and turned his back; and one would-be mugger in London long ago who had failed in his attempt only because of the police whistle I always carried.

Leigh was in neither the peeress nor the purse-snatcher class. So she opened the door wider, bared her teeth in what was meant for a smile, and invited me in with a murmur of thanks.

It was too early for tea, and Leigh was no Barbara Price, to make the social mistake of offering it to me anyway. Neither was sherry on offer today. She simply gestured me to a seat in the drawing room and sat down herself, again with that air of fragility but infinite poise.

"I'm very sorry, Mrs. Martin, if I left you with the impression that I had been offended. You did nothing to offend me. I am quite a busy woman, with charity work and so on, and my time was particularly in demand that day. If I became somewhat impatient, it was because I could not quite discern the purpose for your visit, and you seemed to me to have become somewhat repetitive at a time when I was needed elsewhere. I should at the outset have made clear that my time was limited. If any apologies are due, they should be mine. It seems I was rude. I'm sorry."

Whew! There was chilly politeness with a vengeance. If she was sorry, she sure sounded like she could manage to cope. Well, I could do that, too. I smiled. "A misunderstanding, that's all. I'm glad it's cleared up. So I'd better ask if you have a free moment now. I confess I did come to ask you something, as well as to make amends."

"A moment. Little more. I am expected to chair a

committee meeting at the Women's Institute in"—she glanced at her watch—"twenty minutes."

I took a deep breath and tried to match her extremely formal tone. "I'll try to be quick then. My problem is that when I visited before, you mentioned your sense that Luftwich did not contribute as much to the war effort as might have been expected. That differs so widely from other accounts I've been given that I wonder if you can cite any particular instances. There must be a mistake somewhere, and I'm trying to ferret out where it might be."

"I see. No, after all these years I certainly cannot be specific. It was only a general sense, Mrs. Martin, and might have been colored by my anxiety about the men, particularly my husband, of course. If your other sources have told you differently, they may be right." She glanced away from me, then looked back. "Forgive me. I fear I'm a bit distracted. The meeting—"

I looked where she had looked, probably at a clock. I couldn't see one, but then I, too, was distracted. The rug had just been pulled out from under me. I'd built a whole elaborate theory on her unequivocal statement that Luftwich had been surprisingly ineffective, and now she was taking it back. "Well, the others were pretty definite, I have to say. In fact, they quoted statistics that seemed to prove the Luftwich men had done even more than their share to win the war."

"Well, it may be." Her eyes strayed once more to the fragile, beautiful secretary desk in the corner of the room. "Of course when George was killed, I developed a certain amount of bitterness toward the Air Force in general and Luftwich in particular. Perhaps my memory is at fault."

Somewhere in another room, the telephone rang.

"Excuse me, please." She stood.

"It's time I left, anyway," I said hastily. "I can see myself out."

"If you don't mind. I *am* sorry."

She left the room as briskly as she could, leaning rather heavily on her cane.

The moment she was out of sight I stole across the room to the secretary, blessing the thick carpet. It could be that she was worried about her meeting, and thinking about some presentation that was outlined in that desk. On the other hand . . .

She answered the phone. I heard her speak, though I couldn't distinguish words. I lifted the lid of the desk.

Right on top, neatly centered, was a small black-leather-covered book. On the lower right-hand corner of the cover were the initials WF, in gold.

My ears straining for her voice as she continued to talk, I opened the cover. It was an engagement book. And under it, I saw now, was a road atlas of the United States of America.

I was out the door before she hung up the phone.

I drove off very quietly and turned a corner at random. There I pulled up to the curb and sat while my heart slowed down to normal.

She stole them. Bill's diary and his atlas. That must mean she was the one who attacked Walter.

But she was a frail old lady.

With a cane, a fine, expensive, heavy ebony cane.

I took a deep breath. It was possible. With the diary and the atlas in her possession, it was even likely. But why?

Into my mind came Jane's succinct explanation of Leigh Burton's bitterness. "Bill lived. George died."

It was true, then. It was all true, the fanciful, elaborate story I'd built out of bits and pieces. There had been a fifth-column cell at Luftwich. And Merrifield and Price and Rutherford had all been part of it. The lies I'd heard had been an attempt to steer me away from the truth. But I wasn't the danger. Leigh Burton was.

But what had set her off? If she'd known about the treason all along, and had blamed the people responsible for George's death, why had she waited until now to do something about it?

No, it didn't quite hold together yet, but one thing was certain. Leigh had Bill's belongings. She had stolen them from the museum. She had almost certainly attacked Walter Tubbs.

That was enough to take to the police.

I went straight home. This was a matter for Alan. He could get hold of Derek, and command his attention, far more quickly and easily than I could.

I burst in the door to find him napping on the couch with two cats on top of him. They jumped down in alarm, and he sat up, blinking.

"It's Leigh, Alan. She's the one who attacked

Walter, and maybe the one who killed Merrifield."

He was wide awake in an instant. "Tell me."

"She has the diary, Bill's diary, and his atlas. They're in her desk. I saw them. And she's going to the Women's Institute in a couple of minutes, so Derek needs to know right away!"

He asked nothing further, but went to the phone. When he came back he said, "Derek's on the way. Now tell me the whole story."

"There isn't much to tell. I went over there to try to sort out the difference between her story and the others. She said she must have been mistaken and took the wind out of my sails. But she kept looking at her desk—the most gorgeous little Hepplewhite secretary, Alan!—and I wondered why. So when she had to answer the phone I—well, I snooped. And there they were. And I can't think of any way they could have got there unless she stole them. Only I don't know why."

I ran out of steam abruptly.

"I think, after that, you need a cup of tea. Or something stronger?"

"No, tea is just right. I have to regroup. Some of my ideas are right, but the others must be dreadfully wrong, and I have to think."

"Derek won't rest until he gets the truth out of her, you know. He's very, very good at questioning suspects, and he wants badly to catch this one."

"I know, but I want to figure out where I went wrong."

So while Alan was getting the tea, I marshaled my thoughts, and when he came back with a tray I was ready to think out loud.

"Okay, how about this?" I said when I'd taken a few heartening sips. "Let's go back to the beginning. Bill finds the letter, the coded letter, in a pile of stuff up in the storeroom. He's in the process of organizing, but he's not done yet. He's not sure who donated this particular letter, but he's pretty sure, because it's in a pile of Luftwich memorabilia, that it was from one of just a few people. Merrifield, Rutherford, Price, Tredgold, or Burton. They all donated things to the museum, by the way. They told me so.

"All right. He works out enough of the meaning of the letter—and we know he did because of the marked atlas—enough to be very worried. It looks to him as though someone, someone he knows, someone he served with at Luftwich, has been involved in something very peculiar, if not downright criminal. On the other hand, there could be another explanation. He hopes there is. Now, what would Bill do?"

"He would ask them," said Alan positively.

"Right. That's what I think, too. He wouldn't go to the police, or the military authorities, or anyone like that, until he was sure. He wasn't the kind of man to get a friend into trouble unless he absolutely had to.

"So he phoned them all, told them what he had found, asked for an explanation. And then when he didn't get a satisfactory answer from any of them, he asked them to come and see the letter. Oh! That was what that 'donors' meeting' was all about. Walter said there were no names written down, and I'll bet you anything you like it was because he was so sensitive about incriminating anyone. He probably set aside a block of time and asked them to come in one at a time."

Alan nodded.

"Now. How would they all react to that phone call? I know enough about them that I think I can guess. Mr. Tredgold would go off into one of his fits of remorse over the war. He didn't have anything to do with the plot, of course, but he'd go crazy, as he does at any mention of the war. Merrifield would smoothly deny all knowledge and phone the others to tell them to do the same. But at least one of them would agree to come. To look at the letter, they'd say, and see if they—he—she—whoever—couldn't figure out what it meant. They, of course, would want it kept covered up. Stanley would hug his medals and the stories he's almost begun to believe. Barbara might contemplate some drastic action, but before she could make up her mind to do anything (she's rather muddle-headed), Bill dies and she thinks the problem is solved. How am I doing so far?"

"I'm following you."

It wasn't exactly an endorsement, but I plowed on. "But Leigh—Leigh is different. Bill tells her enough about the letter that her suspicions are confirmed. She agrees to come and look at the letter, and boy, does she want to! She knew something was going on, all those years ago, and now it's proven. And her bitterness, the bitterness over the death, not only of her husband, but of all her hopes for wealth and position, rise to the surface, stronger than ever."

"But Leigh Burton *is* wealthy. What does she want that she doesn't have?"

"Position. A country estate. The respect due the wife of a country squire. All the things she would have had as George Burton's wife. His family left her some money—I don't know how much—but not, of course, the estate. The estate was presumably entailed. If her child had lived, and been a boy, even with George dead she would have had all that. And in her mind, I suspect both George's death and the death of their child could be laid at the feet of the Luftwich traitors. I don't think she's very rational on the subject."

"One can understand why she might not be. But go on."

"Well, then. Leigh knows now that she's been right all along. But she still doesn't know who's involved, and she wants to know, *needs* to know. She wants them exposed, wants to avenge her long-dead husband and the child she never had. She wants reparations for what should have been hers."

"Objection. If she wants them exposed, why did she tell you so little when you first came to the house?"

That set me back. "I don't know. Why didn't she? Maybe—maybe it's because I'm American."

"English by marriage."

"Yes, but Leigh is a snob. She'd think of me as an

American, and would she wash her—or anybody else's—dirty laundry in front of a foreigner? I don't think so! Oh, and not only that, by that time she had attacked Walter, when she was trying to find the letter and other proof at the museum. She knew she was in for criminal prosecution if that was discovered, and that wouldn't suit her at all. She's not the stuff martyrs are made of, and besides, if she were put in prison she couldn't continue with her research and, ultimately, her revenge."

"Sounds positively Greek. *Ancient* Greek."

"A little like that, I think. Leigh Burton is a single-minded woman, and she's not in the least intellectual or well educated. It's a frightening combination. And do you know, I think in a way my visit to her might have been a catalyst of sorts. She hinted something of what she knew, perhaps in hopes that I might learn the truth without it coming from her. But I also started her thinking, and she must have come up with the same conclusion I did: that the man behind the sabotage had to be an officer in charge, had, in fact, to be John Merrifield. And I had further stirred up all her old memories. So she killed Merrifield."

"And today? When she denied her earlier hints?"

"Today she knew she was a murderess. The penalties for that are worse than for simple assault."

"Indeed."

Alan took my hand and we sat in silence, staring at the trappings of Christmas.

THIRTY

WE WERE PICKING AT OUR SUPPER WHEN THE DOORBELL
rang. Alan brought Derek back to the kitchen and,
after a quick glance at him, poured him a glass of
scotch.

"Thanks," he said. "A little water, please, but not
much. I need a stiffener."

"Bad?" asked Alan.

"Fought like a tiger. Literally." He took a long pull
at his drink, and then held out his hands, which were
badly scratched.

"You'll have those seen to," said Alan calmly.
"Humans are among the most germ-ridden animals."

I was shocked and said so. "She did that? The Ice
Princess?"

"Not so icy anymore. I won't quote the language she
used, but it wasn't pretty. Not at all what I would have
expected."

"Did she admit anything?"

"Eventually. Not at first." He took another sip of
scotch and water and settled back in his chair to tell us
the story.

"We caught her just as she was leaving the house.
She did have a WI committee meeting, incidentally.
We sent men there in case we missed her at home, and
the good ladies waited quite a while until they decided
their chairwoman wasn't coming. At any rate, she

insisted she couldn't stop to talk to us, that she had duties to attend to, it was most inconvenient—all that. Then when we insisted—I had Bledsoe with me, Alan, he's a very good man—when we insisted, she gave in with very bad grace, let us into the house, and stood there in the hall tapping her feet. I suggested we sit down, she said there was no need. You know the routine. Eventually I simply ordered her to sit, and she lost her temper. Who did I think I was, ordering her about in her own house, she'd complain to the chief constable, to the Home Office, whoever. I think she'd have got to the Queen if Bledsoe hadn't simply walked over to the little desk and opened it up, and there they were, just as you said, Mrs. Martin.

"Of course she claimed at first they were hers, and then when Bledsoe read out Mr. Fanshawe's name from inside the cover, she couldn't imagine how they'd got there, and so on. It wasn't until I told her we'd have to take her cane in and test it for blood and tissue that she went over the edge. Started screaming, went at me with those fingernails of hers. One wouldn't have thought a woman her age would be so strong."

I shuddered. Alan, without a word, got up and brought some bourbon for both of us. He also refilled Derek's glass.

"No, Mrs. Martin, it wasn't pleasant, but it was instructive. She told us the whole story, or nearly. It dates back to the old air base, Luftwich, during World War II."

And he meticulously went through it, one step at a time, beginning with Bill's discovery of the letter. It all went much as I had surmised, with one outstanding exception.

"And who do you think was at the heart of the thing in the first place, according to Mrs. Burton?"

"Merrifield, of course," I said confidently.

"No. It was the sainted Mr. Tredgold."

"No! That sweet old man?"

"That sweet old man was a pacifist, remember. *Is* a pacifist. If Burton's story is accurate, Tredgold began to spout pacifist doctrine early on at Luftwich. At some point he must have been approached by a German spy—England was rife with them in the early days of the war—who persuaded him that the way to end the war early, prevent further deaths, was an exchange of information and a private nonaggression agreement. They're persuasive arguments, of course. War is never a simple issue of good versus evil, and it's never easy to know what's best. The poor naïve man thought the German line sounded good, so he took it to Merrifield. With all he had to lose, Merrifield loved the idea."

"And that's why Mr. Tredgold refuses to talk about the war," I said. There was a catch in my voice. "Once he began to realize what he had done, what he had unleashed . . ."

"Probably. He's a man with an active conscience. It simply became confused. And he's had to live ever since with what, with the best of motives, he made happen."

"And now there's another murder on his conscience," said Alan, "because Merrifield's death was a direct result of those wartime activities. At least, has Burton admitted murdering Merrifield?"

"Admitted it! She boasted about it. By that time she was treating Bledsoe and me like a pair of naughty schoolboys who were interfering with her duties. She quite patiently explained that we could deal with her later, after she'd killed Tredgold and Rutherford and Price. 'But you do see, surely, that they must be executed?' She used that word. Her rationale was that they were war criminals and deserved to die."

"And maybe they do," I said after a little silence. "And maybe Merrifield did, too. But not at Leigh Burton's hands. She's neither judge nor jury, nor yet God."

"No," said Alan. He sipped from his glass.

"What will happen to them?" I asked eventually. "To Barbara and Stanley and poor old Mr. Tredgold?"

Alan and Derek looked at each other; Derek sighed. "Probably nothing. Rutherford is very ill, I understand."

"Emphysema, he claims, but I wonder if it isn't lung cancer. He coughed terribly when I was there."

"If that's the case, he might well be dead before the cumbersome machinery of the law could be cranked up and set in motion. In any case there's no real evidence against any of them. What have we got to take to a jury? A coded letter that could mean anything. A collection of medals, some of which might be stolen—or might be purchased legitimately. Some statements about Luftwich that may not be true, but made to one person, without a witness. Tredgold would almost certainly confess, if confronted, but given his mental state, who would believe him?"

I looked at my glass.

"We have nothing to support a charge of war crimes," Derek went on. "And they're old. I intend to let them be." He surveyed our faces.

"They caused Bill Fanshawe's death, between them," I protested.

"We can't prove that, either. Oh, I believe he was down in that tunnel to hide the precious original document, just in case one of the people he'd asked to explain decided to destroy it. And I believe the stress of his discovery, and the physical effort involved, led to his stroke. But I can't prove it."

"They'll be facing judgment soon," said Alan, almost to himself. "A truer judgment than any we could mete out."

"And they have been punished and are being punished, Stanley by his miserable existence with his daughter, Barbara by her loneliness and the loss of her fiancé, Mr. Tredgold with his terrible, agonizing memories. Yes," I agreed. "Leave them alone."

"And now who's being judge and jury?" said Alan wryly. "Oh, I think it's the right thing to do. It's only . . ." He raised his hands and let them fall.

"Yes." I tried to reason it out. "We know some things no one else does. The question is, do we have the right to keep them to ourselves? On the other hand, do we have the right to ruin what might be the last few months of life for three people whose crimes were in the distant past?"

"For a policeman, it's simpler than that," Derek pointed out. "It comes down to what it always comes down to, in the prosecution of any criminal: Do we have a case? How often have you, Alan, been forced to release someone you knew perfectly well committed the crime? You hadn't enough evidence to convict him, so you had to let him go. That's the case here. I do intend to go to both Rutherford and Price and tell them what I know. Then if they had any thought of further cover-up action, they'll think again."

"And I suppose," I said, "you'll manipulate the evidence against Leigh Burton so she is tried only for the murder of Merrifield, and that with no mention of motive."

"She has confessed, before a police witness. Unless she recants that confession—and she won't, she's gone right round the twist—we'll have no trouble with a conviction. I don't imagine Her Majesty will have to provide accommodation for Mrs. Leigh Burton very long."

"No." We finished our drinks in silence. There was nothing more to say.

The next morning, early, I went next door. I wanted to give Jane the news before Walter was up.

She had, of course, already heard it. I'll never know how she does it. Perhaps living in a small town for over eighty years has given her antennae for disturbing vibrations.

"So it's over," she said, pouring me coffee without my asking.

"Yes. You heard about Mr. Tredgold being the mastermind behind the whole thing? He's the one I feel sorry for, really. He truly is a fine person, and one horrible mistake of judgment in his youth ruined not only his life, but so many other lives."

"Bill's," said Jane flatly. "Mine."

"Oh, Jane, I'm sorry! I didn't mean—"

She waved away my apology. "Dead, anyway. Last night."

I caught up after a second or two. "Mr. Tredgold? Dead? Goodness, he surely didn't commit suicide! That would be against all his principles."

"No. Just—died. Left a note. Confessed everything."

"How do you know?" This time I couldn't resist asking.

"Friend, nurse at Canterbury House. Rang me up."

"Was it a heart attack, or stroke, or what?"

"Heart failure. What we all die of. Nurse said sometimes they decide to die and do, just like that."

I nodded slowly. "He's wanted to die for a long time, I imagine. If he knew about Mrs. Burton's crimes, especially the murder, it could have been the last straw for him."

"Said he was responsible for everything. In the note. Even Bill's death."

I touched Jane's hand. She accepted the sympathy for a moment and then moved briskly away.

"More coffee?"

"Yes, please. Jane, are you going to be all right? I know this must have come as a terrible shock to you." It was a lame remark, but Jane hates effusiveness.

"Got one good thing out of it," she said, gesturing with her head toward the ceiling. I could hear some sounds of movement upstairs; Walter was awake.

"Walter? Yes, he'll be a companion for you, at least until he finishes at the university."

"More than that." Jane swallowed and cleared her throat, as if what she had to say was difficult. Her face had become flushed. "He's my grandson."

I thought at first I'd heard wrong. "Walter—he—you—" I couldn't find anything sensible to say.

"He doesn't know yet." She sat down at the table, speaking more easily now that the worst part was over. "I had a son. Bill's son. Thought Bill was dead, gave the boy to my cousin. She was married, never able to have kids. Loved having the baby.

"Then Bill came back. Never told him, better for the boy."

"But you kept track of him."

"No. Cousin moved to Scotland. Lost touch. Wanted to forget. No one knew I was teaching—" She let it go at that, but I understood. A single woman with an illegitimate son, in those days, would not have been allowed to go on teaching. She would have had a hard time getting any sort of decent job, in fact. Jane had been forced to make the hard decision to abandon her son. I nodded.

"Cousin did write me when the boy married. Thought I might want to come. Didn't. When I met Walter, name of Tubbs, didn't mean anything to me. Did some checking with the university when he was hurt, trying to find family. Records had father's name. My son's name. Father was dead, mother had remarried, husband, name of Tubbs, adopted the boy. Stepfather dead now, too, mother no better than she should be. Walter oldest of four, neglected . . ." She spread her hands. "I took him in. Only thing to do."

"And you're thrilled. Go on, admit it."

One of Jane's rare smiles broke over her face. I felt I should have heard trumpets, as at an Easter sunrise. "Fine boy. I'll tell him someday. He loved Bill. Would be happy to know he was his grandfather."

Walter came clattering into the kitchen. "*Good* morning! Hi, Mrs. Martin! What's for breakfast, Aunt Jane? I'm perishing of hunger." He gave her a peck on the cheek before turning to bury his head in the refrigerator.

A tear escaped Jane's eye. She wiped it away with one corner of her apron and frowned furiously at me, for my eyes were brimming, too. I waved, not trusting myself to speak, and went out to walk in the garden for a few minutes. I couldn't show Alan tears I wasn't prepared to explain. Not yet. Maybe not ever.

The sky was a dark gray, and as I watched, a few flakes of snow began to fall. Snow for Christmas. I thought about long-held bitterness and new happiness and knew that Christmas, even for the old, was a time of miracles.

Center Point Publishing
600 Brooks Road ● PO Box 1
Thorndike ME 04986-0001 USA

(207) 568-3717

US & Canada:
1 800 929-9108